Praise for That Kind of Girl

THAT KIND OF GIRL

Jacey Bici

JCBC
Publishing

Published by JCBC Publishing, LLC

14621 E SR 70 #247 Lakewood Ranch, FL 34202

Library of Congress Control Number: 9798991813068.

This book is a work of fiction. Names, characters, businesses, organizations, places, events and incidents either are the product of the author's imagination or are used fictitiously. Any resemblance to actual persons, living or dead, events, or locales is entirely coincidental. While the author is a medical doctor, the medical scenarios, characters, and details presented in this story are fictionalized for narrative purposes. This book is not intended to provide medical advice, diagnosis, or treatment. Readers should always consult a qualified healthcare professional for any medical concerns or questions.

Cover design by Spiffing Publishing.

Paperback ISBN: 979-8-9918130-5-1

Hardcover ISBN: 979-8-9918130-6-8

Bespoke Cover: 978-1-969160-00-4

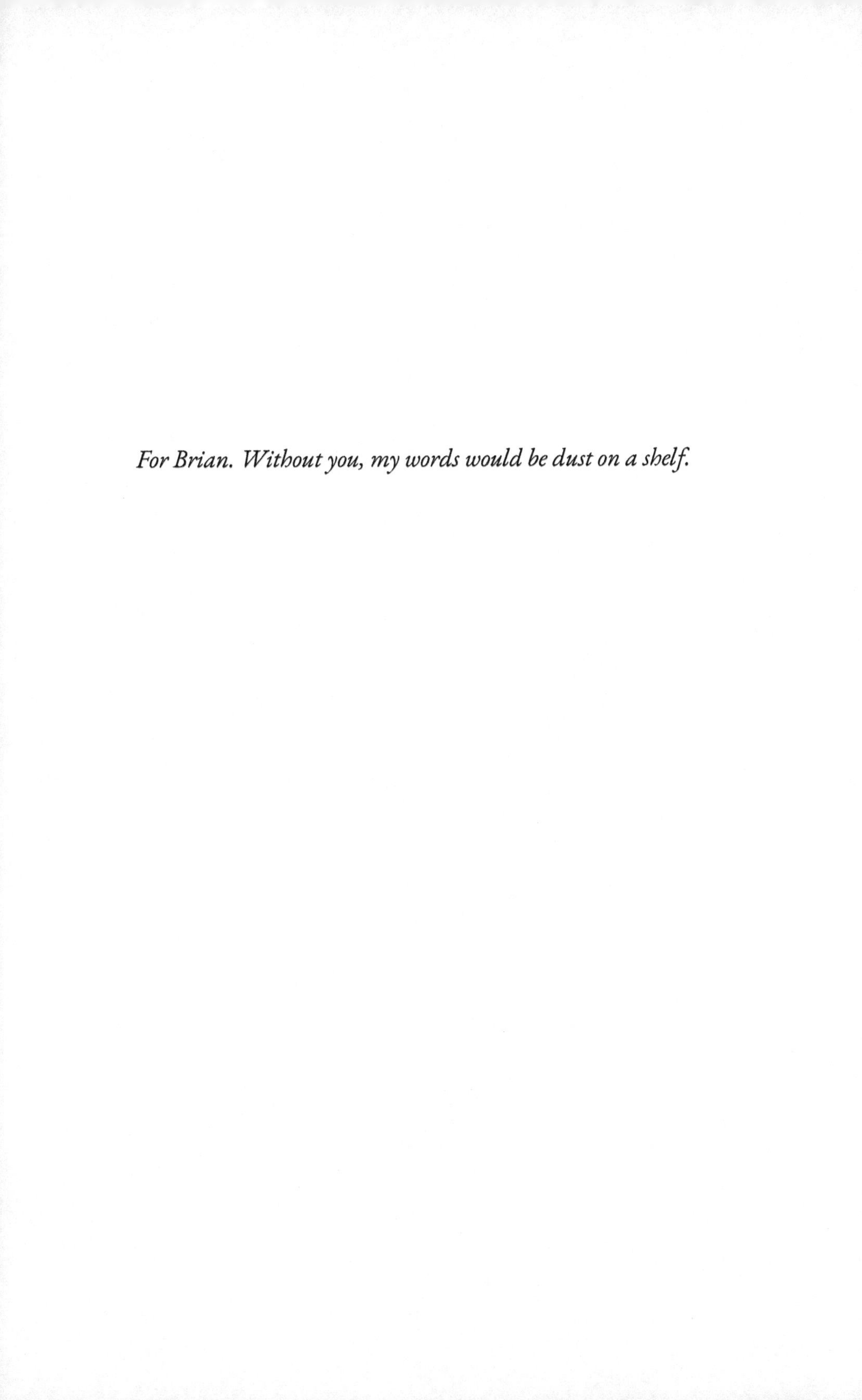

For Brian. Without you, my words would be dust on a shelf.

ONE

2019

OPAL

OUR FLIGHT LEAVES IN AN HOUR. ARE YOU FINISHED AT THE hospital yet?

I knew Fox wouldn't like the answer to his text, so I tucked the phone back into my pocket without a reply. He'd said I needed to get away from this place or it would consume me. I had been swirling in a vortex, fracturing into microparticles of myself for so long, I no longer realized I was sinking. Like debris in an oceanic garbage patch, I was floating through my life, indifferent to rescue or destruction. Fox wanted to be the one to pluck me out of the spiral. He wanted us to go north for a change of scenery. I had no interest in finding myself on the side of a mountain.

"My mother needs me," I'd protested.

"Your mother needs you to be well."

"The children need me."

"The children have your mother."

"The hospital can't function without me," I persisted.

"The hospital should get used to functioning without you," he replied. "Why is this job so important to you, anyway?"

"This job is me," I replied. "Who am I if I'm not the one saving these people?"

I could have been at the airport right now. Dr. Tom Rogers had offered to take the pager, but I didn't let him. I didn't want to be like Karen Chamberlain, the medical director—everyone hated Karen. Then Mr. Harris showed up with chest pain. I still wasn't worried. Chest-pain patients at Ocean Hospital were always quick to interview. Young, no medical history. They just needed reassurance. This one had to be fast—I had a husband and an airplane waiting for me.

Inside Ocean Hospital, the seasons never changed. If you peered out the small window in the doctor's charting room, you glimpsed the pounding rain, blazing sun, and every so often, palm trees whipping in the winds of a tropical storm. Inside, it was always seventy-two degrees with fluorescent sunshine and no chance of rain. The charting room was a sparsely furnished rectangle tucked behind the ICU. From the window, the view was mostly of a parking lot. The clock no longer kept time, and a tiny bonsai tree was the only decoration on the windowsill. In contrast, someone designed the common areas of Ocean Hospital to look like a hotel. They must have hired a designer, because someone thought to install linoleum floors that mimicked hardwood, like the floors at the high-end Walmart. Those floors had seen things: vomit, blood spatter, or worse. It all wiped away. With a little Lysol and a Starbucks next to the gift shop, *voilà*! Hotel Ocean Hospital. Framed artwork of sailboats, beaches, sunsets, and palm trees lined the walls in the corridors between wards. Isabelle Aberdeen herself had designed the entire remodel when Ronald Aberdeen took over the company.

I met Mr. Harris in a private patient room. Decorative cabinets concealed oxygen and suction lines around the bed, and a fifty-four-inch television hung on the opposite wall. Mr. Harris was a handsome forty-something man with the most reassuring, non-cardiac chest pain. He was a talker. I kept track, and I was pretty sure he hadn't come up for air in the last twenty minutes.

I listened intently to his description of the jalapeño cheese sauce that rarely caused this type of heartburn. The longer he talked, the more I became distracted by some sort of rock in my shoe. How did it get there, and would I get it out soon? I needed that rock out of my shoe before I could dash to catch a plane. I glanced at the clock and then over at him lying in his hospital bed. He was describing the new cycling group he had joined. I tried to judge how he would react if I took my shoe off and shook it out while he finished his story.

"You can go ahead and order a CAT scan of my belly while I'm here," he was saying. "And my primary care doctor wanted me to have some blood work. I'll just have you get that too. You can call him and figure out which labs he wanted—"

The rock must have been sharp. I think it was actually piercing the skin on the bottom of my foot. I imagined the tiny prick of blood staining the sole of my shoe. Not wanting to ruin my twenty-dollar pair of flats, I bent over, still locking eyes with my man, and whisked the shoe from my foot. The pungent scent of a ten-hour day in twenty-dollar flats reminded me why I should generally try to keep my shoes on while in patients' rooms.

"Sir," I interrupted. "you're here with chest pain. We may not need to scan your belly right now." I admonished him gently; the patients didn't like it when we were mean. Being mean put us at risk of getting a low patient satisfaction score. He had gotten out of bed and was changing into a hospital gown. Next, he unpacked toiletries from a bag he had brought with him and lined them up on a small table next to his bed.

"No, Doctor," the man persisted. "Wait, you are the doctor, right?" He squinted at me as I held my shoe. Balancing on one foot, I lifted my unkempt toes above the floor. "Who are you, again?"

"Opal Collins," I replied.

Who was I? If he had asked that question before this crazy life, I would have answered that I had come from the Earth itself. Native blood coursed through my veins. I came into the world with strong, angular features that contradicted my delicate constitution. My mother named me Opal in honor of the precious mineral, expecting I would shine. But just as the opalescent gem is built upon the Earth's natural faults, I would carve my path through a series of failures to reach this venerable state in a designer hospital room.

"Anyway," Mr. Harris continued, "I'm going to need you to order that CAT scan. Also, my sleeping pill. And I'll need a refill prescription for the sleeping pills when I leave tomorrow, Dr., uh—"

"Collins," I supplied. "Look, Mr. Harris, you came in with chest pain, but you want a CAT scan of your belly and a prescription for sleeping pills?" I slipped the shoe back on my foot.

"Well, you're the doctor. I just thought everything was about patient satisfaction scores now." Getting into bed again, he took a deep breath and launched back into his story. Just then, the loudspeaker crackled on at the same time as my pager began a frantic *beep! beep! beep! beep!* The operator's voice bellowed overhead, "Code blue, 5A2. Code blue, 5A2."

I cut off my man. "Mr. Harris," I said, pointing at the voice coming from the ceiling. "That's me. Grab a magazine or something because I won't be back for a while."

Two
Opal

Glad to have gotten the rock out of my shoe, I hurried to 5A2, pushing away the thought of our plane taxiing down the runway without me and Fox. I reached the patient room where a crowd had gathered. Betty Smith, eighty-nine years old, had lost her pulse, and my job was to get it back.

If the code blue failed, Betty would die, and I could make my flight. If the code blue was a success, Betty would live, and I would fix her instead of fixing my life.

A flower vase too near the edge of Betty's side table crashed to the floor amid the commotion, bringing my attention back to the woman trying to die in front of me. All thoughts of Mr. Harris and the rock in my shoe vanished. Fox vanished. My children vanished. My mind melted into a state of flow. *Preserve life. Do it, Doctor.*

"Give another epi," I called out to a packed room. A nurse drew up epinephrine from miniature glass vials into a syringe and injected the spidery-thin veins of the old woman. Meanwhile, a man in black scrubs towering over the bed pumped it through her mostly dead body, delivering the rhythmic chest compressions with bone-snapping force.

No fewer than fifteen people crowded the room. I stood in the back, observing with arms folded over my chest. Betty's room was a mess now, with wrappers from IV lines, wadded-up gauze, sheets bloodied by the IVs, and latex gloves scattered underfoot; a battlefield abandoned after the war. The cacophony spilled into the otherwise quiet hallway.

My long white lab coat, with "Opal Collins, MD" embroidered over the left breast, was too big. The hospital had supplied it, with its Doctors Inc. logo. The coat was wearing me. My short legs, appearing shorter with my sensible flat shoes, poked out from the bottom of the jacket. Wisps of hair escaped the ponytail I had fastened more than twelve hours ago, and flyaways fell at will around my face. How did I get this way—cheap shoes, split ends, and clothes that didn't fit? I was just tired. So much of myself had been stripped off and given away, I lacked the energy to have my shit together.

"Check for a pulse," I instructed. As Black Scrubs stepped back, breathing hard from the effort of chest compressions, the others stepped in and pawed at the carotid, the femoral, and the radial arteries, trying to feel the thready beat against their fingers.

My cell phone vibrated in my pocket. It was a text message from Fox.

> Did you leave yet?

> Code blue.

"Dr. Collins!" Black Scrubs snapped. "I'm trying to tell you we have a pulse. Are you done looking at your phone?"

"Yes," I said. "Get me an EKG."

The body in the bed was old to start with. Betty wore her eighty-nine years on a wrinkled face. Her leathery skin stretched over knobby, arthritic joints. Now splayed nude upon the bed, unresponsive, she was a bag of bones, a ship with no captain. It was sad. This didn't seem like a nice way to go. I surveyed the room. Betty's chest continued to rise and fall as they squeezed air into the tube in her throat, but her eyes were dead. Her thin arm slipped off the bed and dangled lifeless in the air. I followed the wires from two defibrillator pads pasted on her bare chest up to the monitor perched on top of the red cart.

A finger tapped my shoulder. I turned to find a nurse from another ward. "Patient Harris would like an update," she whispered. In front of me, Betty's heart had stopped again. I held up a hand to silence the nurse. Was I going to let it go on like this? Every little chime from my phone, every patient request that felt so urgent—they were all distractions. It was like this all the time, getting pulled this way and that. My life was an attempt at sipping water from a fire hydrant. But it wasn't only hurting me; it was hurting Betty Smith right now. No, I was not going to let it go on like this.

"Resume chest compressions," I barked, and Black Scrubs began again. This went on until the bedside monitor showed regular spikes of electricity generated by Betty's own heart. The code blue finished, I thanked my team as they prepared Betty for her short ride to the ICU. They released the brake on the bed and rolled Betty with a heave out the door and into the hallway.

I made my way back to Mr. Harris's room to finish discussing his chest pain. I had no more patience to spare him, but I wanted to stop in and say goodbye. Tom met me in the hallway and gave me a long sideways glance that said, *I told you so,* as he held out his hand for the pager.

"What took you so long?" Mr. Harris asked, hanging up his phone.

I sighed and switched to my nicest voice. "There was an emergency. I'm sorry that happened, Mr. Harris. You can finish telling me about your chest pain now."

"I've been here for over two hours, and I haven't seen a cardiologist yet." He sounded annoyed. He reached over to his nightstand, picked up his wallet, and began looking for something inside.

"Well, that's a good thing," I promised. "Only very sick patients need to consult with the cardiologist right away."

"Well, I'm a very important patient," he replied. "And I expect to see the cardiologist, have my stress test, and go home."

I smiled. "Mr. Harris, all my patients are very important. Dr. Kumar will be available for you tomorrow." I took the card and inspected it.

Rodney Harris DOB 04/23/1977
VERY IMPORTANT PATIENT
Dr. Benjamin Dunsworth cell 904-800-1234
Always on call 24/7/365

I laughed out loud and put a hand over my mouth in a failed attempt to hide my grin. He had an actual VIP card. Betty Smith had a cardiac arrest, and this guy had a VIP card. I handed the card back across the bed.

My phone rang before I could decide whether to respond in my nice voice. It was Fox. I held onto the VIP card and answered the phone, motioning to Mr. Harris to wait a moment. I stepped out of the room and into the hallway.

"We missed our flight," Fox said.

"Sorry, babe." I kept talking to Fox while I started a text message to the number on the VIP card.

> Hey Doc, I have your Very Important Patient, Rodney Harris, here at Ocean Hospital.

"I thought you were leaving before five," Fox said.

> Oh, no! What happened to Rodney?

"I guess that was a little too ambitious," I said to Fox.

> He wants to see a cardiologist right now for his chest pain.

> LOL

"I guess we're not going to get to be those people running like maniacs through the airport," Fox huffed.

"Okay, I gotta go," I said, hanging up with Fox. I went back in with Mr. Harris, who was out of bed, pacing the room.

"Dr. Dunsworth is looking for a cardiologist to see you now," I announced.

"Finally," Mr. Harris said, sitting back on the bed. Finally, indeed. I finally couldn't wait to take the trip to the Poconos I had been avoiding.

"Here's your call bell," I said, handing him the cord with the red button. "Make sure you call if you need anything at all."

THREE
OPAL

Wine. Dine. Make love in a fancy resort. Repeat. Those were the boxes I needed to check to be the wife Fox was searching for. As Fox and I stood in the hotel lobby, I decided I would enjoy these things too. I even deserved them. But I failed to see our vacation in the Poconos as a remedy for a marriage that had shifted from being anchored by love to treading water. Connection was what we needed, and that was what I was after. *Stop checking boxes*, I told myself. Connect with him.

Moss Creek Resort was a monolith at the end of a trail that winded up the mountain and through the forest. Its three-story pillars presented a glamorous portico that promised anything but the rustic experience it advertised. I spotted three or four deer in the woods along the way. Then I noticed the tags in their ears. These were resort deer. I could picture them being poached from the neighboring woods by a man in a Moss Creek polo and sent here to live. The deer would believe their purpose was to inspire the humans to connect with nature when, in reality, the man in the polo only wanted the deer to remind the hotel guests to buy a deer magnet in the gift shop.

Emily had the same doe eyes as the fawn. She was all cuddles and soft blankets. Cal was sharp angles and surprising intelligence. I knew I should get home to them before my absence left an opening for my mother to mold them into something immutably ordinary.

Stop checking boxes, I told myself again. *Connect with him.*

Fox leaned over the reception desk to plead his case for a refund. We lost a night when Betty Smith tried to die. I stood a foot behind, gripping my suitcase handle, rocking back and forth on my heels.

"She's a doctor," Fox was explaining as he pointed in my direction. "She had to save some people."

"That's so great," the manager replied with feigned enthusiasm. "But you booked a package, Dr. Collins, and there is no way to refund a portion of that."

"But, sir—" Fox argued, his voice beginning to rise.

The manager cut him off. "But, sir," he repeated, pressing his hands to the desk. "What I can do is offer your wife a day in our spa." Fox shifted his attention to me. My eyes grew large. I was supposed to take Fox upstairs, perform my duties as a wife, possibly fake an orgasm, and convince him I had my shit together. Getting distracted by a spa day wasn't going to help anything.

"Mountain-water soaking tub, Poconos Pine massage, Fresh Air facial," the manager continued. "It's worth far more than the night you missed."

"That should be fine," Fox relented. He took the gift card and handed it to me. "Go enjoy the spa, honey. I'll get the room ready."

I smoothed my eyebrows before snatching the card from his hand. I scanned the atrium, looking for a place to hide and call the kids instead of going to the spa. Fox mistook my wandering eyes for a geographical deficiency.

"Why don't I bring you there myself?" Fox suggested. He walked with me to the ground floor and checked me in at the spa's reception desk.

Tucked deep within the spa, an employee in a black Moss Creek polo handed me a cool cloth dangling from a pair of little metal tongs. Wondering how long I needed to stay in the sauna to balance my box-checking with Fox's desire to recuperate the lost money, I deposited my clothes in a locker and wrapped myself in a fluffy white towel. I stepped into the sauna, breathing in the dry air. Ten minutes, I decided. I would stay for ten minutes. Sweat pricked under my arms and rolled down my neck. The cedar-planked room was empty except for a woman reclining on the bench with her eyes closed. I settled myself at her feet and pressed myself against the wall.

The woman had a towel wrapped around her waist, and her long, tanned legs were heading straight toward me. There were no traces of sunless tanning lotion around her knees or ankles. I ran my hands over my own legs, taking stock of the constant prick of stubble being pushed out by goosebumps. She had none of that. The woman's chest was bare, and she didn't stir as I gaped at her perfect breasts, each with a wide metal piercing through the nipple.

My eyes snapped to the wall as the woman pushed herself up. Her shadow was thrown onto the wall by a heat lamp hanging above us. The shadow was tall, muscular, and confident. Behind her shadow trailed my smaller, more self-conscious shadow. My eyebrows puffed out of the shadow's forehead and mocked my confidence. The shadow's breasts refused to be perky like those of the woman. They betrayed me with their confirmation that I had old, sagging, flat-nippled breasts.

"Fantasia Maize," she said, offering me her hand. My eyes traced a sleeve of tattoos up her arm. I took her hand and introduced myself. "Are you new here?" she asked. "I haven't seen you around."

"My husband thinks I need a break from my crazy job," I replied, piling my hair into a sweaty bun at the top of my head.

Fantasia laughed. "It's too bad you missed my Ted Talk."

"You're one of the resort speakers?" I asked, my jaw dropping ever so slightly in awe.

"That's how I get all the spa time I want," she replied conspiratorially. "The talk is called 'Why You Shouldn't Have Your Cake and Eat It Too.'"

I wiped my neck with my cool cloth, keeping my towel safely tucked over my body. Curiosity replaced my eagerness to leave. *I must stay*, I told myself. *I must learn why I shouldn't have my cake and eat it too.*

Fantasia wore her platinum-blond hair shaved close to her head on one side, and on the other, white waves cemented themselves to her scalp. The diamond stud in her nostril twinkled in the low light. She had a magnetic pull, as if I had never had a friend in my life and I was discovering friendship for the first time. Fox could wait. I was on to something here.

We were interrupted by a Moss Creek staff member barging into the sauna. I covered my chest with my hands, despite already being covered with the towel. "Folks, we need all hotel guests to exit the sauna and make their way to the campfire on Mountain B," she announced.

Fantasia rose from the bench, covering herself.

"In a minute," I responded. "I'm busy trying to fix my life." I was supposed to have it all figured out by now—how to give myself back to Fox while continuing to feed a cord of my soul like firewood to the ever-more-consuming corporate furnace.

"Sorry, ma'am. Safety protocol. There is a fifteen-minute max in the sauna."

The woman in the black polo switched off the sauna, so I gathered my towel and set off after Fantasia. Relieved, I found her in the locker room stepping into an ironed pantsuit. I pulled my T-shirt and University of Florida sweatpants from my locker.

"My whole life is trying to have my cake and eat it too," I confessed.

Fantasia turned to me, studying my face. Her eyes flicked to my sweatpants. "What's stopping you from finding something better?" she asked.

A text chimed from the locker. Fox.

> Finished at the spa yet? Our room is ready.

"Mostly Karen," I said. "No one likes her."

"Do you want to get facials?" Fantasia asked. "I've got to hear more about Karen."

I swiped Fox's text out of view. "Yes," I said, eager to soak in more of her presence.

"Follow me," Fantasia whispered. We stripped out of the clothes we had just put on and cinched heavy waffled robes around our waists. My phone chimed again.

It was Karen.

I'm going to have you write a discharge summary for Betty Smith.

"Hold on, Fantasia," I said, frowning at my phone. Karen was writing something else.

She died.

"It's Karen," I explained, tapping a reply.

That's so sad. But I'm in the Poconos.

Have it done by close of business.

But she was your patient for weeks. I saw her once in cross cover when she coded. You do her discharge summary.

I'm sure the resort has a business center.

Then Fox messaged again.

Hello?

Tired of waiting, Fantasia rifled through a bag until she found a business card, which she handed to me. The light reflected off the glossy surface of the card and I worked out the hot pink lettering.

Dr. Fantasia Maize, University of Pennsylvania, Department of Psychology.

"Let's not be strangers," she said, pointing to the number on the card. She turned to go. I abandoned my locker and followed behind Fantasia, sending Fox a hasty text in reply.

> Fuck. Fuck. Fuck. Karen wants me to do her discharge summary.

"Can I see you tonight?" I called after Fantasia, my eyes on my phone.

"I have a gig at the Blue Moon tonight," she replied.

I had seen the Blue Moon when we drove in. "The strip club?" I asked, eyeing her pantsuit dubiously.

"I'm also an exotic dancer," she explained. "Therapy and stripping are not mutually exclusive."

I raised my eyebrows. Okay. Fantasia, the Ivy League stripper/therapist. Before I could further contemplate the brilliance of her career choice, a series of messages from Karen began bombing my phone.

> I think you meant to send this to Fox!

> So, I'm deleting it!

> Look before you hit send next time!

I looked at the *Fuck. Fuck. Fuck.* text I'd sent to Karen and not Fox and chewed my lip.

"Can I come to the Blue Moon?" I asked Fantasia, thinking about drinking in her carefully crafted body and life advice.

Fantasia laughed. "Dancing brings me joy. You find something that brings you joy."

"Maybe exotic dancers bring me joy," I said.

Fantasia clasped my arm. "Okay, come see me at the Blue Moon," she said. "But, Opal, you need to find something that's just for you—and keep it all for yourself."

Four

Opal

We made it to the Blue Moon Gentleman's Club later that night. Behind the woman collecting cover charges stood a man in a suit who could have been her father. The only light came from a blinking neon sign, fluorescent green and obscured by a hazy curl of smoke. I craned my neck to see around the bouncer, hoping to find Fantasia. I only found loud music and a dark room.

Fox handed a hundred-dollar bill to the woman. He found it curious that I insisted on spending the evening in a strip club. He didn't know Fantasia. I knew that if I didn't see her again, she would vanish from my life like an apparition returning to the netherworld. I was a moth, drawn to her light by a force outside myself. Everyone and everything else who had their hand out for my attention was going to wait. If this trip was about finding myself—there I was. I would follow her without question into this den of masculinity with questionable stains on curtains that smelled something like tuna. She was that irresistible. When I was with Fantasia, I didn't feel pressured to change my life. I felt inspired to change it.

The thought of going to the Blue Moon excited Fox. We were both eager to bend the rules after I lost my afternoon crafting Karen's discharge summary. But the idea of going to a strip club was so exciting to him, it resulted in a sudden urge to have passionate sex. Hotel sex. Adding-to-the-collection-of-spots-visible-under-a-black-light sex. I liked hotel sex too, but I worried I would miss the chance to introduce Fantasia to him before her set.

"Is Fantasia here?" I asked the woman.

She adjusted the spaghetti strap on her black camisole. "She's on at ten," she replied. "Her husband, Billy, is over there." She pointed to a man whose shirt was unbuttoned too far, revealing a rattlesnake tattoo trying to escape from his chest.

"Who is Fantasia?" Fox asked.

"She's my stripper therapist friend." I beamed. "We met at the spa."

"Opal, we need to talk," Fox said, leaning in and raising his voice above the noise.

"Cool," I replied, taking his hand and thinking only of finding Fantasia.

I caught Billy's attention and waved. We made introductions and he led us to a table already set with rum-and-Cokes. On the nearby stage, a woman with honey-colored skin named Ruby wore a red thong and spun around the pole.

"I want us to grow our family," Fox said into my ear as he pulled out my chair.

I looked at him like he was crazy and made no reply. Was that how he thought a woman struggling to reunite with her lost identity found herself? Fox was a good man, but he was no woman. "How does she balance in those heels?" I asked Billy instead, pointing to Ruby's acrylic platforms.

"The secret is strong ankles," Billy replied over the music. He patted his pocket and pulled out a joint. "I'm glad you guys came," he said, lighting the end of the rolled marijuana and offering us a hit. Fox shook his head as the acrid scent of burning cannabis hit us.

On a whim, I grabbed the joint from between Billy's lips and took in a deep pull of grassy smoke. The smoke seared my throat but I held it anyway. I slowly exhaled a plume toward the ceiling and reached for my drink. Fox coughed as the smoke found his lungs. He turned his head away from the stage, trying to stifle the racking paroxysm.

"I'll step outside to finish this," Billy said, getting up from the table.

As soon as Billy was gone, I narrowed my eyes at Fox. This wasn't fair. The Blue Moon was for me. Fantasia was sitting backstage somewhere, my opportunity to see her slipping away. Buzzing from the joint, I laid in. "Grow our family? Now?"

"No pressure," Fox said, holding up his hands. "You could stop taking your pills, and we could just see what happens." He traced his fingertips up and down my arm. The sexuality of his touch made me uncomfortable, and I twisted my arm away from his fingers.

"Are you kidding, Fox?" I asked. "I wouldn't even bring a dog into my life right now, let alone another child. My life is crazy enough." I whispered the words but knew they fell like a knife. I turned to see how deep they had cut. Somewhere on stage, a thong went flying.

"Not so fast, pretty lady," Fox protested. "You've been avoiding this conversation for too long. It's happening. Just words, Opal. Words can't hurt us. Talk to me."

"No, Fox. Hard no."

He sharpened his tone before flinging words back at me. "Three, Opal. We always wanted three. Climb the ladder, show up at home for once, and slow the fuck down."

"Climb the ladder?" I asked. "What does that mean?"

"Opal, we talked about this the day you got hired. You were afraid the corporate atmosphere would exploit you." He raised his eyebrows. I nodded. "And I said, 'Go for it, Opal. Spend a few years working on the floor before moving up to administration. Take over as medical director.'"

I laughed at Fox as Fantasia took the stage, dancing her way to the pole. She was dancing to an Aerosmith song, garnering cheers from the small crowd. She commanded the room with her asymmetric haircut and her confidence as she spun and delivered the show we had been waiting for. I longed to be like the rest of the customers, with nothing to do but watch the show.

"Do you remember when we were in medical school, and we had that rotation in the homeless shelter?" I asked. I would convince him there were other ways to slow down. He nodded. "There were no productivity markers or patient satisfaction scores. It was perfect."

It was Fox's turn to laugh. "Come on, Opal. We're adults now."

I turned away from him and focused on memorizing every inch of Fantasia's body. "I'm not slowing down. I'm not quitting my birth control, and we are not having another child."

Our server approached cautiously and leaned over our table, her cleavage spilling between us. I downed the rest of my drink, and she collected the empty glasses. I let the alcohol and cannabis melt my thoughts as Fantasia stripped down to her black lingerie. When the server was gone, Fox continued.

"Is giving your life to Ocean Hospital worth losing your family?"

"I'm afraid," I admitted. "I'm afraid that if I peel off any more of myself for you or a child or Ocean Hospital, there won't be anything left."

"Opal, you're going to find yourself," he promised, squeezing my hand. Fantasia's song ended, and the room fell silent. Fox continued gazing into his drink until the next song started. My eyes flitted to Fantasia's thong as it sailed through the air.

"I need things to change," he whispered. "I can't take any more late nights or missed flights."

"What are you saying?" I asked.

"I thought our family would resemble the family I was raised in. But I haven't seen the Opal I married in a very long time."

"I love your family," I argued. "We are like your family."

"My dad has a job for me in New Haven." Fox pushed out his chair and stood up. "I'm canceling my return flight."

I jumped from my seat, rum and Coke rolling in my gut. Wanting to be worthy of something better, I called after him. "I do want to be the medical director, Fox." He turned. "But I don't think I'm good enough."

Fox waited for me to continue. His shoulders slumped. His eyes were holding back tears. His face had given up trying to smile. He wasn't a bad guy. He looked so sad.

"I'm not good enough, but I'll try," I said. "I'll try to be medical director, and I'll try to grow our family." I steadied myself with a hand on the table. What he wanted made sense, right? He wanted to nurture our marriage and my career at the same time. I loved him enough to do it, right?

Fox inched back, shoulders slumped, and took my hand. "Three months," he said finally. "We'll spend the next three months trying to get pregnant while you figure out how you're going to get that job."

I let out a breath, nodding to myself. "What if I can't do it?" I asked.

Billy returned to the table. He slid into his chair and pointed at the stage. "Fantasia's up," he announced with a grin.

"You missed most of it," I replied. Fox looked away, wiping his eyes with the back of his hand.

"It's okay. I know how it ends," Billy replied.

I leaned over the table and kissed Fox on the cheek, plucking a twenty-dollar bill from his wallet in the same motion. Signaling the end of the worst talk we ever had, I turned my attention to Fantasia. She was the real Fantasia, all oiled muscle and shimmer lotion with a scent like warm vanilla. Fantasia was like a brightly colored doll dropped in the Pocono Forest by a child whose mother had taken hold of their hand and led them home after an afternoon picnic. But unlike a discarded doll, Fantasia was a piece of art. Fantasia was bold. I was understated; Fantasia was comfortable in her own skin. I wondered what lay beneath my skin.

This was who I wanted to be. Beautiful, confident, commanding. She winked at me as she slid into a split so I could reach her garter belt and tuck in the money.

FIVE
RONALD

WAS IT THE INCESSANT THROBBING IN HIS HEAD OR THE alarm clock that woke him? Ronald brought a hand to his temple, where his fingertips found the bounding vein of another headache. The air outside the blanket was crisp, and he drew in a frigid, air-conditioned breath. He rolled onto his side, propping himself on an elbow as he scanned the bedside table for his pill. Pill, water glass, phone, lamp. He found the small pill and put it on his tongue. He raised the water to his lips. The pill slid down his throat and was gone. Soon, he would feel the headache melt away, and by the second cup of coffee, it would be gone.

Without looking, he knew a woman lay beside him, eyes covered by a black mask, lips parted. For forty-four years, they'd awakened together in the same bed. He picked up his smartphone and lay back on the pillow. The screen was too bright for his current state of headache, so he abandoned the phone and switched on the television.

CNN ran through the news of the day, and Ronald's eye landed on a congressman standing at a podium. The banner identified him as Allen Collins, a Democrat from New York. Ronald sat up, rubbing his eyes and inspecting the screen. Allen Collins was the head of the Science and Research Committee. Ronald's gut twisted as he thought of his own science and research abandoned by force in New York.

He pulled back the cover and swung his legs out of bed. According to Isabelle, the bathroom lighting was supposed to mimic natural light, but when he threw on the switch, the light was cruel to the pain behind his eyes. His reflection was of an aging man blinking in the mirror. His hair was still black, his jaw still strong, but the skin on his neck and chest was beginning to sag; coarse black hairs poked from his nostrils, and a new skin tag was forming in his armpit.

Ronald ran the water hot until steam warmed his face as he shaved off yesterday's stubble. Allen Collins was familiar. Had they met?

Isabelle's reflection appeared in the mirror as a stream of black flecks wound down the drain. "We have the thing with Jamie tonight," she said.

"Is she hair or makeup, honey? I can't remember."

"He's the stylist, dear."

"You have a stylist?"

"We have a stylist," she said with a laugh. He could see the corners of her lips turning up in a smile. "Remember, Ron? You agreed it would be good for your image."

"I don't think people have stylists here in the South, honey," he countered.

She squeezed his shoulder, then whispered in his ear. "True. That's why I flew him in from New York."

"Can we cancel?" Ronald called as she climbed back into bed.

"He's styling you for the press conference," she replied, pushing the mask over her eyes.

His heart leaped like a startled rabbit at the word "press." "Do we have to do the press conference?" he asked. "I'd rather be at a bench doing research."

"But you're so good with the press and so boring doing research," Isabelle chided as she lay back in bed. She said it casually, but Ronald knew—oh, how he knew—how fiercely Isabelle clung to his corporate rise and loathed his academic ambitions. Her answer was unequivocally no. But Ronald knew the trouble he tended to have with the press. He would find a way to avoid them and return triumphantly to New York, where he was sure the cure for cancer was within his grasp.

Ronald snapped his fingers. He realized why Allen Collins was familiar. He looked like Fox Collins, the husband of one of his doctors. Opal, was it? Allen Collins was Opal's brother-in-law. How serendipitous. As Ronald drove to the corporate office through the back streets, he tapped a button on the steering wheel to call his good friend, Karen. Her chipper voice greeted him through the car's speakers.

"Karen, we should discuss the doctors impacted by the situation," he said.

"Oh, I have a few ideas."

"What can you tell me about one of your docs—Opal Collins?"

"Collins?" she replied. "She's a disaster. Why do you ask?"

"I need to keep her."

"Hmm," Karen considered aloud. "Did she file a complaint about me?"

"No idea. What do you mean, 'disaster'?"

Karen sighed. "She never pulls her weight. Her numbers are always twenty percent below her peers. She's constantly nagging me to help her finish her work."

"How are her patient satisfaction scores?"

"Well, she always scores well on those," Karen admitted.

"Do we need to cut her with the others?" Ronald asked. Karen chuckled. Ronald continued. "How would her peers answer that?"

"Her peers? Her peers love her," Karen said. "The nurses too. And her patients. She spends way too much goddamned time talking to her patients."

"Why do her peers love her if they're always picking up her slack?"

"Because she always takes the problem patients. She likes to take care of homeless people and alcoholics and drug addicts," she explained with a note of disgust. "Don't ask me why." The line was quiet for a moment while Ronald waited for traffic to clear. "Can we cut her?" she asked.

"No!"

"Seriously, Ronald," Karen argued. "Let me do it. Let me fire Opal Collins."

Opal's connection to Allen Collins felt too important now. He couldn't have Karen firing his ticket out of the corporate monster he had built. "I'll get her out of your hair, Karen. Give me a few days."

"Bye-bye, Opal," Ronald heard her say under her breath.

Six
Opal

With a gentle tap, I pushed open the door to Gloria Halloway's hospital room. She was a favorite, and I was both dismayed that she had returned and comforted to know I would see her. They say the first thing you should do in the morning is "eat your frog." That is, accomplish your most revolting task early in the day in order to enjoy the remainder of the day. But whoever was eating frogs didn't know Ronald Aberdeen. He was the king of frogs. I would speak to him, but before I crossed his path and suggested a reordering of administration, I needed Gloria to imbue me with positive energy.

As I stepped into Gloria's room, my phone rang. I stepped out and pressed my back to the wall. The din of the hospital ward continued around me as I answered the call from Fox.

"Cal's class party is today," Fox announced.

"Shit!" I cursed.

"I took care of the poster-board thing," he said. I heard the sounds of his hospital, Bonne Santé, dinging and chiming in the background.

"Did you draw stick people on the poster board again?" I asked.

"The character parade starts at five," he said instead of answering.

"Parade?" I asked, furrowing my brow.

"Emily and Cal have a costume parade," he intoned, as if explaining to a child. "The kids dress up, and the parents stand in the heat and take a lot of pictures."

"I will definitely be there," I promised.

"Just making sure," Fox said. We said, "I love you" and hung up.

With a hand to my brow, I did the math and recalibrated my time per patient at negative twelve minutes apiece. This sum resulted in a long sigh. I was swimming upstream in the river, paddling against a current that carried me farther and farther from the bank where my family waited impatiently. It was impossible for me to spend the day making small talk with Gloria, or even Dr. Aberdeen, for that matter. However, I possessed exceptional multitasking skills.

Another bout of bronchitis had led to Gloria's third admission in as many weeks. Gloria lay sleeping, her gentle snoring breath taking in the oxygen being delivered through the prongs in her nose. She was an old woman, frail in every way. Her weathered face was peaceful, and her spindly arms lay limp beside her barrel chest.

I approached her bed and gently shook her shoulder. "Gloria, it's Dr. Collins. Wake up."

Without opening her eyes, she sneered, "Well, I hope you brought cigarettes!" We broke into laughter. "Are you going to be my doctor this time?" she asked.

"I am. How are you doing this morning? Feeling better?"

"Thank God. I thought I was going to have Dr. Tang again," she said. She opened her eyes and looked me over.

"Oh, Gloria. Dr. Tang is good," I argued.

"Dr. Tang is always telling me to stop smoking." She snorted. Her voice sounded as if it were going to give up if she smoked one more cigarette. She sat up and took her phone from the bedside table, unaware of my scheduling dilemma, and started to show me the latest pictures of her grandchildren.

"Hush now, and let me listen to your lungs," I said. I sneaked my stethoscope onto her back while she had it turned to me. The familiar scent of tobacco emanated from her gown. Tight wheezes gripped her chest. Her breathing sounded terrible today. She pulled up the pictures. How could I not indulge her?

"And how are the Collins children?" Gloria wheezed.

"They're in a parade tonight," I replied.

"Well, what are you doing wasting your time talking to a corpse? Skedaddle! Go finish your doctoring and get to that parade!"

I laughed. "Fine. If you say so. I'll check on you tomorrow."

As I shut her door, turning toward my next patient's room, I collided with a tall man in a dark suit. Oh, fuck, I thought. Ronald fucking Aberdeen. "Afternoon, sir," I said, looking at my feet. Still investigating a piece of pleather peeling itself away from my shoe, I added, "I'm glad you're here. I want to speak with you."

"Dr. Collins," he began, grasping my shoulder. The warmth of his hand surprised me. "I need to speak with you too. Can we pop over to the office?"

I looked up and down the crowded hallway, satisfied that we were alone. "I'm swamped. Let's do it here."

"I've created a new position called the patient advocate liaison," he said, releasing me from his grip. "Or PAL, for short. I want you to test-drive it."

My face pinched, and I was quiet. Anything related to patient advocate made me itch. Why was he saying this? Was I being punished? "You call all the patients who've filed complaints," he explained. "And salvage the patient satisfaction score."

"I had something else in mind—" I said, but I stopped short when I spotted Karen Chamberlain's teased-out hair bubble making its way to us from the elevator.

"The PAL position is remote," Dr. Aberdeen continued. "You will be working from home. Good for someone who's 'swamped.'" He stopped as Karen approached and nodded a greeting.

"Hello, Ronald and Opal," Karen gushed.

I regarded her with suspicion. Sure enough, she pulled the Doctors Inc. pager from her belt and held it out to me. "I need you to take the pager so I can go to the mall for a little shopping."

"I'd love to," I replied, turning to Dr. Aberdeen for support, "but my kids are in a parade."

"Oh, I see," she patronized as she jiggled the pager. "Well, those things happen." We fell silent for a beat, the pager suspended between us.

"I need to be getting to my meeting," Dr. Aberdeen announced. "What did you want to tell me, Opal?"

That I would make a better Karen, I thought. That Ocean Hospital would be better off without her. I swiped the pager from Karen's outstretched hand. "Nothing," I replied. "It was nothing."

"Okay," he replied, already walking away with Karen by his side. "You can tell me about nothing Wednesday at four. Corporate office."

I looked at the little door prize in my hand. The pager. Before I could flush it down a toilet or test its resilience to the microwave, Gloria came to the threshold of her room, breathing hard. "That's some bullshit," she wheezed.

"Gloria, get back in bed," I complained. "Your lips are blue!"

"That PAL job sounds like a shit job kissing shit brick's asses," she continued. I smirked at the quip coming from her cyanotic lips, validating my repulsion at the suggestion. What would Fox say? Would he be so repulsed by an offer that would bring me home and slow me down? Fox didn't have to know. Some secrets were for the best.

The pager trilled, and instead of throwing it against the wall, I said goodbye to Gloria and found a phone. "Hello?" came the voice of a woman.

"Doctors Inc.," I replied.

"Doctor, this is the Risk Management department," explained the woman in a heavy Southern drawl. "We need you to come down here. There has been a complaint."

My stomach dropped out of obligation after hearing the phrase "risk management." I contemplated the idea of throwing the phone and the pager at the wall, but I caught a familiar tone in the caller's voice. "Nassrin?"

"Opal?" came Dr. Nassrin Fahadi's normal voice. "I thought Karen had the pager! I was trying to prank her."

"Karen is shopping," I explained. "Now I'm holding the pager instead of going to see my kids' parade."

Nassrin hung up and appeared from around the corner, her long black skirt swishing around her ankles as she approached. With an outstretched hand, she said, "Give me the pager. You get to your kids' thing."

"What? No, stop, Nassrin," I demurred.

"Seriously, Opal," she insisted. "Tallahassee canceled our dinner date."

"What? Why? Is he going to that boxing gym again?" I asked.

"Huh? No, no—he said he has the flu."

"And do you believe this?" I asked.

"Opal!" She laughed. "Pager." She jabbed her open palm at me. Handing over the pager would mean my colleagues were picking up my slack again. It would make me more like Karen than different. My children would say it was for the best. When I handed her the pager, she leaned in close to whisper. "I have the drugs you asked for. Want me to shoot you up quick?"

Fox's suggestion that we get pregnant had sent me into a panic. It felt like a downward spiral from autonomy. I'd called Nassrin while I was still in the Poconos and asked her to procure a depot injection of birth control that would buy me months of blissfully failed fertility attempts. I wavered now. The irreversibility of the injection felt like another path in the downward spiral of control over my body and my life.

"No," I replied under my breath. There was another way. Surely, a smaller secret was for the best. "I'm sticking with the pills."

SEVEN
OPAL

THE CROWD OF PARENTS CLUSTERED AT COCONUT GROVE Elementary was thick and restless as I approached. The parade must have already been underway, their excitement was so high. Fox, with his crop of copper hair and surgical scrubs, was easy to find among the parents. I trotted up to the throng of people and inched through until I was beside my husband, slipping my hand into his. I settled into appearing to be a perfect mother. My job was to stand here and be present. The humidity left over from midday still clung to the air. I shifted on my heels. Fox squeezed my hand.

"You made it," he said. "Strong work, Momma." He slipped his hand from mine and put his arm around me, kissing the top of my head.

"Did you think I would miss it?" I asked, poking him in the side.

Fox looked down at me, frowning. "Yeah, Opal. I thought you were going to miss it."

I cleared my throat and attempted a smile. He wasn't being mean; he was only letting me know he was struggling.

"You missed Cal," Fox said. "He's already gone through."

I winced, wiping at the sweat on my brow. "I'll still get to see Emily."

"She doesn't need that witch hat, right?" he asked.

"Yes, she does! Without the hat, she looks like a five-year-old misanthrope in goth!"

"What about the toy gun from Cal's police officer costume?" Fox asked. "I just assumed he would need that."

"Fox!" I cried. But when I saw he was laughing, I pretended to punch him.

Classes continued to file out of the school, all the little ghouls and goblins being led by their teachers. My mother, Tanya was a kindergarten teacher, and I spotted her first. She wore an astronaut costume and led a class of tiny kindergarten cuties dressed in wigs and face paint. She caught my eye and waved excitedly.

Emily came next, carrying a witch hat in one hand, dragging it along the sidewalk. When she spotted Fox and me, she tried to make a run for us but was stopped by the long arm of a teacher's assistant. She rejoined the class with a wide grin. "You made it, Mom!" she yelled. A whooping cheer rose from overly enthusiastic parents as the school principal, Wendy Windsor, closed out the parade. She marched down the sidewalk, dressed as a lumberjack in a red flannel shirt with rolled-up sleeves and overalls, waving a balloon ax at the crowd. Her flawless black skin had not betrayed her with an ounce of sweat. The pixie cut must have kept her cool.

As children were being returned to their parents, I found Cal holding the hand of another child's mother. "Mom, you missed it!" Cal said with pouting lips.

"Sorry, honey. I—"

"Jackson's mom came," he announced, turning to his friend. This lady couldn't outdo me. It wasn't fair.

"Because my mommy loves me," Jackson added. I glanced at Jackson's mother, expecting the worst. She held both boys by the hand. Just as I suspected, her Coconut Grove T-shirt was covered in rhinestones and knotted at the waist. Her jeans with high heels had PTO written all over them. She handed over Cal without a greeting.

I scooped up Cal and kissed his sweaty head. Damage control.

"Any movement on the medical director thing?" Fox asked.

"I meet with Aberdeen on Wednesday at four o'clock," I replied, winking at him as though I had done something right. Wrong again.

"You can't do Wednesday at four," Fox complained. "That's when the arborist is coming."

I cringed as I recalled the giant oak tree behind our house. For the last century, it had thrived unchallenged, and now I had absolutely no capacity for its demise. Fuzzy little patches had popped up on its trunk and the leaves were falling before their time. There were, as it turns out, doctors for trees, and it seemed I was expecting one on Wednesday. I couldn't waste this opportunity with Aberdeen though. Not unless I wanted Karen Chamberlain and Ocean Hospital to snuff out my marriage. "Fox, I can't. . . I can't do the tree."

Fox took Cal from my arms and swung him onto his shoulders. With all the leeway that comes with a decade of love, he smiled. "It's okay, Opal. It takes a village."

Before I could respond, my mother and sister Amber approached us, Emily skipping along between them.

"Fox, Opal," my mother said. "I have some news."

Amber stood beside her, doing a giddy clapping thing.

"What is it, Mom?" I asked.

"Wendy Windsor is promoting me to assistant principal," she said. She let go of Emily's hand, and Emily wrapped herself around my leg.

Trying to keep my knee from buckling under her weight, I said, "Mom, congratulations!"

"I know, I know," she said, shaking her head. "This means I can't watch the kids after school anymore, Opal. After winter break, you're on your own."

I swallowed hard against the news, a dark cloud coming over me. Across the sidewalk, I stared at her. The physical resemblance was striking. If I looked carved from the earth, she was the earth itself. Her dark eyes twinkled with delight in herself. I should have felt delighted too. But my hope for saving myself was dissolving.

My mother touched my arm. "Surely you can work your schedule around this, Opal. I can't be responsible for your children forever."

The way she said it. *I can't be responsible for your children forever.* As if she didn't trust me to raise my own children. She would never let go of the past. I would always be a disappointing child, cowering under her moral superiority. *Girls like you get people in a lot of trouble*, she had said to little Opal.

The quicksand of overwhelm caught me by the throat. The numbers didn't add up. Flashes of nannies crowding my kitchen, frowning at my jug of expired milk, tumbled into pictures of day cares crawling with children and germs. I looked from one adult to the next in our "village" and didn't bother to ask why I was the one who had to make it work.

"Is there a way you could work from home?" Amber offered.

I gave my sister the side-eye. She didn't realize Dr. Aberdeen had tried to push that very idea a few hours ago. She didn't understand the patient advocate and the shit bricks. Neither did Fox. They didn't have to. "I'll just fucking quit," I said under my breath. "That ought to make everyone happy."

"If you resign," Fox interrupted, hearing my tantrum through the noise of the crowd, "you'll never be able to come back to clinical work." I touched my fingers to my eyebrows and rubbed at the salty crust of dried sweat that had formed there. "Remember Rose Thomas?" Fox asked.

"Rose Thomas," I repeated, nodding. Rose was a gastroenterologist who traded endoscopes for baby wipes and had since been turned down by every hospital she'd applied to due to her "lapse in clinical skills."

Fox peeled Emily off my leg and swung her up to his other hip. The witch's hat fell to the ground. "There's no other option. You need to nail your meeting with Aberdeen," he whispered. "Whatever it takes to get medical director."

Eight
Opal

As we drove home from the parade, I thought back to the day I'd first interviewed with Doctors Inc. It was a long time ago now. "Remember the sweater?" I asked Fox.

"The blazer was more, uh, memorable." He chuckled.

After we got married, Fox and I had decided to stay in my hometown, Gilbert. Vacationers called it *Gill-bert*, but it was pronounced *Zheel-bare*. At any rate, my grandmother had passed down the farmhouse to me. When we moved in, working at Ocean Hospital became a foregone conclusion. Doctors Inc. was eager for me to start work, a fact that should have alarmed me—or at least given me pause.

When I called about the job, the woman from Human Resources asked, "Can you come this afternoon for an interview?" My mind was more on settling Grandma's estate than being thrust into an interview, plus I was driving.

"I. . . I. . . I don't even have a copy of my resumé right now," I replied, taken aback and pulling the car over.

"No problem. We can get all that later. Just come into our corporate office downtown and ask for Miranda."

Ocean Hospital was the newer of Gilbert's two hospitals, built on the west side of town. Before the massive influx of citizens, Gilbert was all farmlands. The other hospital, Bonne Santé, was older and in the center of town. Now, the area around the hospital had a bustling Main Street with skyscrapers rumored to have ocean views from the upper levels. The pastures in east Gilbert became sprawling masses of track homes. The pastures in the west became golf courses with palatial country clubs. West Gilbert was the jewel of the town because of its proximity to the Gulf of Mexico. Ocean Hospital was built to serve this area.

My empty stomach turned over with a loud groan as I drove. If I didn't get this job, we'd have to move the family to New Haven, where Fox could work for his father. Where we would be miles away from anything I had ever known. Fox and I had already discussed this. Interviewing at a moment's notice wasn't the plan, but I would make it work.

Dressed in a tired red sweater that had become the usual during the haze of raising toddlers, I stopped at the first clothing store I passed along the way. Like most of my wardrobe, I'd pulled the ugly sweater from the hamper that morning. Kids' snot and breakfast crumbs from the day before were brushed off when the garment passed the sniff test. The store was called Fifi's, and I wondered if Fifi was going to have something suitable for a momentous career shift. I shoved flamboyant tropical blouses down the rack, causing the hangers to screech as I flipped through what looked like the mature ladies' section. I frowned, ducking as if a passerby would find me unfit to be Fifi's clientele. But giant palm tree patterns or not, I had to arrive in clothes that were actually clean. When I found a black blazer, I purchased it hastily to conceal the ugly red sweater, even though it had big gold pilot buttons.

As I approached the parking ramp for Doctors Inc., I realized the blazer was far too tight, pinning my arms to my sides and threatening to burst a seam as I reached for the steering wheel. Flopping around the car like a T. rex, I heard the seam rip. Sweat beaded over my lip, undeterred by the air-conditioning vents aimed straight at my face. Would it be toddler puke or T. rex? Giving up, I tore out of the blazer like I was the Hulk and threw the tattered garment into the back seat. Maybe I wouldn't be meeting anyone important.

Miranda put me in an enormous conference room and left me alone while she went in search of the boss.

"The boss?" I asked before she left.

"Dr. Aberdeen," she replied. "You'll be interviewing with the president of Doctors Inc."

I furtively glanced around the room for security cameras. I imagined myself as the subject on the officer's screen, picking at the snot on my sweater while the company watched and laughed. I spotted it up in the corner. I knew it. How was I going to clean myself up now? I left the crusted snot on the sweater and opted instead to apply the lipstick tucked in my purse for emergencies. I wasn't normally the type to wear lipstick, but judging by the bold color on Miranda's lips, cosmetics were the sort of thing that would impress this Aberdeen character.

If I had been hot in the car, I was ice cold now. The thermostat was set way down low, and a vent blew chilled air into the room where a row of leather swivel chairs surrounded a long marble table. As I blew a warm breath into my cupped hands, the door burst open, and a tall man wearing a black suit came barreling in. He focused on the smartphone he held in one hand and didn't look up as he pulled out the chair next to me and sat down. I waited for him to finish, and when he did, he set the phone face down on the table and turned to face me.

"Ronald Aberdeen," he said, extending his hand. I placed my icy fingers in his grip. His handshake was firm and brisk as he said, "I'm the president of Doctors Inc. Why do you want to work here? What have you heard about us?"

My heart thumped. I had heard nothing about them. I'd merely searched online for doctor jobs near me. Was I supposed to do a research project on an hour's notice?

"Um. . ." I stalled. "This interview was kind of last minute." I dropped my hands into my lap, hoping that would be a sufficient explanation for the vomit on my sweater, and made the decision then and there to stop wearing things out of the house that had puke or snot on them. New rule.

"Do you think you can handle a volume of twenty-plus patients per day?" he asked.

"Of course. I've been doing this kind of work for the last four years—"

"That's not much experience, is it?" he asked. "Can you handle complex medical cases? We see a wide variety of patients at Ocean Hospital."

"I can handle whatever you need me to handle," I said, hoping it was the right answer.

An hour after my interview, Miranda had called and offered me the job. "We need you to start seeing patients next week."

The quickness of it had shocked me. The whole thing felt rushed—deceptive even. What was I getting myself into?

"We're going to expedite hospital privileges for you. The sooner you can start, the better."

"I was thinking next month, actually," I'd countered. "I'd like time to talk to your doctors before I commit."

Miranda had sighed. "Do you want the job or not?"

It really came down to a matter of geography. It was this or New Haven. Doctors Inc. was desperate, but I was desperate too. I told Miranda I would let her know by the end of the day.

"I'm afraid Dr. Aberdeen is going to squeeze me like he's trying to get blood from a turnip," I told Fox later.

Fox kissed my hand. "Bonne Santé has an opening in the interventional radiology department. They want me for the job, but I don't have to take it. If you won't be happy at Ocean Hospital, we might as well go to New Haven."

Connecticut. Connecticut, with its hoity-toity Yale and Izod sweaters. Its utopian communities and impossible expectations. Its lack of palm trees and blood relatives. I could compromise on Ocean Hospital and work myself up to a promotion. Yes, that could work. I emailed Miranda my resumé that afternoon.

Once Doctors Inc. hired me, Fox and I had willingly embedded ourselves in the corporate wheel, all in the name of clinging to Gilbert. Me at Ocean Hospital and Fox at Bonne Santé, grinding it out day after day—returning home to a hand-me-down farm so the Ronald Aberdeens of the world could perch high in a skyscraper with a view all the way to the sea.

NINE
OPAL

A SOLITARY DEW-COVERED BMW OCCUPIED THE DESERTED Ocean Hospital parking lot. As expected, I found Tom in the office, sitting in the dark glow of his computer, looking haggard. Tom stretched, arching his back before turning his chair to face me. His scrubs were rumpled, and he had traded his contact lenses for glasses. His forehead gleamed, greasy after his long shift. In twelve hours, I would look like him.

"You're here too early," Tom said. "I'm still admitting patients from overnight." The clock on the office wall read 5:05 a.m.

"Tom," I said, sliding into the chair beside him, "I want to be medical director, and I want your support."

Tom brought a hand to his mouth, but his eyes gave away the grin. "And replace Beehive?" he asked, referring to Karen's hair. "Sure, Opal." He dropped his hand and laughed out loud, slapping his knee. "Why would you want to be the medical director?"

"Someone who wants us to thrive should lead our group," I replied. "I'm tired of being pushed around by a woman who cares more about her nail polish than her colleagues." I wanted better hours too. And I wanted to stay married, but I kept that to myself.

"Are you sure you want to be beholden to Ronald Aberdeen?" Tom asked, the name coming out of his mouth like spoiled milk.

He had a point. Ronald was gruff and dismissive, but he was also obscure and seldom at Ocean Hospital. What would it be like to take orders from him? "I meet with him on Wednesday," I confided.

Tom set down the patient list he was holding. "Don't wait until Wednesday." He lowered his voice. "Things are going on behind the scenes. If you wait for Aberdeen to come to you, it may cost your job."

I recoiled from Tom. He had been doing this job forever, guiding me every step of the way. Tom may as well have been my father. He was surviving here, somehow. His rich brown skin was wrinkle-free. There wasn't so much as a crow's foot stamped on his face, despite the grueling pace of this job. But he had to be wrong about this. Aberdeen just offered me a job doing patient-advocate things—the PAL, he had called it.

"You must be mistaken. Dr. Aberdeen is trying to help me." I patted his shoulder as if he were confused and gathered up my stethoscope to start seeing patients.

"No. Opal. Karen wants you out. I heard her on the phone with Human Resources."

A ball of flame shot up my throat and left my cheeks burning red. No one had ever fired me in my life. What had I done but give my heart and soul to Doctors Inc.? Family dinners, soccer games, and class parties, all thrown on the pyre in the name of my career. I wasn't going to let Karen take it all away. Over what? A discharge summary and a text with a few four-letter words?

Tom was right. I had to get to Aberdeen.

"How do I get to him before Karen does?" I asked.

"Well." Tom laughed. "You'll be seeing Dr. Aberdeen in person this morning."

"Aberdeen was here yesterday. I think you're tired. Go home and get some rest," I offered, reaching for the pager.

"Can't," Tom replied. "The staff meeting starts at eight."

Staff meeting? Tom read the question on my face. "We have a general staff meeting this morning. I'd skip it, but Aberdeen is coming down for this one."

The flush in my cheeks receded, replaced by the gusto of a woman on a mission. How would I gain an audience with the president? Should I stand in his designated parking space and wait for him to arrive? Perhaps something bolder? I could sneak into the men's room and catch him at the urinal. Men made the most important deals there, did they not? Two men in a pissing contest?

Tom caught me plotting and pushed his phone across the desk. He had pulled up Aberdeen's contact card. "Call him," he said, pointing to the phone.

"Tom, it's five in the morning," I reminded him.

"Opal, your job is on the line," he countered.

I snatched Tom's phone from the desk, jabbing the call button before I could talk myself out of it. As the ringer hummed, I ran through my opening line. *Karen Chamberlain is a snake.* No, not that. *Karen Chamberlain is not the person you want in charge of your doctors.* That was better. *Doctors Inc. will be far more profitable with me as the medical director.* Yes, that was it. The call picked up.

"Tom?" came a woman's voice.

"No," I replied. "Is this. . . is this Isabelle?" I hadn't spoken more than a few words to her over the years. I was surprised I even remembered her name.

"No," the woman replied sarcastically. "It's Ronald's mistress. Of course this is Isabelle Aberdeen! Who is this?"

I fumbled for words. "I. . . it's. . . This is Opal Collins. I'm sorry."

"Well, ask a stupid question, and you get a stupid answer," she said. I heard a man far away tell the woman to be nice. I had to press on.

"May I speak to Dr. Aberdeen?" I asked.

"No!" the woman exclaimed.

"All right." I waited for her to say something else, but she didn't. "Can you please give him the message that I need to speak with him before the staff meeting?"

She sighed, as if being her husband's secretary was exhausting. "I'll let him know, but his schedule is tight."

At eight o'clock, doctors of all sorts began to arrive for the staff meeting. I never made it to Dr. Aberdeen's parking spot, and I'd changed my mind about the men's room, so by the time the meeting started, I still hadn't had my chance. I could catch him after the meeting.

Doctors Inc. employed generalists, specialists, subspecialists, inpatient doctors, outpatient doctors, and every kind of physician one could think of. Now, they were filling the auditorium and taking their seats for the mandatory meeting. Most of them wore long white lab coats, but the surgeons stood out in their surgical caps and scrubs, with ID badges clipped to their pockets and pagers attached to their waists. Others wore sport coats and ties, and still others arrived in jeans and flip-flops.

As Tom, Nassrin, Alex Tang, and I settled into our seats, balancing mocha lattes, pumpkin-spice skinny iced drinks and bagels, Karen joined us. Our row was conveniently full, so Karen had to take a seat across the aisle. She wore a burgundy suit with matching lipstick, and her hair was teased around her head to twice its natural height. An expert on high heels, her pumps didn't so much as wobble as she slid into her seat and folded herself into the small space. "Good morning," she whispered across the aisle. "Opal, are you okay?"

I looked myself over. It wasn't as if I'd bothered with makeup this morning, and my white coat wasn't exactly ironed, but other than that, I thought I looked all right. I patted my head, trying to remember if I brushed my hair before I left home. "I'm fine."

"I know about the little meeting you set up with Dr. Aberdeen," she whispered. "Is there something you want to tell me?"

"Oh," I said, waving her off. "No big deal."

"I know about the PAL too. Congratulations. I hope you take it."

Before I could ask what that was supposed to mean, a bald man with a suit that wore him instead of the other way around tapped the microphone at the podium. "Okay, folks. We're going to get started. Here today is the president of Doctors Inc., Dr. Ronald Aberdeen, to discuss the items listed on our agenda. I'll turn it over to you, Ron."

The president stood from his chair and took the podium. He adjusted the microphone upward for his height, then laid two gigantic hands on the podium, scanning the auditorium before beginning to speak. The red scarf in his jacket pocket matched his tie, and his hair was short. He was a king preparing to address his subjects.

Shockingly, the meeting was boring. I tried to pay attention to blah,

blah, Medicare cuts and blah, blah, Medical Home, but my mind was elsewhere, focused on bringing down Karen Chamberlain.

"And for everyone in the room, but especially the hospitalist division," Dr. Aberdeen emphasized, "this especially affects the hospitalist division." He enunciated the words one at a time. I looked to my left and my right and realized I was not the only one in outer space. Alex had dragged a computer on wheels into the meeting and was charting rather than listening. Nassrin had stepped out to return a page, and Tom, who was usually the one taking notes at these things, had actually fallen asleep. "Blah blah blah. Blah blah blah," Dr. Aberdeen was saying. I looked over at Karen, who was nodding her head and taking notes. Alex stopped typing and squinted his eyes toward the front of the room. I jabbed Tom with my elbow. He opened his eyes in time to hear the phrase repeated, slower this time. "Blaah blaahh blaahhh. Blah. Blah."

"I have a big announcement coming up at the next staff meeting, so mark your calendars, folks," Dr. Aberdeen went on. "We will consolidate the hospitalist division."

What now?

Dr. Aberdeen repeated, "We are consolidating the hospitalists. There will be layoffs."

Stunned, I turned to Tom to interpret. Was he right? Was I about to lose my job? I couldn't. I was trying to grow my career, not chop it off at the head.

"Go get 'em," Tom whispered, pointing at the stage.

Dr. Aberdeen had stopped talking, and the crowd was already beginning to push out of the room. He left the podium, heading straight for me and me straight for him. He had an entourage of audio-visual technicians, doctors, and administrators in tow. No matter. When the president stopped in front of me, the crowd stopped too, bunching up like an accordion. Karen was right behind me, hovering like an insect. My heart sped up, and my breath caught in my throat as Aberdeen met my eyes. The clarity of his dark irises and the humanity I did not expect to see there surprised me.

"Looking forward to our meeting, Opal," he said, taking me by the shoulder and leading me out of the auditorium, his staff still in line behind him. My voice stuck in my throat instead of saying what I needed it to say. I submitted to his grip, once again feeling warmth radiate from his hand. "I'm sure you'll come around to my way of thinking about the PAL position." And with that, he released my shoulder and was gone, his entourage following.

Karen looked as though she were going to say something, but I scowled at her and hurried in the direction Dr. Aberdeen had gone. On a hunch, I circumvented the entourage and ducked into the men's room. It was blessedly empty and, thank God, smelled of lavender. Only Ocean Hospital could keep a men's room from smelling like piss. The mirror was clean, and my reflection was of a woman who looked frightened. I leaned over the sink and smoothed my hair. I wiped the sweat from my brow and waited.

The door pushed open, and Ronald Aberdeen stepped inside. When he saw me, he didn't miss a beat. "Isabelle said you called." He stood at the sink next to mine and turned on the faucet.

I stared into the mirror and waited until we locked eyes there. "Karen is a snake," I said.

He took wet fingertips to an errant strand of hair, pushing it back into place. "I might be a snake too."

"If she's trying to get me fired—"

He put his hand up. "You don't need to worry about Karen Chamberlain."

My shoulders slumped in relief, and I started panting as if I had been running. "Thank you," I said. "This job means everything to me. I was thinking—"

He shook the water from his hands. "You need to worry about yourself," he remarked. He turned, opened the door, and said as he left, "We'll continue this Wednesday."

TEN
FOX

FOX FOUND THAT THE DRIVE TO WORK WAS THE BEST TIME to call his mother. From memory, he dialed his childhood phone number while the light was red. Opal's efforts to take Karen Chamberlain's job while trying to get pregnant had caused so much change. Good change, yes, but something nagged still, left over from vacation. It was the way Opal had latched onto the stripper—no, not that. It was the way she'd tossed him aside for the stripper. Another sacrifice she'd asked of him.

Fox expected his mother to lean into him about moving to New Haven, but her monologue would be supportive rather than selfish. Right now, New Haven didn't sound so bad.

"You didn't come home for Christmas last year, honey," his mother said. "Your father says you need to bring his grandkids up to see him."

"Mom, I was working on Christmas last year, remember?"

"Remember that job your father offered you? The one at Collins Radiology? The one with paid holidays?"

Fox smiled at her reliability. "I'll see what I can do about Opal, Mom."

"Fox," she continued with an unaccustomed edge to her voice.

Something was wrong. "Your father's business is. . . struggling. Your father is under a lot of stress, and I'm beginning to worry."

Fox worried about his father too. Medicare had cut reimbursement, forcing Collins Radiology to stretch its resources thin. The family business, once eternally waiting to take him in, probably couldn't absorb an interventional radiologist like himself. Breathing life into this fact by mentioning it was not going to be helpful.

"Dad didn't say anything to me," Fox replied. He pulled into Bonne Santé, told his mother not to worry, and ended their call.

The Interventional Radiology Department of Bonne Santé Hospital was ice cold, but Fox stayed warm under his lead vest and sterile gown. A tray of stainless-steel instruments was set out before him, and the CT scanner greeted his first lung-biopsy patient with an electric hum. His nurse practitioner poked her head through the door, holding a telephone receiver to her ear.

"Clyde Jewel wants to meet with you at five thirty in Conference Room B," she whispered.

"Why on Earth does the president of Santa Rosa Medical System want to meet with me?" he asked, resting his sterile, glove-covered hands on his chest.

She shrugged.

"Can you ask him?"

"His administrative assistant was the one who called," she explained. "But your meeting is only nine hours from now. You'll know soon enough."

Fox sighed and resigned himself to concentrating on his procedures. He plunged the needle through his patient's chest and pulled back a core of lung tissue. Like a worm, it floated lazily in the specimen cup's solution. Mr. Jewel had to have good news. Fox was sure he hadn't done anything wrong. Working fast, he could make it to the conference room by five and still have time to prepare.

No receptionists appeared to usher him in, and there were no refreshments on the conference-room table. The room looked like it had been forgotten since the 1970s. Fox had to flick on the lights before choosing a seat at the table. He brushed a thin layer of dust from the arm of his chair and the one beside it. He would have brushed the dust from all the chairs—there were ten—but he assumed the meeting was private and there would be no need.

The elderly Mr. Jewel arrived ten minutes late, waving his cell phone in the air. "Can't work this blasted thing," he complained.

Fox hurried to his feet to pull out a chair for the aged man. He had always enjoyed working for Clyde Jewel. The man's slight build was accentuated by a stoop. He always opted for short-sleeved shirts, never bothering with ties or jackets. Fox recognized that despite his frail appearance, Clyde was capable of running the region's largest medical group.

Clyde waved Fox away and sank into the chair. Once settled, he removed a pair of thick glasses from his face, wiped them with a handkerchief he pulled from his pocket, and put them back on. He blinked at Fox through the spectacles.

"Son, do you know why I asked you here today?"

"No idea whatsoever, Mr. Jewel. What can I do for you?"

"Before we get into things, can I trust you to keep this meeting confidential?"

"Absolutely, sir. Nothing leaves this room."

"Just a moment, son," Clyde replied. He removed his phone from his breast pocket and held it up in front of his face. Fox sat still while Clyde fumbled through the information on the screen realizing he would need help. He lifted it from Clyde's hands.

"What are you trying to do?" Fox asked.

"Trying to find the redial button," Clyde replied.

"Okay, let me see," Fox said, pulling up the recent-call menu. He clicked on the top number and handed the phone back to Clyde.

"He said he's willing to hear our pitch," Clyde said into the phone with a smile. As the door opened, a tall man in a black suit and a wide grin entered. He was swinging a briefcase, which he allowed to crash onto the table next to Clyde Jewel. The man gave Clyde a rough slap on the back and took a seat beside him. Still with an energetic smile, he reached across the table and shook Fox's hand.

"Ronald Aberdeen, president of Doctors Inc."

Fox's mouth hung open, and his guard went up. "I know," he replied. "We've met."

Ronald squinted across the table at him, considering this. "Of course. Yes."

Fox had never liked Ronald. The man walked around like he was God and treated his employees, including Fox's wife, like robots programmed to improve his bottom line. A clandestine meeting in the bowels of the hospital felt somehow deceptive. He wrapped his arms around his chest.

"Fox, you come from a line of hardworking, intelligent men," Clyde continued. "Your father owns a radiology practice with over twenty franchise locations, and your brother is a United States congressman. The Collins men are doers. Men of action."

"How do you fit into all this, Ronald?" Fox asked, narrowing his eyes.

Clyde answered for him. "The companies are merging, Fox. SRMS and Doctors Inc. are merging. We're going to need strong leadership for success."

Ronald jumped in. "Of course, there have been no announcements yet."

Fox put his hands up. "I won't say a word."

Ronald continued. "We have you in mind for Radiology Department head. Bonne Santé, Ocean Hospital, and thirteen outpatient centers. You'll work for me."

Fox leaned back in his chair, considering this. The air in the room was stale, and the temperature seemed to climb, as if the air conditioning had no need to make its way to this forgotten section of the hospital. The accolade was tempting. The Collins men naturally floated to the top; Clyde was right about that. But if he were the head of radiology, wouldn't he be cementing himself to Gilbert? It would, in essence, cut one more string from his dream of returning to New Haven.

"If I wanted to be an administrator, my father would love to have me at Collins Radiology," Fox replied.

"Listen, Fox," Ronald said, leaning forward. "Health care is going the way of big corporations. It has been for some time. That's why you signed up with SRMS instead of going to work for your dad. That was the right move. And now, with all the new legislation coming, it's going to be impossible to be a private guy like your dad and survive. Your brother would tell you that. Your dad would tell you that. I bet they have told you that. What I'm getting at, Fox, is that you're going to want to ride this wave with us. Interventional radiology will not be what it used to be. You're going to be spending your days staying late to drain abscesses and coming in early to tap lungs just so you can pay your mortgage."

"You're a fine doctor, Fox," Clyde added. "I've been watching you over the years, and I'd like to expand your role in the company. Like I said, you were born for it."

Fox rubbed his temples. Why had Clyde Jewel teamed up with Ronald Aberdeen? To say yes to Jewel was easy. Saying yes to Aberdeen was like choking on a chicken bone. And what about Opal? If Fox were promoted, would Opal still need to be promoted? In theory, he could take on the role of slowing down and spending more time with the kids. Fox coughed. That wasn't what he'd had in mind. "What's your offer?" he asked.

Ronald opened his briefcase and tore off a small portion of paper. With a pen in hand, he swiftly wrote something in small print and passed it to Fox. Clyde Jewel sat back with his hands folded over his belly, his eyes closed for the moment.

Fox lifted the corner of the paper and peered at the writing. That couldn't be right. He held the paper close to his face. He read the number and silently mouthed the figure.

"That's a lot of money," Fox said. "You know, I have to think about it."

"It's perfect timing, with Opal transitioning to the PAL position," Ronald said, rising from his chair.

Fox dropped the tiny paper. "What PAL position? What is a PAL?"

"Oh," Ronald said, pausing in midair. His eyes grew bright, and he sank back into his chair. "The patient advocate liaison is a work-from-home job I created for Opal. She'll be answering patient complaints, raising our ratings, and balancing that work-life juggling act."

"So Opal knows about this?" Fox asked.

"Of course. We meet Wednesday to finalize it." Ronald cocked his head to the side. "She didn't tell you?"

Fox clenched his teeth. The muscles in his jaw tensed under his cool exterior. She'd lied. Despite being handed a solution to everything that was wrong with her job, her marriage, and her life, she didn't even bother to tell him. Her ambition was more important than their relationship. Clyde rose from the table and started for the door. Ronald followed.

"Nothing is set in stone," Clyde whispered.

"Head of Radiology is a stepping stone, of course," Ronald added. "We'll promote you to chief of staff within three years."

His eyes snapped to Ronald after hearing "chief of staff."

"You're right, Clyde," Fox said, picking up the paper Ronald had offered. "Nothing is set in stone. My brother taught me a little about politics, and my father taught me a little about business." He reached over, picked up Ronald's pen, and scratched out Ronald's number. Above it, he wrote an even higher number and slid the paper back across the table.

"If you'll excuse me, gentlemen, I have to get back to the suite. I have another abscess to drain." With that, Fox left the giant men to their giant plans.

ELEVEN
OPAL

I FOUND MYSELF RACING AGAINST TIME. I HAD NO ONE TO
blame but myself. The formal meeting, the corporate office, the
company president—they had coalesced into a three-headed monster.
I'd built the day up to such importance that when it came, I pushed
back with equal and opposite force. Resistance, I think they called it.
My resistance had a name. Higgins Beach. The sounds of waves crashing
on the shore, the salty air, and the sun on my skin prepared me. I
brought my children with me, giving their absence from school no
second thought. Oh, how they loved the beach. I let time evaporate into
the humid air, regrettably with no way to get it back now.

My car skidded to a stop in front of Amber's house. True, I hadn't
asked her to watch the kids yet, but Amber lived on my way to the
corporate office, and she never had plans of her own anyway. When I
pulled up to the yellow bungalow, I saw her green station wagon parked
in the driveway. A Lexus sedan, unfamiliar to me, was parked beside it. I
left my engine running as I climbed the porch steps with my children
close behind. Amber opened the front door as we approached and knelt
with arms open wide to receive Cal and Emily.

"What are you doing here, Opal?" The surprise was evident on her
face.

"I need you to watch the kids," I said, pushing them through the threshold.

"What makes you think I'm available?" Amber stood and crossed her arms.

"Is someone here?"

Principal Windsor emerged from the kitchen, joining us at the threshold. "Hi, guys!" she exclaimed. "Nice to see you!"

I rubbed my eyes with my fists in disbelief. When I opened them again, Wendy was still there. Of all days, Amber was entertaining a friend today? My job was too important to unravel for a girls' day watching *Ellen* reruns.

"My meeting with Dr. Aberdeen starts in fifteen minutes," I pleaded. "I just need you to watch the kids for an hour."

"They aren't staying," Amber said, turning to Wendy.

"That's today?" Wendy exclaimed. "Wasn't she going with the high heels?" Wendy hissed to Amber while gawking at my beach attire.

In my bedroom lay a pair of brown slacks—the ones without stains —a cream sweater, and the black-lacquered heels with the ankle straps that I hadn't worn since I was single. The ensemble would have to stay laid out on my bed. Time was up. I had thrown my swimsuit cover-up, a purple terrycloth romper, over my freshly sunburned skin. A thick crust of sand still clung to my flip-flops. I inspected myself from head to toe. I would need to add a second request.

"Oh, and Amber, I'm going to need you to lend me some clothes that say, *Promote me to medical director*," I added with a wink. By this time, my children had let themselves into Amber's house, and I could hear them pulling open kitchen drawers and rummaging for snacks.

"So, no clothes and no shower either, huh?" my sister asked.

I glanced at my watch. It wasn't good. "Tick-tock, Amber!"

"I can't do this," Amber groaned. "I have nothing to lend you anyway."

"Okay," I acquiesced in defeat. "I'll cancel the meeting." I turned toward my car. "Come on, kids. Let's go." I motioned for my children to follow before taking one more stab at Amber. "Doctors Inc. announced layoffs. I have to get this promotion."

Wendy shrugged out of the tweed blazer she was wearing and draped it across my shoulders. "Take this for good luck," she said. "I need to leave anyway."

My heart squeezed in my chest for Wendy's generosity. I loathed having resorted to juvenile behavior, pestering my big sister to save me from myself. What excuse did I have? Wendy gathered her purse and keys and blew a kiss to Amber before walking to her car, her heels clicking against the driveway with each step.

"Wait!" Amber exclaimed. "Opal, if Wendy agrees to stay, I will watch Emily and Cal."

"Deal!" Wendy exclaimed, turning back.

"Thank you! Thank you both so much," I cried, shoving my arms into the blazer. I hugged Amber, and while I had her tied up in my embrace, I implored one last favor. "Can you make Emily's All-About-Me poster?"

"Opal! Really?" she scolded.

"Come on, sis. It's due tomorrow, and you are *so good* at Pinterest stuff."

"Emily should be the one doing the work," Amber argued.

I gave her my pleading hands and pulled a $100 Staples gift card from my purse. "Amber, you know as well as I do it's the parents who make the All-About-Me posters," I contended. "Does it really matter which adult makes it?" I backed away and mouthed a thank you before she could answer.

"Opal!" she called after me. "This will not cost $100."

"Use the rest for school supplies for your classroom," I suggested with my hand on my car door, surveying the road ahead. The hard part was only just beginning.

TWELVE
Fox

Fox pressed the accelerator harder than he should have. He had to beat the arborist. Hospital, arborist, kids, dinner—none of it stopped weighing on him. Opal didn't own overwhelm; they both lived in it. His foot crushed the gas pedal—a poor substitute for control —but the neighborhood's carefree shouts and bursts of laughter called him back. Brake lights flicked on. He only had to make it home alive. He didn't have to make it home on time.

The arborist could hold off, the tasks would get finished, and Opal would come back from her meeting with a promotion as impressive as his. Then Fox wouldn't have to confront her about the lie.

Whispering Way unfolded, quaint and wrong. The track homes jutted into land that once belonged to Opal's family. Developers had cleared the ancient oak tunnel, leaving trees like skeletons over dead land. Then they burned them away, the smoke rising as if from pyres to a cloudless sky. Only one stood now: the oak behind the old farmhouse, its branches a survival statue.

As Fox pulled into the driveway, a bumper sticker greeted him: *Are you breathing? Thank a tree!* Rust coated the arborist's truck, and its open tailgate spat out tools. The smell of stirred warm pollen scratched under Fox's eyelids, drawing his fist to his watering eyes.

Fox caught sight of the arborist leaning into the back of the truck. He wore wire-rimmed glasses and was squinting through them at something in the truck's bed. He had fastened his greasy brown curls into a ponytail. Fox called out, and the tree man wiped his hands on his corduroys before reaching out to shake Fox's hand.

"Sorry I'm late," Fox said. "Have you seen the tree?"

"Dr. Collins?" asked the tree man.

"Call me Fox."

"Jimmy. Arbor Day Foundation." His handshake was delicate. "You have quite a tree," he said. "She's a real beauty."

"We estimate it's about eighty years old," Fox offered, wiping the moisture from his face.

"Try a hundred. Let's have a look."

Before they could head for the oak, car doors slammed. Fox's kids piled out with their Aunt Amber. She offered the usual mock cheer. "Special delivery!"

Fox's relief curdled. He checked his watch. "She's supposed to be home by now," he muttered.

"She left dressed to kill. That meeting had better end with a tiara for her, right?" Amber called after him, already ducking into her car.

The kids wouldn't survive long without candy-fueled distractions. His afternoon unraveled before his eyes, but he guided them toward the backyard. The oak hadn't changed outwardly, its sweeping moss and timeless girth still turning sunlight into sanctuary. If the family had paid more attention, they might have cared for the tree as they would have a family member. Now fungus had taken hold, and to Cal, it was asthma incarnate.

"Stay off the tree," Fox warned as Cal shot toward the swing. Velvety brown patches crawled outward from the roots, stubborn and spreading. "Take Emily inside and put on *Power Rangers*," he instructed Cal. Emily wandered off, turning on the hose. She had already soaked her clothes.

The branch clutched in his hand felt like a bad omen. Opal hardly glanced at the sick bark when they first made the discovery. She thought it was nothing to worry about. That was until Cal had choked awake the following night.

"You allergic?" Jimmy asked, noting Fox's watery pink eyes.

"Yeah. Cal too."

On cue, Cal began a rapturous paroxysm of coughing. Fox jumped to intercept him, pulling an inhaler from Cal's pocket. Thank God Opal had remembered to put it there. The inhaler hissed, silencing the incoming wheeze. Fox nudged him toward the house before turning back to Jimmy.

"Well, your tree seems to have a case of Phytophthora ramorum," Jimmy announced. "We can't be sure unless we send a sample to the tree lab, which I recommend."

"Is that like a fungus?" Fox asked.

Jimmy scratched his chin, frowned, then turned back to Fox.

"Sudden oak death," he said in a low voice.

"So that little patch is going to kill this tree?"

"We can send a lab sample, apply phosphorus treatments—but the truth is, she's already failing."

A spray of hose water rained down on the men. Emily stood triumphantly, laughing, her finger pinning open the nozzle.

"Thank you, Emily. So helpful," Fox grumbled.

Jimmy adjusted his glasses.

"So, Jimmy, you're predicting this tree will die?"

"Yes, sir. Dr. Collins, sir," Jimmy stammered. "You're probably going to lose her."

Fox frowned at the tree in disbelief. "Emily!" Fox called. "Bring that hose over here." He wasn't ready to give up. There had to be a way to save the tree.

"Dr. Collins!" Jimmy pleaded. "If the tree is keeping your son from breathing, you need to—"

"Bring the hose," Fox repeated. "We're watering it."

At the same time, Jimmy exclaimed, "You need to cut it down!"

THIRTEEN
OPAL

The hushed interior of the corporate offices of Doctors Inc. seemed to whisper, *It's fine that you're late.* There was an absence of chaos. A slowing of time punctuated with potted plants and candy dishes on the desks of the receptionists concealed the lion's den that it was. It did not seem possible that entire companies were being run behind the closed doors, coming in and out of view while the elevator ascended. Trapped in beach clothes and Wendy's blazer, I pushed back against the serenity and clung to my self-consciousness as Miranda, a receptionist with a sharp nose and pencil skirt, led the way to Dr. Aberdeen's office.

Pulling the blazer tighter around my body, I considered bolting from the building, back to the safety of my family. Miranda's spiked heels made tiny indentations in the speckled carpet as she walked. My flip-flops smudged out her trail as I followed behind. I didn't want to be like this anymore. I wanted to be the one with a smart bun and exceptional time management. It was time to shake off my dread and face my fear.

"Dr. Aberdeen will see you now," Miranda said, opening a door before leaving us alone.

Dr. Aberdeen sat behind a desk appropriately massive for his frame.

The wall of windows beyond overlooked the city. "Please, have a seat," he said without getting up.

I chose the chair farthest from him and pressed my back to the wall. "You're being laid off."

His gruff words came like an arrow, piercing my chest suddenly, out of nowhere. "That is, unless you've reconsidered the PAL position we discussed."

Anger crashed over me like a wave cresting on the shore. I might have been late and dressed like a twelve-year-old, but I wasn't ready to give up. "Sir," I argued, crossing my legs. "You can't fire me. You have to promote me to medical director."

His eyebrows leaped in surprise. "Replace Karen? Opal, you sound like a politician. You have one in the family, right?"

"Allen?" I asked, confused by his change in direction.

"He's a congressman, right?" was his response.

"Oh," I said. "Yes. New York."

"You know, I'm from New York," he said, sipping from a water bottle. "What. . . um. . . what committee is he on?"

I laughed nervously. "Sir, I don't even know what I had for breakfast."

"Science and technology," Aberdeen said before capping the bottle again. "Anyway, tell me about your sudden itch to be a supervisor."

"Being a doctor is putting a real strain on my family," I replied. I adjusted my throat. Maybe my voice would stop squeaking.

"Why?" Ronald asked, bemused.

I shifted on the acrylic chair, pulled in a breath, and pictured Fantasia on stage. "The patient-advocate stuff doesn't interest me, and I'm a better leader than Karen."

"You aren't ready for medical director," he said quickly. "And as your ally, I want to be clear. If you pass up the PAL, you could end up losing everything."

Fuck, he hated me.

He beckoned for me to sit across from him. I avoided his eyes and gazed instead at an expensive watch and gold wedding band. He leaned forward, elbows on his desk, his dark eyes searching me, waiting for me to continue. I had to come up with something, or I would become the next Rose Thomas, trading my stethoscope for baby wipes. When I said nothing, he patted my hand with his. It should have felt patronizing, but I relaxed under his touch.

"I can do it, obviously. . ." I trailed off.

Ronald rested his chin on his fist and considered this. Then he leaned back, studying my purple romper and flip-flops. I waited for him to respond, but he didn't.

"I want to see fewer patients and have more time with my family."

At this, he laughed out loud. "Are you a banker?" He continued to laugh as I died on the inside. Finally, he recovered. "Opal, I know being a doctor is hard. And it's getting harder, right?"

I nodded.

"There are more patients and paperwork, and everything has gone electronic with the medical record, right?" I nodded again. "And it's frustrating, too, right? Because the patients nowadays have this sense of entitlement, right?"

"Sometimes," I whispered.

"And they expect that Dr. Collins is going to prescribe a pill or wave a magic wand," he said, waving his pen through the air, "that's going to put them back together again."

I had grown distracted, my mind wandering back to his wedding ring. But he was still building steam.

"So you have to fix the patients, stay within the quality guidelines, keep your satisfaction scores high, and then, on top of that, your bosses are always coming up with more work."

When I stared at my feet and didn't respond, his face relaxed. "At the end of the day, it's as though you've gotten away from the essence of practicing medicine."

After a long pause, I met his eyes. "It's exhausting," I replied. I imagined my son's sweet face and my daughter's smile. They didn't care how many patients I could see in a twelve-hour shift. Hell, they didn't care if I brushed my teeth.

"Then why do you want to be a doctor?" he countered.

Does he already know? Had he seen into my core and found the gossamer thread that tethered me to my profession, no matter the pressure?

"Because what I do is amazing," I replied firmly.

"Right!" he exclaimed. "You're on the front lines with these people. You comfort them. Nobody spends more time with the patients than you, Opal. This is your gift. Come," he said, beckoning me with his finger. "Come closer." He bent down to a filing cabinet as I leaned over the desk.

I held my breath, wondering if he would see the sand on my feet or admonish my sunburn. Why did I suddenly have the need for sandless feet and perfect skin?

His head reappeared, a lock of hair falling over his eye. He opened the file and rifled through the papers. I studied the upside-down photocopied pages. He chose a paper, held it up, and began reading.

" 'Dear Dr. Collins, thank you for taking such good care of me. You really listened to me. You are a wonderful doctor.' "

He set the paper down and chose another. " 'Dr. Collins, you took care of my mother. I knew she was in good hands. You have a wonderful bedside manner.' "

Warmth spread to my cheeks as he read the flattery.

"You're one of the best, Opal. You have the highest patient satisfaction scores and the lowest readmission rates." He smiled, handsome despite his age. "You're going places in this company." He paused, leaning over his desk. I threw myself backward instinctively, but he motioned me forward as if sharing a secret. In a low voice, he said, "Doctors Inc. is growing, Opal. Take the PAL, and soon you'll never worry about workload again, I promise."

"I thought we were downsizing," I replied.

He sniffed the air in the small space between us, squinted, and sniffed again, rolling the scent around his nostrils. I froze, mortified. "Is that—" he asked, sniffing the air once more. "Suntan lotion?"

"No!" I jumped back. "No! Yes! Yes, it's sunscreen," I stammered. A shrill beep and the sound of Miranda's voice through a speaker on the desk rescued me.

"Dr. Aberdeen, your four twenty is here."

He pushed a button on the phone. "Thank you, Miranda."

He stood to usher me out. I allowed him to guide me to the door by my shoulder. His hand was warm, as it had been the last time he touched me. An uncomfortable truth was settling over me. I wasn't like these people. I was Dr. Frumpy Flats living in a stiletto world. I could have bedside manner all day long, but I was the weakest link on my team. Yet there I was, expecting a promotion. There I was, stinking like Coppertone, covered in sand and ugly clothes in the president's office, where people wore suits and four-inch heels, and I expected a promotion. Dr. Aberdeen's encouragement was merely to squeeze a little more from the problem child. He could see what a disaster I was. Anyone could see it. I shriveled, deflated and humiliated.

He held the door open for me. "You've got to get your numbers up, Opal," he said as I retreated with my head down. "If you want to keep your job, find your inspiration. Rediscover what makes this profession gratifying."

He planted a tiny seed within me, without invitation. I recognized it and called it by name. Desire. Would Ronald Aberdeen's admiration make this profession gratifying? Desiring approval was normal, right? Desiring the warm hand on my shoulder was not. "Thank you, Dr. Aberdeen," I said. "I can do better. You'll see."

"Ronald," he corrected. "Call me Ronald." His grasp loosened, but his hand lingered. His fingers were heavy, but his touch was light. "I know you'll make me proud," he whispered before closing his door.

FOURTEEN
OPAL

I hated working the night shift. The food was old and gross by the evening, and it was lonely. Today, however, was different. The food was still old and gross, but I wasn't lonely. Fox insisted on visiting me at the hospital because he said he had big news. I eagerly intercepted him in the doctor's lounge, but he told me we should eat before the custodians threw away the food. Ice had formed around the side of the cooler, and I leaned in to find a salad whose lettuce wasn't brown and wilted. Fox was behind me, carefully arranging his tray with bottles of water and a plate piled high with meatloaf and mashed potatoes that had dried out and were flaking at the edges. As I wedged the salads onto a small table, it wobbled on its uneven legs, threatening to send the meatloaf to the floor.

"I have some great news," Fox said as I dropped into my chair. He avoided my eyes and fidgeted with his fork.

"You have my undivided attention," I promised.

"It's all hush-hush right now." Fox lowered his voice and leaned close to me, but before he could share his secret, my pager began a parade of long, loud beeps until I pulled it from my waist and found the button to silence it. The room fell still, the only sounds coming from the hum of coolers and the buzz of lights. I dropped the pager back into my pocket.

"Do you have to answer that?" Fox asked.

I waved my hand casually as if I could brush off the summons when, in fact, I couldn't. But I had to make it at least seem like Fox was my priority. "In a minute. Let's finish eating." I drizzled more dressing onto my limp salad and took a few quick bites. The pager chirped again and, this time, sounded impatient.

"Answer that, honey," Fox said, scooping up the last of the mashed potatoes from his plate.

"Fine, but I want to hear the news as soon as I get back." I crossed the room to a wall-mounted phone and dialed the number listed on the pager. It was the emergency room. As the doctor at the other end of the line described the patients, another distraction walked through the door.

Ronald Aberdeen strode into the doctors' lounge in discussion with the surgeon on duty. What was he doing here? Dr. Aberdeen had stopped seeing patients years ago. He was the boss now. Not to mention the late hour. Was it possible he was there to see me?

I stopped hearing anything said over the phone and stood frozen, watching the two men cross the room. Why did the sight of him make my heart take off beating wildly like the gallop of a spooked horse? Was I afraid or infatuated? I knew that heartbeat, the sweat on my palms, the pull between my legs. This was lust. I knew it well. I bit my lip. Lust was a tricky beast. It had built me up to the top of the world. But it had also smashed my world to pieces. Decades later, I was still rebuilding. I willed myself to focus on Fox, but my eyes betrayed me and followed Ronald to the couch in front of the television.

I was still watching Ronald when I realized the phone pressed to my ear was dead. The ER had disconnected the call. I hung up my end and walked back to the table where Fox was waiting for me. He was looking down at his plate and had become strangely quiet.

"What were you about to tell me, honey?" I asked absently. Could I listen to anything Fox was saying while I had my head turned toward another man? I had never seen Ronald in scrubs before. The scrubs somehow made him appear even more powerful than his three-piece suit. The sleeves stopped just above his biceps, and I followed the muscular arms down to his hands with those manicured fingernails—

"Opal!" Fox was snapping his fingers now to get my attention. I tore my gaze from Ronald and looked Fox in the eye. He leaned across the table and whispered, "We need to talk."

Before I could reply, Ronald crossed the room to us. As he shook hands with Fox, the operator announced overhead with surprising volume that there was a rapid response on 3A. I sprang from my chair. Curiously, I found myself restrained by my wrist. Fox had taken hold of me. Did he not understand that big news or not, I was responsible for whatever disaster was happening on 3A?

"Let Dr. Aberdeen take this one, Opal," he said. "He's a doctor too."

You've got to get your numbers up. That's what Ronald had told me.

The loudspeaker boomed the announcement again. "Rapid Response on 3A."

Fox let go of my wrist and searched me with pleading eyes.

"I'll be right back," I promised before breaking into a run.

"I'll come with you," Ronald added, catching up to me with ease. We left Fox alone with his mashed potatoes and the surgeon on duty.

FIFTEEN
OPAL

WITHOUT A WORD, I DASHED UP THE STAIRS, NEARLY colliding with Ronald's stout frame as he lingered in the doorway of 3A, waiting for me. I pushed past him, opened the door, and continued dashing down the hall until I found the room where personnel had taken on a frenetic buzz, as if inside a wasp's nest.

As I slowed to a stop, a nurse rushed past me, pushing a bright-red crash cart. I followed her inside. The hospital was dark, but the room was bright, all the lights having been thrown on. Another group of nurses rummaged around a bed that held a young man sitting straight up, clutching his chest with his fist.

"What have we got?" I asked the room.

Tammy, the nurse in charge on 3A, was connecting wires to the patient's bare chest for an EKG. "This is Reggie Jackson, forty-three years old, admitted yesterday for chest pain. At 11:04 p.m., he alerted his nurse to an increase in pain."

"I know who you are. You're Dr. Fahadi's patient," I said to him calmly as I scanned the monitor for his vital signs.

"It hurts, Doc," he panted as beads of sweat formed on his forehead.

Ronald appeared and strode to the bedside like a cock taking stock of his hens. He leaned over me and pulled me to him, whispering in my ear, "If you save this guy, I could never get rid of you."

I forgot about watching Reggie's monitor, his crushing chest pain, and the room full of people. Was Ronald crazy? I wasn't saving Reggie to save my job; I was saving Reggie to save Reggie.

"Who's running this?" the charge nurse interrupted with irritation.

"I am," I snapped, embarrassed to have succumbed to distraction. Determined to regain focus, I elbowed Ronald before barreling on. "Let's give nitro and pull up 25 mics of fentanyl," I instructed the pharmacist who had arrived to man the crash cart. I held my hand out for the EKG as it rolled out of the machine. As I scanned the paper, Tammy slipped a nitro tablet under Reggie's tongue. "The EKG looks nasty," I reported. "Who's on call for cardiology?"

"It's Dr. Kumar," came a voice from the hallway.

"Get Dr. Kumar on the phone," I barked. "Tammy. Aspirin. Now."

"I have it right here," she confirmed, holding up a small plastic cup. Reggie rocked back and forth as she tipped the cup to his lips and told him to chew.

"Pressure's dropping, Dr. Collins," announced the floor nurse at the patient's other side.

"Let's bolus a liter of saline," I replied.

Reggie stopped rocking. His eyes rolled back as his body went limp. He collapsed on the bed with a groan. I glanced at his monitor and saw the lethal waves of ventricular tachycardia. Gulping back the surge of panic rising in my chest, I placed a hand on his neck and dug my fingers in until they found a thready pulse.

Ronald joined me once again, IV kit in hand. "He needs a second line," he said while looking for an external jugular vein. Ronald's hands worked to insert the IV, his brawny arm pressed against mine as I ripped open the defibrillator pads.

"Make it 50 mics of fentanyl and let's shock him," I said calmly despite a fine tremor that had started in my hand. Flashes of Betty Smith blinked through my head. *Don't die, Reggie. Please don't die.* Tammy ripped open a foil package of wired stickers connected to a defibrillator that someone had handed to her from the crash cart. While passing the syringe of fentanyl from one hand to another through the room and up to Reggie, we heard the defibrillator sound a shrill beep. The battery was charged. The fentanyl hadn't made it.

"Clear!" I called, stepping back from the bed. The nurses stepped back, their hands raised in unison. "Sorry, Reggie. This will be the worst part of your day," I told him. Then, "Shock."

"Shocking," came a voice from the defibrillator. The sound of the beep stopped, and Reggie's chest jumped, then flopped back down.

"Motherfucker!" Reggie yelled, eyes wide. The nurse at the IV received the fentanyl syringe, and she eased the painkiller into the line. He sucked in quick, shallow breaths.

"Dr. Kumar's on the phone," came a voice from the hall. Someone handed me a cordless phone across the room. Relieved, I pressed the phone to my ear and explained the situation.

"Activate the cath lab," she instructed. "I'm driving there now. I'm eight minutes out."

I relayed the plan, and Tammy released the brake on Reggie's bed.

As he was wheeled off to meet the cardiologist and the 3A staff drifted back to their posts, I accompanied Ronald down the hall.

"I'm impressed," Ronald said.

"Thank you," I mumbled, looking at my feet.

Ronald took me by the shoulder. "Let's speak in private," he said, leading me into the stairwell. We sat on the landing, and it felt like we were the only two people in the world. He's going to let me have Karen's job. This was it. I did it. I got the job. I fixed my family.

But instead, Ronald said, "There's something I need you to do for me."

"What do you mean?" I asked, turning toward him. His chest rose under his thin scrubs as he took a breath. Every hair on his head was neatly combed. The scent of his cologne mingled with the stale air in the stairwell.

"If you want a promotion, there's something I need from you."

I drummed my fingers on my knees. So, he was that kind of man. The spark wasn't just in my head. I should have taken offense, told him to take his promotion and go fuck himself. But I wanted that job. Fox wanted me to have that job. Ronald was powerful. Dangerous. The decision should have taken more than a fraction of a second. But who was I kidding? I'd made it long ago. I'd always been that kind of girl.

I lifted my chin, met his eyes, and nodded.

Sixteen

Opal

Looking back on that day, I would see the line I had been straddling—one foot planted in the light and one foot inching into the dark. Had I been paying attention, I would have recognized it as the moment that changed everything. But at the time, I saw none of that.

I gathered my stethoscope, motioned for Ronald to follow, and marched off the ward to a call room at the end of a dark and empty hallway. Maybe I thought I was already there. Maybe I thought I belonged there. After all, I was already broken. What had started as a crack a long time ago was now a chasm where the old me vanished and the new me came to life.

At the time, I saw an open road, poorly lit by tired fluorescent lights, where I could slip into the sparkly new life I suddenly could not do without. One more door held me on the side of fidelity, and with a nonchalant swipe of my badge, I unlocked the final step across the great divide.

Once inside, I slammed the door shut. Ronald reached over my hand to turn the lock. The heavy bolt fell with a loud thud.

"Is that okay?" he asked, brushing past me.

I nodded, and he led me across the closet-sized room past a computer whose screen saver displayed the Ocean Hospital logo bouncing back and forth in neon light. A plastic ficus gathered dust in the corner. Ronald stopped and rotated me until I was facing the wall. Someone had hung a poster in a cheap frame behind plexiglass. Wonder Woman. Stepping behind me and clasping his hands on my shoulders, he asked with breathy words, "Do you want this?"

"Tell me I got the promotion," I replied, keeping my eyes on Wonder Woman.

"I'm going to let you tell me," he said in a low voice, pressing his thumbs firmly into the palms of my hands. "Is this something you want?" he asked again, brushing the hair from my neck and tucking it behind my ear. His breath was sweet and smelled of cinnamon.

I gulped, heart pounding. He hadn't promised me anything. Could I throw away a decade of happy marriage for nothing? But in that moment, nothing felt like something. I held power in his erection. Sex was like autonomy. An orgasm would be like finding a lost identity. "Yes," I replied firmly.

"It's really important," he continued. "Because we both need to want this. There's so much at stake."

"I know," I breathed. With fingers gently pinching my arms, he turned me around to face him. He lifted my chin until our eyes met. "I know," I repeated. I leaned in and kissed his lips gently. He returned the kiss, gently at first and then more urgently. My chest found his, and I wrapped my arms around his waist. I clung tightly to him as my tongue found his warm, wet cinnamon mouth. His cheeks were smooth and his jaw strong. I raked my fingers through the hair at the nape of his neck and squeezed, yanking his mouth from mine.

His eyebrows raised in surprise, and I felt the twitch between his legs. I pushed him away to drink him in with my eyes. We paused, both of us panting. A burst of noise erupted from the phone in my pocket.

Yay! Time to get back to work! my ring tone announced. Ronald chuckled.

I cringed. "Ocean Hospital number," I explained, ending the call and tossing the phone on the desk.

Ronald reached out and caught the bottom edge of my scrub top. He lifted it slowly, exposing my waist. He pulled me to him by my shirt and I peeled it off as his hand slid across my back. A fire lit between my legs, quiet for too long. Desire was swelling there that I needed him to fill. I put my hands between his legs, exploring on top of his scrubs until I found what I needed.

He pulled the tie on my scrub pants, dropping them like a rock to the floor. I kicked them off. I stood there in a new bra and matching panties, and he told me I was beautiful. He turned me around once more, and I steadied myself with a hand against the wall. Still dressed, he untied his scrubs and moved the crotch of my panties aside.

I emptied my mind as he jammed himself between my legs, past the little friction that remained. We moved in a slippery rhythm with his breath on my neck as I forced myself to swallow the sounds that begged to escape my lips. Wonder Woman stared at me from the wall. *How could you?* her eyes demanded. But I didn't answer to her.

Yay! Time to get back to work! the phone cried again, but this time no one was listening.

I met his thrusts with wet acceptance. He squeezed my breast and breathed into my ear, "This is the end of meritocracy, Opal. You can have whatever you want."

I squeezed my eyes shut. Why did he have to say that? His words changed everything. I was suddenly a teenager, not pressed against the wall but pinned to the floor. Not receiving delicious thrusts so much as being torn apart. But it was all delicious, wasn't it? He wasn't smashing my face against the floor now. I wasn't being torn apart. I was in charge. I was Wonder Woman.

I should not have climaxed when he said it, but that was the version of me that got off on taking what I wanted. Breathing hard, I noticed an inscription on the poster. *To Mom. Not all heroes wear capes. Love, Jackie.* I slapped my hand over the words as Ronald twitched and jerked his way to finishing.

Yay! Time to get back to work! The phone had crossed a line and was no longer funny. These nurses needed to stop calling for every little thing. Still entwined with Ronald, I answered the Ocean Hospital call.

"This is Dr. Collins. Listen, I won't replace everyone's potassium at night, but Dr. Fahadi adores electrolytes and will be here in the morning."

"Opal, it's Fox," said the voice on the other end. Fuck! My dear husband was now with us in the room. My clitoris still convulsing, I pulled away from Ronald and a splash of white slime dropped to the floor. Just two minutes of being a whore and I already had to answer for myself.

"Shit, Fox!" I cried. "You're still here?"

"You said you'd be right back!"

I leaped into my scrubs in an instant, like I suddenly had Wonder Woman powers. My eyes darted to the dead bolt on the door, as if Fox were on the other side.

"I left my phone in the car, Opal. I had to call from the doctor's lounge. Are you coming back?"

My gaze shifted to Ronald, who was patting the bed beside him. Shaking his head, he mouthed "no." But now I had the power. I had taken it straight from his erection, which lay shriveled in his lap.

"Of course I'm coming back, Fox," I said. "I love you."

I turned to Ronald and shrugged, my fingers unbolting the door with a satisfying click. Feeling my way back along the dark and empty hallway, I left him alone in the call room.

Seventeen

Opal

Once the night in the call room had ended, I was alone with my guilt. I had done something so terrible, I couldn't even picture Fox without feeling like I'd been punched in the gut. It was worse when I thought of my kids. What kind of person betrays a six-year-old? But there were butterflies, too. What was I supposed to do with that?

I called Fantasia and told her I was into something deep. Amongst her frenetic schedule of patients, pole dances, and lectures, she booked the next flight. It made sense that when I needed talk therapy, she brought me to a strip club.

Starship Gentleman's Club just north of Gainesville would have been empty on a Wednesday afternoon if Fantasia hadn't borrowed a key from an old sorority sister to get us in there.

"We're going to stretch first," Fantasia said, leading me to the stage. "Then we'll get you on the pole."

Fantasia and I sat across from each other, sliding into straddles. She rested with her long legs rigid and toes pointed, as if her torso were grafted onto Barbie's legs.

Ever since I cheated on Fox in the call room, the memory of a man named Michael McMillan pressed my thoughts, insistent and unresolved. I had become a doctor to fix other broken people—penance for my guilt. I married a respectable man to cover my shame. My conscience was supposed to be clean, but my hands were dirty.

The Starship felt ordinary with the lights on. There were no strobe lights or raucous music—no dollar bills being waved in the air. Fantasia's T-shirt dropped off her shoulder as she reached for her toes. Her platinum hair fell gently around her face with no gel to cement it in place.

Fantasia unfurled until she was upright. "What's happening with your job? How's Karen, or whatever her name is?"

I swung my legs in front of me and reached for my toes, hiding my face in my knees. "Karen's job is mine if I want it," I said with my face down.

"Okay, wasn't expecting that," Fantasia said. "Here, grab the pole." She helped me to my feet. "Now, plant your toe and spin."

I turned slowly, looking out at the empty tables and the bar.

"How did that happen?" Fantasia asked as she corrected my posture.

"I slept with the president of the company," I replied. She was a therapist, and a stripper. She took off her clothes for money. I never would have guessed that she'd have problem with that.

"Opal, what the fuck?"

I stopped my awkward spin mid-pole, humiliation flooding my chest. I thought I knew the woman covered in tattoos who stripped for men, but I had misjudged her. In the past, when things happened with Michael, my friends had accepted me. Encouraged me, even. Things were different then. We were kids. I thought about how things had started Michael.

We were all competing for the affection of a stupid boy named Cody — Tracy, Daphne and I. That stupid boy had started everything. Michael, Tracy's father was an ER doctor and volunteer gymnastics coach. He used to throw parties at his lake house, and the overnight retreats led to the inevitable chaos of teenage romance.

Everything had unraveled at one high school party.

"Daphne!" I'd exclaimed, scanning the field for my friend. We caught sight of one another and rushed to an embrace of giggles and shrieks.

"Let's go to my room and get our swimsuits on," Tracy had suggested. We weaved through the adults who were busy finding space on the counter for their crocks of potato salad and bowls of chips and dip. Someone had turned on the stereo, and classic rock was being pumped through speakers in every room. Tracy's mother, Gabby, stood in the periphery, directing her guests. We passed by a bedroom where her father, Michael, held a telephone to his ear, inviting more guests to stop by.

"Do you think Cody is here yet?" I asked the girls. We took turns sitting at a vanity in the corner that held a small mirror. I leaned close to the mirror and smoothed down my eyebrows. I sucked at my braces and checked my teeth.

"I get Cody this time," Tracy announced. She bumped me gently with her hip and took my place in front of the mirror.

"Not so fast," Daphne teased. "It's my turn to have Cody." We laughed as Daphne pushed Tracy off the stool and began applying dark lipstick.

In the morning, my tongue had been thick from the cheap booze we had sneaked from abandoned coolers.

The door to Tracy's room creaked open. Cody poked his head in, his hair a wild and tangled mess. He scanned the room and whispered, "Where's Tracy?"

I froze, heart sinking. "No boys allowed!"

"Whatever, Sasquatch," he jeered, nodding toward my eyebrows, and left the room.

Tracy stirred and rolled on her side to face me. "What was that?" she murmured.

"Cody," I replied.

She closed her eyes as she smiled and breathed in through her nose, hugging her pillow. "You know, he kissed me last night, Opal," she said, opening her eyes and catching mine in the mirror.

My heart had sunk like a stone, and I ran from the house. My best friend had betrayed me. I had to go to the lake, desperate for refuge.

If only her father hadn't seen me run, a poor little gazelle in the sights of a lion.

"What's wrong, Opal?" Michael had asked, looking straight ahead instead of at my tearstained face. He dropped into an Adirondak chair facing the placid lake with an all-too-casual invitation for me to join him.

I sighed. "A girl kissed my boyfriend."

"Ah, I see. And you like this boy?"

I nodded.

"Cody?"

I nodded again.

"Fuck him," he'd cursed. My eyes widened at the curse. No one in my house ever cursed. We were the tight-lipped, confrontation-avoiding, passive aggressive type of family. "He's a child. You're too mature for him."

I pivoted to face him. "I am?"

"For sure, Opal. You're so grown up for your age." Michael had turned to face me, his eyes gentle as they searched mine.

"It was Tracy," I admitted.

"I figured. You're more grown up than Tracy too," he'd confided. "Practically a woman."

Then Michael did some rearranging of plans behind the scenes. Suddenly, he'd had to drive back into town to cover for a doctor calling out sick, and he took me with him. He said this was so he could get me to church, where I was scheduled to volunteer at the second-best sale. His wife, Gabby, had regarded him suspiciously.

I'd grabbed a pancake for the road and mumbled a quick goodbye to Tracy. Michael was waiting for me in a red Jeep. His eyes went from me to the road and back to me again.

"Thanks again for the ride, Dr. McMillan."

He chuckled. "Call me Michael," he said. "What do you want to be when you grow up, Opal?"

"I want to be a social worker," I replied.

Michael scoffed. "Well, you're not buying yourself a lake house like mine if you're a social worker," he retorted. "A social worker? Why a social worker?"

"Because I like helping people," I replied.

"Why not be a doctor if you like helping people?"

"Me?" I'd asked, surprised. "I thought you had to be a superhero to be a doctor."

"Opal!" he exclaimed. "That's you, superhero. You could do it. You could definitely be a doctor."

"Hmm," I replied, turning the idea over in my mind.

We were quiet for the rest of the ride. As we'd neared the northern edge of Gilbert, I'd pointed out the road leading east to the church. "Turn there."

"We're not going straight to the church, Opal. I need to stop at home first."

"But I'll be late," I protested.

He waved me off. "It'll be okay. I need my coffee. Stat."

I bit my lip, unsure if I should protest further. I didn't talk back to grown-ups. I decided against it and sat in silence. The pastor would be so disappointed if I was late, and he would tell my mother.

"Do you drink coffee, Opal?" Michael had asked.

"Oh, yes," I replied, thinking of the instant coffee that my stepfather Louis and I sometimes stirred into mugs of microwaved water. After the coffee dripped into the carafe, Michael poured two mugs and handed one to me along with a bowl of sugar.

"I just remembered," he said, setting his mug on the counter. "I have something for you." He disappeared down the hall and came back with a large shopping bag.

"What's that?" I asked.

"I bought some new clothes for Tracy, but I got the wrong size. It's too much effort to return them. I want you to have them," he'd said, handing me the bag.

"Wow," I'd breathed, peering into the bag. It was heavy, brimming with more new clothes than I had ever held at one time. "Thank you so much!"

"Let's keep this between you and me," he said, his smile hinting at our growing bond.

It had been something special that brought me joy. Something I had kept all for myself.

So was Ronald.

Now, at the Starship Gentleman's Club, I dug my heels in and threw it back at Fantasia. "I found something that brings me joy like you told me to." I pointed my finger at her. "And I'm keeping it all for myself."

Fantasia started past me, careful not to meet my eyes as she exchanged places with me and spun around the pole. Painful seconds ticked by without conversation as she spun, letting my corroded morals hang between us.

"Do you have feelings for your boss?" she asked.

"Fox deserves a bigger piece of me," I explained, crossing my legs. "If I'm the medical director, Karen won't control me, and I can give him that."

Fantasia waited for more.

"Ronald is merely a means to an end," I added.

"But you just said he brings you joy," she whispered. And before I could admit she was right, she changed the subject. "Did you know Billy joined a band? Can you believe it? He's playing the guitar."

I winced. She had abandoned me in my confusion and closed the door on the subject. Fine. I didn't enjoy her criticism anyway. "Wow," I said of Billy. "Your husband does have a rock-star vibe."

"It's very sexy," Fantasia said. "Can you jump onto the pole like this?" She leaped onto the pole and squeezed it between her outstretched legs. Once she had dismounted, I clumsily threw myself at the pole, then slid down it like a dead insect smashed against a windshield. Fantasia laughed and turned the conversation back to me. "Pleasing old men makes you happy?"

My old skeleton rose up then, begging me to expose it. "I assumed the conversation was about Billy now," I said.

Fantasia shook her head.

"I made a mistake with an older man from my past. I believed that being a doctor and a perfect wife would redeem me," I explained instead.

"But it didn't, so you gave in and slept with your boss," Fantasia analyzed.

I whipped my head around to her. "Exactly, Fantasia. I liked it and I'll probably do it again. If that's okay with you."

Fantasia shrugged and hopped off the stage, heading for the exit.

Before she had made it halfway, she turned and replied, "Hey, I have no skin in the game. But whoever you're sleeping with—" Her face held a grave expression.

I bit my lip. I didn't want her to be angry, but then she broke into a broad grin.

"Just don't show him your pole dancing!"

I met her laughter with my own. "Fair," I replied as I hurried to catch up with her.

EIGHTEEN
RONALD

It wasn't a corporate office day; it was an Ocean Hospital day. Ronald constantly found reasons to be there now. It was where Opal was. They hadn't seen one another since she'd left him in the call room. The affair was a mistake, for sure. Such a thing could completely ruin his life. Ronald frowned. People took things very seriously, he remembered.

He'd come to Ocean Hospital that day to meet with Karen and finalize the list of doctors they were going to fire. He took a seat across from her now and twisted his wedding ring while he stared through the nest of hairspray and bangs atop her forehead.

"What's wrong, Ronald?" Karen asked. Ronald stopped twisting the ring and fumbled for words.

Karen took herself very seriously, always applying for the next promotion. She would have made a fine internist, but ambition tugged her to the executive suites. Inevitably, she'd become the medical director at Ocean Hospital. Her drive made sense to anyone who knew her husband: Brad Lessons, the billboard-famous attorney whose smile beamed from bus stops and park benches across town. With a partner like that, Karen's hunger to keep climbing didn't just seem reasonable—it seemed inevitable.

"Expect some rumbling when this deal happens," Ronald warned as Karen settled at her desk. "Doctors never understand what it's like to manage a business."

"Well, I can appreciate that," Karen added. "You can't make everyone happy."

"Especially the board of directors," Ronald continued, although there was only one person whose happiness he cared about in that moment. "You know the saying. Happy board, happy life."

"I'd be a great board member," Karen chirped with a bat of her eyelashes.

"Do you have the numbers I asked for?" Ronald asked without indulging her.

"Right here," Karen replied, pulling a file from her drawer. She set the file in front of her, opened it, and picked up the top sheet. She handed it to Ronald for his inspection. "Alex Tang. His numbers are excellent. He's one of our top docs." Karen handed him the next sheet in the stack while he scanned Alex's stats. "Nassrin Fahadi. Even better numbers. Well-liked by nurses and patients." She kept going. "Tom Rogers. Highest number of admissions. Highest patient-satisfaction scores—"

"Didn't administration get some complaints about him?" Ronald interrupted.

"Tom?" Karen paused. "I don't know of any issue with Tom."

Ronald didn't answer as he pored over Tom's numbers. They were impressive, he had to admit. The man was a machine.

Karen kept going. "Tom's been with Doctors Inc. a long time, Ronald. Longer than you have, actually. He started when this was still Sunshine Medical." She handed him the next sheet. "Opal Collins. Her numbers stink. She's always behind, and I'm always picking up her slack."

"Dr. Collins delivers excellent care. Anyone else?" Ronald asked.

"We need to fire someone, right?" Karen asked. "It has to be Opal."

Ronald closed his eyes and rubbed his temples. This meeting was headed nowhere. He imagined himself informing Karen she was going to be replaced. Opal would never be content with mediocrity, and leaving her in a mediocre position was no longer an option. Despite this, she was distinctive from the people lined up requesting increased pay, additional benefits, and elevated status. He was like that himself. At sixty-seven, he should be slowing down. He should be drawing Social Security and enrolling in Medicare. He should be lining up for the early-bird special at the Beachside Diner, if Isabelle would ever let him. Isabelle wanted more. From her perspective, Ronald was only getting started. He was president of Doctors Inc. But Doctors Inc. was only one of the health-care giants in the region. Why not own them all?

"Headache?" Karen asked.

"I have a feeling my blood pressure is up again," he replied.

Karen opened a drawer in a gray metal cabinet, pulled out a blood-pressure cuff, and strapped it to his arm. She nestled her stethoscope buds in her ears and placed the stethoscope on the inside of his elbow. She continued talking as she inflated the cuff.

"Listen, Ronald. I could have emailed you these numbers," Karen said, waving to the rest of her stack of papers. She paused as she let the air out of the cuff. "186 over 115," she reported without comment on the absurdly high blood pressure. She continued. "I assume the reason you drove all the way down here is because you want my opinion. My opinion is that Opal Collins is weak. Period."

The discussion ended with a knock at the door. Karen rose to answer while Ronald grasped his wedding ring again.

"Well, speak of the devil," Karen said with sugar in her voice. Ronald turned and found Opal standing in the doorway.

"Um," Opal mumbled. "I saw Dr. Aberdeen come here, and I wanted to discuss my numbers."

Karen gave Opal a quick nod and fake smile, then left the two of them in her office. Opal tiptoed to Karen's desk and smiled as she sat in Karen's chair, as if she were already the medical director.

Where did they stand now? Ronald found himself desperate to be wanted. He jumped from his chair and his stride was fast and direct as he approached her.

Opal's hair was curled and brushed to a shine. She wore dark-red lipstick that revealed her white teeth when she smiled up at him. Even if her productivity didn't improve, at least her appearance had.

"Dr. Aberdeen!" she exclaimed, as he took her by the hand. "What are you doing here?"

"Dr. Collins," he started.

Her chin fell, and she whispered, "I thought we were on a first-name basis now, Ronald. Are you here to check on me?"

"Of course I'm not here to check on you," Ronald lied, moving his hand to her arm. "I've already seen that your numbers are up for September."

"I believe it's these new shoes!" she said, pointing to the dressy shoes on her feet. "I'm so much faster making rounds in them."

Ronald cringed at the bad joke. Was it the awkward conversation or the deep fear of the consequences of what they had done that gave him the urge to flee?

"I'm not here to see you," he said, dropping her arm. Why was he doing this? "I came to meet with Karen."

Blood rushed to her cheeks, giving away her disappointment. Good —he enjoyed seeing her crave his attention. Yet the satisfaction faltered. Why did he need to twist the knife?

Opal tucked a pen into the pocket of her white coat and pushed herself up from the chair. "I've got patients to see," she mumbled and turned her back to him.

Maybe he had gone too far. If he offended Opal, his shot at a connection with Congressman Allen Collins could be over before it began. And no Allen, no research in New York. As she pushed past him and walked away, he said in a low voice, "Wait!"

She turned to face him. His heart thumped in his chest. His finger beckoned her back. Opal narrowed her eyes at the gesture. This was going all wrong. Forget about Allen Collins. If Ronald didn't keep Opal happy, she could blow up his life like a bomb. It would be a repeat of New York. Ronald folded his hands and mouthed, "Please."

She stepped back into the office where Ronald had perched on the desk, now filling the small room with his limbs. He wanted to touch her, but not here, not out in the open. When her hips brushed against his legs, the two of them crowded in the room, it sent a rush of excitement through his body. "You look very pretty today," he said in a hushed tone.

Opal met his eyes, the nervous humor having left her expression. "Call-room pretty?" she asked.

NINETEEN
OPAL

TWO DAYS HAD GONE BY SINCE THE INCIDENT WITH RONALD in the call room, yet I had somehow avoided any serious conversation with Fox. Unsure if I could face him after what I'd done, I lingered at Ocean Hospital far too long before finally heading home. Fox was waiting for me in the kitchen. When I cracked the door and eased myself in, he extended a glass of sweet tea.

"Thanks," I said, taking the tea. He had brewed it sickly sweet today.

"We haven't discussed the tree guy," Fox replied, flipping on the light above the table. The shadows of sunset fell away.

"There's a lot we haven't discussed," I said, taking the chair across from him. The ever-present undertow of conversations left unspoken loomed between us.

"Have you heard of sudden oak death?" he asked gently.

The mention of death, even the death of a tree, jarred me. The subject could derail my good news—that I had all but sealed my promotion. I sighed, tugging at my eyebrow. "I have."

"That's what the arborist thinks."

"Well, I guess we've got firewood for the winter," I teased, masking the punch of his revelation with a wink. Rising, I grabbed kale for the salad, intent on pivoting the conversation away from loss. No one here was losing anything. This family was rising.

"Firewood?" Fox repeated, his voice tinged with disappointment.

"I'm kidding. Listen, we probably need a permit to cut that thing down."

His hand tightened on the glass. "Opal, 'that thing' is a tree. It has been here for a hundred years. It was your grandmother's tree, and she used to push you on its swing. Now it's our children's. Shouldn't we fight for it?"

I faced him, a stalk of kale dangling in my hand. "Honey, sometimes you have to know when a tree is worth fighting for and when to let go."

Fox's expression hardened. "Opal, I love you, but you're being careless with something valuable. If you don't protect it, the tree will be gone. And once it's gone, you can never get it back."

"Okay," I murmured, retreating. There were bigger battles to fight.

"Mom, I'm hungry!" Cal interrupted, wandering into the kitchen. "When will the fish sticks be ready?"

"Lasagna. Thirty minutes," I replied, waving him off. I turned back to Fox as Cal lodged complaints about lasagna under his breath. Time to turn on parental selective hearing. "Fox, we need to talk."

"I need to tell you something too," he said, smiling faintly.

I raised an eyebrow. "It's—"

"I need help wiping!" Emily called from the bathroom.

"You know how to wipe yourself," Fox called back.

Ignoring Emily, I pressed on. "Dr. Aberdeen offered me a remote patient advocate liaison role. I told him no."

Fox stepped back, his face twisted in disbelief. "What the hell?"

"Language!" Cal chimed in from another room.

"Take the damn job!" Fox exclaimed. "That would solve everything."

He'd never yelled like that, not at me. My jaw tightened, indignant. "Medical director is still on the table," I countered.

"So is getting fired," he snapped.

"I'm not going to—"

We glanced down as Emily traipsed into the kitchen, her pants around her ankles, holding a roll of toilet paper. "Wipe me!" she screamed.

Fox took Emily by the hand, a threat to close the discussion.

I kept going. "The medical director job matters. The PAL is bullshit."

"I heard about the PAL position!" Fox yelled suddenly. "And I've got news—I got promoted. Head of Radiology." He was already halfway out of the room.

His words hung in the air, chilling me. Promoted? How? And how did he hear about the PAL? What else did he know? I slumped into my chair, queasy. Before I could gather myself, a shrill sound pierced the air —the smoke alarm. I bolted for the oven as black smoke rolled out. The lasagna was on fire.

Fox was there in an instant, gripping me and whisking me away with a single motion. He sprayed the fire extinguisher with precision. "Stay back," he commanded. "You might be pregnant."

Knowing that was impossible, but welcoming the lie, I allowed myself to be saved by his embrace. His arms were as strong and soft as always. This felt like home. I pushed away thoughts of deep conversation and rested in the warmth of his chest.

Fox lost no time, trailing his fingertips along my arm. Why did resting in the warmth of his chest instantly mean foreplay to him? Cringing, I twisted my arm away. "I'm not pregnant." I rejected Fox's seduction, throwing a thumbs-up toward Cal peering curiously from the hallway. "I need to be honest with you. I thought I could do this, but I can't. Growing our family is out of the question. You understand how important my work is, Fox. You, more than anyone."

"Our children are important work. Our marriage is important work," he pressed. "You won't have to give up your work forever. But fight for us first."

The air left the room, the smoke all but dissipating, and I softened. When he spoke again, his tone was gentle. "Before you know it, Cal and Emily will be in college. And I'm going to get old, Opal. I'm gonna get really old," he teased.

"Are you going to get weird moles with hair growing out of them?" I asked, a smirk creeping up my lips. Clasping his face in my hands, taking in his rich smile and beautiful red hair, I sighed with content. They were mine, and I was glad.

He nodded in mock solemnity. "Thick glasses. A cane. Maybe a monocle for full effect."

"Are we going to grow apart?" I asked quietly.

Fox tilted my face to his. "I'm not going anywhere. I'm not your father. I'll never leave you."

My resolve cracked. "Okay. We'll try," I lied.

Lust rose in my chest. I sucked in a breath as I followed the idea of making love to my husband with an image so cruel, it sent a spasm between my legs. A snapshot of Ronald Aberdeen would blister into frame while I fucked Fox.

I plunked burnt lasagna in the trash, poured cereal into bowls, and set them out for the kids as if I were feeding stray cats. Then I led Fox to the bedroom. Actions would bury deeds. Actions would fix this mess. I pressed hard on his chest, flattening him to the bed. He pushed his briefs to his knees. I tossed my panties on the floor and grabbed him. He was already hard. I climbed on and my mind replaced his face with Ronald's.

It was over quickly for us both. We lay side by side, breathing heavily. "See, babe?" Fox said. "This is going to be fun."

"Yes," I lied through my teeth. For the first time since Ronald, I felt calm. Fox would never know. What I did had saved us. "How'd you know about PAL?" I asked as we lay in the dark.

"The merger. Ocean Hospital and Bonne Santé are merging."

I squeezed his hand, shocked. I knew what that meant, but I couldn't bring myself to say it. What I couldn't say, Fox did.

"I'm going to work for Ronald Aberdeen."

"He's some boss," I whispered. And before the house returned to chaos, I asked, "Do you want to check on the kids, or should I?"

TWENTY
RONALD

PILL. WATER GLASS. PHONE. LAMP.

Ronald navigated the bedside table with his hand in the dark until it found the small pill. This morning there was no headache, only adrenaline. Today he would announce the merger. He was going to put on a show in front of Opal and she was going to revel in his power.

"You're wearing the red tie, right?" Isabelle asked, stepping behind him as he shaved.

"I thought you picked that one," Ronald replied pointing to a blue tie dotted with golf clubs.

"Ronald, no!" she snapped. "You need to look like a president, not a jackass."

He smirked; he enjoyed teasing her. Merging Doctors Inc. and Santa Rosa Medical System was Isabelle's idea from the start. She wasn't satisfied with a husband leading one firm; she wanted him to own them all.

What Isabelle didn't know was that Ronald had been secretly communicating with Allen Collins. She wouldn't approve of his plans to return to research in New York, somewhere prestigious like Sloan Kettering. He'd never get his foot in the door without Allen's help, thanks to his old boss, Jerry Winterfeld. But with Allen, he could reclaim his research and publish breakthroughs that could get cancer patients the treatment they deserved. That legacy meant more to him than corporate mergers ever could.

"I'll show you what I think of your stupid tie," Isabelle said. She lifted the tie from the door handle and yanked Ronald's arms behind his back.

"Isabelle, I don't have time for this," he protested as she pulled him toward the bed.

"Lie on your back and put your hands up," she commanded. He did as he was told, his erection growing and straining against his boxer shorts. "You're not going anywhere."

"I need to assemble the teams at Ocean Hospital and Bonne Santé," Ronald said.

"I didn't think Ocean Hospital had anybody worth keeping," Isabelle replied, tugging down his boxers. She laid the golf tie over his crotch, slipped off her panties, and straddled him.

"Ocean Hospital needs an overhaul. There's one doctor, a total train wreck—"

"Your golf tie is dirty." She pulled it out from between her legs and settled him inside of her.

Ronald's heart raced as she used the damp tie to bind his wrists. She slipped her hands around his neck and squeezed as her hips began to move. He met Isabelle's eyes. "Opal Collins," he grunted. "Married to Fox Collins—"

"Who you want for head of Radiology," she finished. "If you want to keep him, you've got to keep her."

"I need to go, Izzy," he said as she fucked him.

"Not until I'm finished," she said.

Pinned beneath her, overwhelmed by her intensity, his old medical student Trisha's face flashed in his mind. Ronald rolled away from Isabelle. He covered his face with his hands as he remembered. It was so long ago now...

"The hospital is letting me go," Ronald told Isabelle in their New York City apartment. Nearly twenty years ago.

"Letting you go where?" she had asked, concern etched across her face.

"I no longer work for Good News Hospital," he declared, fist clenched.

"They can't just let you go! What the fuck happened?"

Ronald squeezed his eyes shut. "We have to leave New York."

"What are you talking about?" Isabelle persisted, shaking her head. "We are New York!"

"I think we should go to Rebecca in Phoenix," Ronald said. It would be good to be near their daughter. "University Medical Center has a good research program. I can move my cancer research there."

As her hands froze in understanding, he knew he'd reached a breaking point.

"What did you do?" she asked, her voice filled with accusation.

"Nothing," he replied calmly.

"You're chief of surgery. Your portrait is hanging in the hospital lobby." Her voice became shrill and frenzied. "Tell me, Ronald. What did you do?"

Silence.

"The hospital's letting me go because of a medical student," he admitted. "She didn't like her grade."

"What does that have to do with Arizona?" Isabelle shot back.

"I slept with my medical student."

Her face fell, the only indication she gave that his news devastated her. "Arizona is not going to work," she insisted, her voice firm.

"I want to escape," he whimpered.

"You don't have the connections to be a chief of surgery there," Isabelle said slowly.

"I need my research," he had pleaded. "It'll save lives."

"Ronald, listen to me. I didn't drop out of medical school to raise your kid just so you could run away and pout when something doesn't go your way."

"It's more complicated than that, Izzy," he argued.

She held a hand up to silence him. "I don't need you to be a nobody, Ronald. I need you to be a somebody."

***

It was a point he couldn't shake. Even now, twenty years later. He was having trouble keeping his erection. Determined to reclaim his past but troubled by thoughts of Opal, Ronald drew a deep breath as Isabelle coaxed his erection back with her mouth. "Opal Collins. . ." A guttural utterance. Opal terrified him. Not butterflies. Only panic. She was someone he could love. Maybe he already did.

"Go see her," Isabelle said, defeated. She untied Ronald's hands, flopping down beside him.

"She's a disaster," he continued. The best lies were half truths.

Isabelle chuckled. "I know who you're talking about. The Walmart dress at the Christmas party."

"Yes."

"Mousy brunette. Mismatched shoes last year?"

"Uh-huh."

"Oof. You're right. Poor thing is a disaster."

"I couldn't agree more," Ronald said, sitting up. He was getting a headache, after all.

"But you can't get rid of her if you want Fox," Isabelle said. She left the room and returned with the red tie. "Make her feel special," Isabelle said. "Butter her up so you can get Fox."

"I think I can do that," Ronald agreed.

TWENTY-ONE
RONALD

THE PRESS WAS EVERYWHERE AT OCEAN HOSPITAL AND OPAL Collins was nowhere to be found.

Pain clambered up Ronald's temples and seized his forehead as he anxiously tried to find her. He didn't want Opal anywhere near the press without him. Taylor from public relations had called all the local outlets, and now clusters of reporters and their cameramen swarmed the hospital's front entrance.

Ronald would give a statement after the meeting—as would Clyde at Bonne Santé—but for now, he ducked into the side entrance, dodging the flashing lights and microphones thrust his way.

Inside, he headed to Karen's office to wait for the meeting to start. Karen left him there as she hurried out to the wards to make sure her hospitalist team attended the announcement alert and on time.

Fidgeting, Ronald stood from Karen's desk and buttoned his suit jacket. He smoothed the red silk tie and straightened the American flag pinned to his lapel. His shoes were shined, his hair was combed, and his face was freshly shaved.

It was time.

Before he could leave Karen's office, the door creaked open. Opal slipped inside.

"I wanted to wish you luck," she said, running his tie through her fingers.

His chest filled with pride. He wanted her to think he looked powerful and that his words were impressive. He wanted her to know he was important, and he wanted her to be a part of it.

"Will you be watching?" he asked.

"Wouldn't miss it," she said with a wink before disappearing back to the ward.

Ronald took a steadying breath and walked to the auditorium. The podium was waiting. The mic was on and ready to go as he took the stage. Static crackled impatiently over the wire as he gripped the stand, leaning forward and surveying the crowd. White coats and black suits filled the room. He scanned each face, looking for the one he couldn't get off his mind. His eyes stopped midway across the front row, where Isabelle sat looking up at him with anticipation on her face. Ambition dripped from her clasped hands. Power coiled between her tightly crossed legs. She was his queen.

His guilty eyes moved to the back of the room, where he finally caught sight of Opal.

A rock of disappointment formed in the pit of his stomach. Opal was looking down, fumbling with her beeper. She wasn't paying attention to him. She probably didn't even realize how badly he wanted her to glance up. The silence lingered, and now he saw Isabelle wringing her hands nervously. Opal was in her own world. Finally, Ronald cleared his throat.

"Doctors Inc. has been a leader in health care for the last fifteen-plus years," he started. The crowd stilled. "But as of January 1st, that will come to an end."

Gasps traveled like a wave through the rows of chairs followed by whispers, low and hissing. Opal had left her seat and was walking out a back door. Red heat began to creep up his collar to his neck and his cheeks.

"I'm proud to announce that starting on January first, Doctors Inc. will merge with Santa Rosa Medical System and become Health Solutions South."

Right on cue, the room's projector switched on and the giant screen behind Ronald was filled with the image of Clyde Jewel. His warm, beaming smile streamed live from Bonne Santé out to the room of shocked faces. Ronald turned toward the image to greet the president of SRMS and spotted Opal, newly returned and now standing a few feet from his wife. He smiled to himself, relieved and giddy. She watched him intently, and an excited smile spread across her young face. This was his show.

The speech went splendidly. He said all the usual things about mergers. He paused in requisite silence while Clyde Jewel made the announcement that he would retire and leave Ronald Aberdeen to be president of it all. And when Clyde finished delivering the short speech, Ronald flashed his white teeth in a camera-ready grin for the first wave of photographers from Ocean Hospital.

In front of the palm-lined entrance to Ocean Hospital, Ronald found Isabelle amongst the throng of cameramen and motioned for her to stand beside him. Ronald stepped up to the microphone, practically knocking over Clyde Jewel, who had arrived from Bonne Santé. "I'll take questions now," Ronald said.

A middle-aged man in a short-sleeved button-up and drugstore reading glasses moved to the front of the crowd with a handheld recorder and a clipboard. "Terry Knowls. *West Florida Observer.*"

"Good morning, Mr. Knowls," Ronald replied, smiling as he looked out over the crowd.

"Congratulations on your merger of Doctors Inc. and Santa Rosa Medical System this morning. How does it feel to be taking the reins at Health Solutions South?" the reporter asked.

"I have been preparing for this moment behind the scenes for a long time," Ronald said. "The next step in the company's evolution feels completely natural and we're excited to offer the community an expanded network of health care."

"How do you think the community will respond to the expansion in light of your sordid past?"

Ronald froze. Clusters of men and women in expensive clothing and sleek sunglasses had started to gather—board members and their families. Ronald recovered and looked at the reporter quizzically. " 'Sordid past,' did you say?"

Terry Knowls looked down at his notes before locking eyes with Ronald. "Ronald Aberdeen, you purchased Sunshine Medical from Adam Winterfeld in 2003. Prior to that, you were the chief of surgery at Good News Hospital under the leadership of Jerry Winterfeld, Adam Winterfeld's brother. You were dismissed from Good News Hospital in 2003 after allegations of sexual harassment."

Ronald stood in excruciating silence. His headache pounded in his ears. Lightheaded, he was unable to continue.

Isabelle jumped in front of him and quickly lowered the microphone. "That won't stand up to the fact-checking, Mr. Knowls," she said with a smile through clenched teeth. "Next question."

"Who is Trisha Brown?" the reporter asked.

"I have no idea. Next question," Isabelle replied.

"Did your husband sexually harass Dr. Brown, then a medical student under his supervision, and retaliate against her rejection by assigning her a failing grade?"

"Mr. Knowls," Isabelle interrupted with exasperation, "it was only an allegation. No evidence was ever discovered, and no charges were ever filed. We're not here to discuss the smut that inevitably follows a visionary like my husband. We are here to celebrate the success of Doctors Inc. and Santa Rosa Medical System and prepare for the joyous birth of Health Solutions South. End of interview!" She waved him off as if he were a gnat.

When the press conference at last came to an end, Ronald dashed through the crowd and into the men's room. Heaving the contents of his stomach into the toilet, he gripped the porcelain, palms slick with sweat. Thank God Opal Collins was nowhere in sight.

Twenty-Two

Opal

I was the first to arrive at the Rest Rite Motel. Gilbert was short on luxury, but still, I was expecting something with a grand entrance, something tidy with working fixtures. My imagination had nowhere to land but on Moss Creek Resort, which this was not. I'd watched the route snake across my GPS in a blue line, heading east beyond Gilbert into a run-down neighborhood. I had been this far east in a distant past. There were shelters not far away where I used to volunteer in soup kitchens. As a child, I'd trolled every shelter in Gilbert looking for my father. My pastor brought me to all of them, thinking only that I was unusually socially conscious for a nine-year-old. Most of those places were gone now, the buildings empty.

As I drove down the street looking for the neon Rest Rite sign, I passed a mobile home park, a strip club, and a pawn shop. They all appeared sleepy and deserted in the midday heat. I found the place and pulled into a nearly empty gravel parking lot. Sitting alone in my car, I wondered for a moment if I was safe.

I couldn't carry on with Ronald in the call rooms of Ocean Hospital forever, but this place? The undeniable filth matched the state of my soul and cast a harsh light on my betrayal. The neon "R" blinked fruitlessly, refusing to stay lit, as if mocking my obsession with Ronald Aberdeen.

The tired row of rooms had private entrances from the parking lot. Each door was numbered, most with peeling black paint that revealed rusted iron beneath. Some of the porch lights were still on despite the late morning hour, their bulbs surrounded by thin clouds of insects. A fat man with tattoos covering his arms and legs leaned against the building outside the office, smoking a cigarette.

I closed my eyes and thought of the grandeur of Moss Creek—and of Fox. Putting my car in reverse, I backed out of my spot and pulled up to the road, heart pounding. Jesus, I wanted to run back to Fox. I looked up and down the street one last time for Ronald's car, but it wasn't there.

Instead, a pack of police cars came flying down the road toward the Rest Rite, lights and sirens screaming. I put a guilty hand to my mouth instinctively, as if the police knew what I was about to do and were coming for me. But instead, the cruisers descended on the gas station across the street. They spilled out into the road, blocking my exit from the Rest Rite. I sighed and re-parked my car at the motel.

I tucked my phone under my shirt as if it were safe there, and kept one hand in my purse, gripping my wallet, as I shut off the car. As I approached the man with the cigarette, I looked over my shoulder at the spectacle of lights across the street. The scent of the man's tobacco permeated the sidewalk.

"Do you work here?" I asked.

He looked me over as I stood on the sidewalk, feeling exposed. "You need a room?" he asked.

"Yes," I replied quickly.

"You paying by the hour or by the night?" he asked.

"How much for the night?"

"It's fifty bucks for an hour or sixty for the night," he replied.

My eyes darted around the outside of the motel as I pulled out my wallet. Near the street, a tall man in a dirty baseball cap pushed a shopping cart that contained a blanket and a suitcase, unfazed by the criminal commotion. The wheel squeaked at the top of every rotation.

Room 4 of the motel opened, and a woman called to him. He paused, yelled something back, and kept walking.

I handed the man with the cigarette three twenty-dollar bills. He disappeared in the office and came back with a plastic key ring with a faded number seven printed on it. He motioned for me to follow.

At the door with the seven screwed in place, he pushed the key roughly into the lock. The key stuck and the knob stayed stubbornly fixed as he tried to turn it. A part of me hoped he wouldn't be able to open the door.

What was I doing here?

The police cars made room on the road, and a Gilbert city bus pulled up and stopped with a hiss in front of the motel. Its diesel engine chugged as the door folded open. I watched a row of people descend onto the sidewalk and disperse to places nearby.

The man threw the butt of his cigarette on the sidewalk beside us and bent forward to inspect the lock. I reached my foot past him and stamped out the cigarette with my boot. The knob turned, and the door to my room opened with a creak like the groan of old bones.

"Thank you," I said as I hurried past him into the room.

I flipped a switch on the wall by the door, and a ceiling light blinked before turning on. I looked around for any roaches or hypodermic needles. To my relief, I seemed to be the only living thing there. I let out a breath and nervously reached into my shirt to retrieve my phone. I pulled the curtains closed and carefully removed the linens from the bed.

Motels washed the sheets, but they never washed the quilt, I could hear Michael McMillan explaining from a distant motel in a distant past.

I crossed through and inspected the bathroom. The light was harsh, and the white tiles harbored too many layers of dirt to ever pass for clean again. The mirror caught my reflection and forced me to consider how this looked. Tension creased my brow, and my mouth pulled down in a frown. I smoothed down my eyebrows and reminded myself how excited I was to be there. I forced a smile and rummaged through my bag until I found a bottle of deodorizing spray. I pressed the nozzle as I swept it back and forth across the room until I was satisfied with the aroma of lavender masking stale smoke. With nothing else to do, I pulled a chair over to the window and peered through the curtains, waiting for Ronald.

He eventually pulled his car into the lot and parked beside mine. The police were gone, and the motel was sleepy again. My pulse quickened as the engine cut and he stepped out. I watched with curiosity as he approached a man who sat on the curb nearby.

Ronald, dressed in linen pants and a light short-sleeved button-up with a shiny watch and expensive shoes knelt beside the man and began speaking to him. I couldn't hear what they were saying, but I could see Ronald clap him on the shoulder, take him by the hand, and help him stand up.

The sound of their laughter drifted through the parking lot and into the room where I waited as the two men walked to the office. Ronald held the door, and the feeble old man shuffled in ahead of him. A moment later, they emerged—the elderly man holding a sandwich and a soda.

I thought of myself hoping for Moss Creek luxury and the president of Doctors Inc. stopping to help a stranger. Heart squeezing in my chest, I flung off my pride and longed for Ronald to be in my arms.

The rap at the door startled me, even though I had seen Ronald approaching. I dragged the chair away from the window, opened the door, and pulled him through.

The man from the parking lot had disappeared. Ronald said nothing about him, as if he weren't worth mentioning. We both pushed the door shut and Ronald turned the lock and slid the dead bolt in place. He took me in his arms and smiled at me warmly. My nerves vanished, my heart melted, and a very real smile replaced the forced smile I had worn before.

"I missed you," I whispered.

"I had to see you again, Opal," he replied.

We undressed where we were, leaving our clothes in a pile next to the door. We moved in tandem to the bed. If our first time had been urgent and fast, our second was slow and languid. I wanted to explore every part of him. I traced his biceps lightly with my finger, then ran my fingertips down his chest. His limbs were firm, but his middle was soft.

My lips grazed his hairless chest and the soft mound of flesh around his waist. The pale skin was warm, doughy, and vulnerable.

He was an alligator with a topcoat of armor—the dark scales and sharp teeth protecting a soft underbelly. I studied his face for signs of a leviathan beast, but Ronald showed no signs of being reptilian.

This is the last time, I promised myself as I kissed his soft belly. But I was already thinking about how I could blend into his world and capture his heart.

Twenty-Three
Ronald

Several miles from the Rest Rite Motel was an auto repair shop that looked as if it needed repairs of its own. A small food truck was parked off to one side. The trailer was trimmed with what used to be a white-and-red awning and was now more of a worn, mildewed gray. A poster board spelled out *Tacos* and beside the open window leaned a handwritten menu.

Ronald parked in the dusty lot. At this point, he and Opal had been to the Rest Rite on several occasions, but this was the first time they'd left together. There was a beat-up pickup truck and a dusty minivan that the 1980s might want back.

Then he saw a shiny green car with tinted windows.

It was the same one he had seen at the gas station across from the Rest Rite and the same make that Isabelle drove. If he didn't know that Isabelle was having her nails done today, he might have been nervous. As it was, he wasn't thinking about Isabelle at all. He was thinking about what it was going to take to keep Opal from losing interest in him.

Ronald studied her face for signs of disappointment and found her grinning across the air-conditioned seat. "I love this place!" Opal beamed, as if he had passed a litmus test. "I haven't been here since my grandfather was alive. I can't believe it's still here!"

Before Ronald could respond, she had jumped out of the car, heading for the trailer. He tossed his suit jacket in the back seat and followed her. He laced his fingers into the belt loops of her jeans and held onto her hips. As Opal stood on her tiptoes and ordered fish tacos, Ronald scanned the parking lot.

"I've been meaning to ask you something," Opal said as they collected the fish tacos and returned to the car, where the vents blew ice-cold streams of air into their faces.

Ronald forgot about the green car and braced himself. "What is it?"

"The other day, I saw you talking to a homeless man. You bought him a sandwich before you came to the room."

He nodded. "That's Bernie," he explained.

"Did you know I was watching?" Opal asked.

"No. Why?"

"I didn't know if you were trying to help him or trying to impress me." Opal wiped the salsa off Ronald's chin with a napkin.

Ronald scoffed. "Opal, I'm a good person even when no one is watching."

She raised her chin. "That's what I thought."

"Let me tell you a story about me and a homeless man." Ronald finished his taco before settling into his well-worn anecdote.

It was 1978. Ronald was an intern at Good News Hospital. His overnight call had been dragging on forever, it seemed. He had already admitted eight patients to the hospital, and his ninth—a John Doe—was proving to be a real challenge.

John Doe had been found face down in the street. His body wasn't even on the sidewalk. When police picked him up, he was unconscious, with a bluish lump on his forehead the size of an egg. His T-shirt was dirty, and there were holes in his pants and shoes. He smelled of urine and sour breath.

"Who is this?" Ronald had asked.

The nurse at the bedside shook her head and rolled her eyes. "Another bum."

"Well, what are his vital signs?" he asked.

"I wouldn't know. Haven't checked them yet."

Ronald laid a hand on the man's chest. The man had been changed into a hospital gown. Ronald felt the man's ribs through the thin fabric. He gently shook the man. "Hey, mister," he called. "Wake up, mister. You're in the hospital."

The man didn't respond. Ronald pulled a penlight from his pocket and carefully lifted the man's eyelids. The pupils were large but reactive. The man's breathing came in regular intervals. "Can we get a set of vitals?" he asked the nurse.

"Can you move?" she replied impatiently.

Ronald had gone back to check on John Doe every hour throughout the night. He drew blood from his arms, collected his urine in a Foley catheter, delivered fluids through an IV, pushed on his abdomen, checked his reflexes, and monitored his breathing. By the morning, John Doe remained unconscious.

A group of interns and residents had gathered for morning rounds. Ronald pushed back his wild hair, rubbed the dark circles under his eyes, and began to recite the condition of each of his patients. The attending, Jerry Winterfeld, who would go on to be chief of staff at Good News Hospital, listened patiently as he tapped the ashes from his cigar into the ashtray mounted inside the hallway's handrail. Ronald described a patient with a bowel obstruction, one with a gangrenous toe, one with a respiratory infection, two patients with chest pain, one getting a blood transfusion, one with a tumor in his lung, one with diabetes—and John Doe.

"His bloodwork is normal, his urine was clear, his respirations are adequate," Ronald said. "I could be wrong, but I think his abdomen is becoming distended—"

"Dr. Aberdeen," Jerry interrupted, holding up a hand, "he's homeless. This is the best night's sleep he's had in a month. You're doing a great job."

The doctors moved on. Jerry puffed on his cigar, making the tip sizzle in a fiery little ring. Rounds finished. Another intern took over the admissions. Ronald was dismissed. Instinctively, he circled back to the ward where John Doe was roomed. At the sight of him, a nurse, younger and fresher than the nurse on duty overnight, rushed to meet him. She grabbed Ronald's forearm.

"That John Doe," she said, "you were right. There's something wrong with his belly." She pulled the sleeve of his white coat until they were at the bedside. "Feel," she directed.

Ronald lowered the sheet and pulled up the gown. John Doe's abdomen now ballooned from his body. Ronald sank his palm into the skin. Like a drum, the belly resisted his hand, and a grimace crossed the man's face.

"This is a surgical abdomen," Ronald confirmed. "Get the operating room on the line," he instructed the nurse. They hurried to the nurses' station. "Get me a room," Ronald said into the phone.

"All the rooms are booked with cases today," the clerk told him.

"Well, unbook one," he replied, hanging up the phone.

The nurse handed him another receiver. "It's Dr. Winterfeld."

"Ronald," Jerry barked, "what the devil is going on? The nurse says you're sending someone to the operating room?"

"It's John Doe," he explained. "He has a surgical abdomen. He needs an emergency laparotomy."

"I'll decide who needs an emergency laparotomy!" Jerry fumed.

Ronald stayed calm as he watched a gurney containing John Doe wheel past the nurses' station on the way to the operating room. "You can decide in the OR. I'll meet you there."

John Doe had a cancerous tumor in his intestine. It had grown so large, it had obstructed the passage, and the tissue had become necrotic. Ronald and Jerry worked in tandem. The tumor was removed, and the intestines were repaired. Jerry let out a victorious whoop and left Ronald to suture the incision closed.

"He would have died if it weren't for you," Jerry would later say.

John Doe remained unconscious for the next two days. He was treated like a VIP—and Ronald, like a hero. When John Doe eventually woke up, he gave the clerk his real name: Lester Banks, and he had, in fact, been homeless.

Now, in the parking lot, Ronald rubbed the rest of the salsa off his chin and marveled at the woman who wanted to be here with him. He ran a hand over the soft skin of her arm, lingering. Opal calmed him, slowed him, rooted him to a foundation he hadn't realized he had slipped from.

He glanced in the rearview and found the green car still idling nearby. Now he could see the driver—a woman with shiny black hair and perfectly manicured nails—and he knew in his heart that it was Isabelle, sitting alone with her heart breaking.

Isabelle was so different from Opal. For one thing, she wouldn't be caught dead eating at this taco stand. She was more of a Chez Poisson girl. Isabelle was the wind that blew him gently upstream, gliding past each achievement and on to the next like salmon leaping up a fish ladder, always wanting him to do more, get more, be more.

He had leaped without thinking from chief of surgery to Doctors Inc. president, to merging with SRMS. He was trying to leap back to New York. He was almost home. But here he was, tangled in a switch-back named Opal—a sharp bend in the stream. He grasped the weeds along the bank and held on.

Ronald imagined himself leaping from his car and running to Isabelle. He could take her in his arms and beg to hold onto the life he knew. On the other hand, with Opal beside him, it was all he could do to keep from peeling out of the parking lot and running away with her. Who was he going to hurt today?

"What is it?" Opal asked.

Ronald sighed. "It's Isabelle," he admitted.

"Oh," she said softly.

"No, I mean it's Isabelle in that car over there." It was time he put some distance between himself and Opal—safer that way.

"Oh!" Opal gasped, sliding down in her seat.

"Don't hide, Opal," Ronald said. "That will make it worse."

"What are we going to do?" she asked, her voice a panicked high pitch.

Ronald pressed his thumbs into his eyelids. "Get out of the car," he said.

"I'm sorry?" Opal asked. "What?"

"Get out of the car. Walk to the taco stand, and don't look back," he said.

"You're not serious. And get home how?"

"Just wait at the food truck."

He opened the driver's side door and climbed out, leaving Opal alone. He heard the slam of her door as he crossed the dusty parking lot to Isabelle's car. He didn't look back. Ronald raised his fist to tap on Isabelle's window, but the window lowered before he could rap. "Hello, Isabelle," he said.

"What is going on here?" she asked. She gripped her steering wheel, her fingers laden with rings. He looked her up and down. Her skirt was hiked up and he could almost see her panties. She wore high heels, the right shoe kicked off so her foot could maneuver the pedal. Ronald reached through the window and put his hand on her leg.

"You told me if I wanted Fox, I was going to have to get to Opal," he explained.

"This isn't what I meant!"

"It's not what you think," he said, pressing his hand between her legs.

"I saw you two leave that sleazy motel," Isabelle insisted. But she let her legs fall apart.

"Then you know how to find her car," Ronald said, smiling. "Take Opal back to the Rest Rite," he whispered, leaning in for a kiss. He moved his hand up her skirt, inside her.

Isabelle closed her eyes and stifled a moan. "Fuck you, Ronald," she said, but she put her hand on top of his.

"Unless you want me to take Opal back to the sleazy motel," he said. They both studied Opal standing at the taco stand. "I could get a room for you and me at the Rest Rite," Ronald added. "I wouldn't know, but I hear it's newly refurbished."

Isabelle slapped his hand. "Get out of here, Ronald. I'll take care of Opal. Leave before I change my mind."

TWENTY-FOUR
OPAL

I told myself that Ronald's decision to abandon me in the parking lot of a taco truck wasn't cowardice. It was inevitable. Isabelle had smirked as she delivered me back to my car at the Rest Rite, triumphant as she reveled in my humiliation. I should've been grateful —Fox didn't catch us. I could slip back into my marriage unnoticed, safe. But that wasn't the ending I envisioned. Each passing day, I dreamed less of returning to Fox—and more of crashing back into Ronald.

If I wanted him, nothing was stopping me.

I had become a middle-aged cliché—a paunch around my waist, thighs speckled with cellulite. My shoes were old. My clothes were stained. But today was different. Today, my lips gleamed a bold red and my hair bounced in disciplined waves. If I couldn't be like the polished women of Ronald's world, fine. I deserved more; perhaps Fox did too.

It was Allen who'd given me fashion tips. He explained that wedges were a good transition from flats to heels. He taught me about Kate Spade bags, Tory Burch shoes, and Nordstrom Trunk Club. His wife, Katy, began texting me links for retinol cream, nail polish, and body butter. I started waking up early to brush my hair, pluck my eyebrows, and apply lipstick.

But it was more than lipstick and shoes. Ever since things started with Ronald, I was young again. The energy was a creature in my chest that pounded along with my heart, lifting the corners of my lips into a smile as I powered through my days. I smiled at patients, laughed with nurses, and even stayed long past the end of my shift to lighten the load for my coworkers. They noticed. Tom thanked me. Could I keep up this frenetic pace day after day at Ocean Hospital? I hoped so. Ronald would like this version of me.

Refreshed, I prepared to attack the day. Gloria had returned with another breathing exacerbation. I met her nurse, Tammy, outside the room, and she filled me in.

"Still smoking," Tammy reported woefully. "She came in hypoxic, and they nearly had to tube her in the ER."

"How is she doing now?" I asked.

"Better. We have her weaned down to four liters of oxygen. She'll likely be released soon."

"Thanks, Tammy." I pushed through the door, switching on the light.

Gloria blinked at me over the nasal canula hissing in her nose. She coughed and pulled her sheet over her chest.

"Gloria!" I said, glad to see my good friend after a long absence. I wrapped my arms around her. "My son has asthma. I know how scary it can be when you can't breathe. How are you?"

She pushed me back and coughed. "Get away from me!" she rasped. "That hairspray will finish me off."

I laughed, half stunned. "Gloria, you've smoked a pack a day since the Reagan administration, and you think my hairspray is going to kill you?"

"Doesn't take much," she muttered. "Why are you so fancy today, anyway? Who're you trying to impress?"

I bristled. "No one." I fumbled my stethoscope onto her chest. The wheeze was tight, and her frail chest struggled to rise and fall.

She squinted at me and wheezed again. "Too late for me to change. But not too late for you."

Her words caught me mid-breath.

"Not too late for what?"

"To be better than this," she said, coughing. "To stop pretending."

"You want to know a secret?" I asked, moving closer to her despite my toxic hairspray fumes. "This is me. This isn't even my first affair," I whispered.

"Do you want a medal or something?" she croaked.

"I'm telling you," I explained. "This is just who I am."

"Sit down," Gloria instructed. "Open that drawer. Get that bottle of nail polish."

I pulled out a bottle of bright-pink polish. "This looks like Nassrin's favorite shade," I said.

Gloria smirked. "I made her give it to me last time she was my doctor. Now, let me see me your hands."

"What are we doing?" I asked.

"If you're going to be fancy, at least do it right," she coughed. She rose and swung her legs over the bed. "I'm going to fix your fingers, and you are going to envision a new version of yourself."

"If you say so," I replied, placing my hand in hers.

"You can repent. I believe in you." Before painting, she picked up a tiny wooden stick from the table and began pushing back my cuticles.

"Ouch!" I complained. "What is that?"

"Don't you ever get manicures?" she asked. "I'm prepping your nails."

I closed my eyes and tilted my head back as she worked. After the pinching came the cool touch of the polish brush. My breathing slowed as she squeezed my fingertips, rolling them this way and that. I didn't look up when the door opened and snapped shut again.

"Dr. Aberdeen!" Gloria cried, dropping my hand.

An imposing shadow swept itself across the floor before Ronald's voice sliced through the room.

"I take it there are no patients left to see, Dr. Collins?"

My breath caught like a knot in my chest. Behind me, Gloria chuckled dryly. "Relax, Doc. We're just painting our nails. Haven't you heard? It's therapeutic."

Ronald's eyes flicked over the scene, his mouth hardening at the corners. "Therapeutic? It looks like a beauty salon to me. Dr. Collins, we need to talk when you're finished here."

I didn't like his tone. He seemed to be in a mood, and I preferred to keep Gloria around to shield me from it. "You can tell me now."

He retrieved a folded piece of paper from his coat and held it out. "Patient complaints. All yours."

"They couldn't wait?" I asked, waving my tacky wet nails. The tension in his shoulders squeezed his face until his brow furrowed. The wrinkles were like canyons. Why had I never noticed them?

"This hospital runs on appearances," Ronald snapped. His tone cut deeper than any memory of the taco truck or Isabelle's smirk.

"Appearances." I took the paper with beautiful, angry fingers. The list was long, topped with the chest pain patient Rodney Harris, and below his name, a pair of expletives.

Funny he mentioned appearances. Did he realize how it had appeared when he'd abandoned me in the bad part of town with his wife? It appeared as though I wasted my time convincing Gloria—convincing myself—I deserved it. I didn't though. Who was I?

Something in me balked. "You're under pressure," I said coolly, meeting his eyes. "But I'm not your scapegoat."

Ronald straightened his tie and cleared his throat. "You know how much pressure I'm under," he murmured before leaving. His retreat was victorious.

Gloria broke the silence. "You can do better than him."

"I don't know what you're talking about," I lied.

TWENTY-FIVE
OPAL

RAP MUSIC SEEPED THROUGH THE MOTEL WALLS, ITS BASS rattling the sticky air. Familiar. Too familiar. I swore I wouldn't come here again—not after Isabelle caught us, not after Ronald turned icy. But here I was, under the guise of a "business meeting," folding back into our secret routine.

The Rest Rite was unchanged, its peeling stucco and lazy charm a constant on the outskirts of town. For strangers, it was just a run-down motel. For us, it was something else entirely: a cocoon of bad decisions, pulsating with a rhythm we couldn't shake.

Bernie wasn't outside with his shopping cart. Good. I was out of patience for Ronald's misplaced benevolence. The sandwiches and Coke, a room for the night. Bernie got the five-star treatment and somehow, I was an afterthought. My dreams of our future revolved around climbing the ranks at Ocean Hospital. Fair hours. Coming home to healthy children and a satisfied husband. I hadn't envisioned a rising stack of patient complaints, escalating tension with Fox, or surrendering control of my life to an old man.

Ronald entered the room, keys clinking on the table. I stayed at the window, arms crossed. "I'm not happy," I said flatly.

He leaned in, pressing a kiss to my hair. "I'm not Freud, but I think that goes beyond me. You're projecting daddy issues." His grin caught the light.

"That's not funny," I snapped, but my curiosity betrayed me. "What makes you think I have 'daddy issues'?"

His smile deepened as he loosened his tie. "Because you're sitting here waiting for someone to give you all the answers. I could be wrong." He sat on the bed and patted the space beside him, coaxing me closer.

"Quit doing that."

"Doing what?"

"Dodging," I said. "I'm telling you I'm not happy."

He leaned back, his shirt half unbuttoned. "Then finish the thought. What exactly do you want me to fix?"

I flinched at the challenge. My hesitation only made him bolder. "Let me guess," he said, peeling his shirt off. "Your dad left, and you've been chasing stability in men who look like they already have it together. That sound about right?"

My voice wavered. "My dad was an alcoholic. He hit rock bottom. Lost custody."

Ronald stayed silent, waiting.

"He's a flight mechanic now," I added, more defensively. "Lives in Gilbert, I think."

Ronald rubbed his chin, and appeared thoughtful. "And you haven't seen him because. . .?"

"I haven't made the effort," I admitted.

"Maybe you should," he said matter-of-factly. His hand traveled absently over the belt of his slacks. "If he's anything like me, he wants to be in your life. Trust me."

Frustration bubbled over. "I didn't ask you here to play therapist!" I snapped, standing abruptly. "I wanted to talk about how this is going to change—us. This mess."

He tilted his head, studying me coolly. "What do you want? Flowers? Champagne?" His sarcasm sharpened the air between us. But when I didn't answer, he stood, adjusting his slacks. "Fine. You deserve a promotion."

I blinked, caught off guard despite having waited for him to say it for weeks. "I know that."

"Doctors Inc. is going through some restructuring." He coaxed me to the bed and stretched out on his back. I climbed on top of him, ready to talk. "Karen Chamberlain is better suited for the PAL," he explained. "The medical director role needs someone sharp. Someone like you."

"Ronald," I gasped. "Karen will kill me if you make her the PAL!"

"No one cares what Karen thinks," Ronald replied. "And if her feelings get hurt? That's my problem, not yours." He smiled and pulled me toward him. "You're good, Opal. Better than you think. It's time you started letting everyone see it."

He kissed me softly. I wanted to believe him.

My thoughts tangled as I pulled off my shirt, feeling him get hard. "Is this the death of meritocracy?" I wondered aloud. Beneath me, he was both my lover and my conduit to ambition—the lines blurring.

We pushed the rest of our clothes to the floor. I pulled him inside me, covering his mouth with my hand.

Ronald thrust his hips, his breath becoming ragged. He moved my hand from his mouth. "You're ambitious," he murmured, stroking my hair. "Smart. Talented. This is your moment. Everyone knows it."

I pulled away, doubt creeping in, and rolled off him. "I want to be medical director, but you can't move Karen to the shitty PAL job. Not after what just happened in this bed."

He laughed darkly and pulled me closer. "What just happened in this bed has nothing to do with the medical director position, understand?" His hand found his dick and stroked it until his erection was back.

I watched with curiosity.

"It's important that you understand what's going on here." He paused to be sure I was listening. I furrowed my brow and gazed up at him. "Here," Ronald said, spreading his hands to imply the room, "we're just two friends having fun. Out there"—he gestured toward the door—"it's a multimillion-dollar corporation where people get in a lot of trouble over any confusion about what's going on here, okay?" He lifted my chin and coaxed me onto his lap.

I was wet.

"What happens out there?" he added. "That's where reputations are made. Trust me. I won't let this touch you."

For a moment, I believed him.

Pinning him to the bed, I held his thick wrists with my small hands and leaned into his face. "Ronald," I whispered, "don't ever say the word *money* while I'm fucking you."

He smiled as we started again.

"Everyone's going to hate me," I said, resuming the slow roll of my hips.

"No," he assured, his voice thickening. "They'll envy you."

His words were intoxicating—the kind of promise that fogs judgment. But even as I climaxed, clinging to his shoulders, a seed of doubt lodged itself deep.

Afterward, I straightened my clothes, and my voice was hollow. "I need some time off."

Twenty-Six

Opal

After securing three days off for Thanksgiving, I surprised Fox with a trip to New Haven. His eyes lit up when I told him. "I love you so much," he said, and those words pierced my heart. I loved him too, but they felt like a weighted promise as he asked, "Why New Haven? Why not spend time with your family?"

I was getting in too deep with Ronald, who was revealing a version of me I barely recognized—and didn't want. I yearned to focus on building a future with Fox. "I miss your parents," I replied, digging my heels into the deception. The lie felt preferable to confronting the truth.

As our flight descended into snowy Connecticut, hope and anxiety blended inside me. Allen and his wife Katy awaited us at the terminal, having detoured from Washington, DC, to New Haven. Allen, with his ginger hair and handsome features, looked just like Fox, both dressed in matching cashmere sweaters. Katy carried her growing belly with effortless grace.

"Aren't you cold?" I asked her from the back. Emily, Cal, and I had on puffy winter jackets, hats, scarves, and gloves.

Katy laughed. "I haven't been cold in thirty-two weeks. I'm a human furnace."

The drive was filled with comfortable banter. Katy described the nursery she was decorating for her soon-to-arrive daughter, prompting a flood of advice from me. Surrounded by the warmth in the car—with Emily's head resting on my shoulder and little Cal's hand in mine—I finally pushed Ronald from my mind. I began preparing to announce my promotion to medical director. We had exactly what we wanted.

The warm scent of apple pie and soft classical music greeted us as my mother-in-law, June, threw open the door. She scooped the kids into her arms while Fox's father, Calvin Sr., shook hands with his sons. Fox was named after his father, another Calvin Collins, but his nickname had taken root long ago after flipping through one of Calvin Sr.'s medical journals and landing on an illustration of Foxglove in an article about the cardiac medication digitalis. As Emily and Cal rushed past us into the house, June wrapped me in a hug, breathing deeply, as if I'd long been lost. It was a motherly embrace I wasn't used to. Stiff and awkward, I eventually relaxed, melting into her arms. Night had fallen, and our breath was visible in the porch light. June ushered me inside, insisting on carrying my bag. The house smelled not only of apple pie but of lavender candles, adorned with a Home, Sweet Home cross-stitch beside the coat closet. I lingered in the foyer, hanging up coats, while Fox remained by my side.

"Is it good to be home?" I asked.

"It's good to be home."

We gathered around the table and drank red wine. June handed Cal and Emily each a paper sack filled with toy cars, stuffed animals, and candies. They played boisterously on the carpet in the next room.

"Watch the plant!" I called to Cal as he barreled toward a plant stand. The green mound of leaves rocked dangerously before settling back.

Fox peeked into the next room. "I gave Mom that spider plant when I was in second grade."

June nodded. "It was just a little thing then."

"It's like our oak tree," I mused.

———

In the morning, I walked to the garage, carrying a mug that read But First, Coffee by the handle. Fox's dad was outside shoveling the snow that had fallen overnight, and I wanted to spend time with him. Not to mention that snow was a novelty for me. I leaned over a gasoline jug and shop vac to reach a folding chair. The garage overflowed with odds and ends collected over a lifetime. A cold gust of wind whipped through the open garage door, billowing up my pajama top as I pulled the chair free. I took a sip of steaming black coffee, glad for the warmth, and watching Calvin shovel chunks of snow from the driveway. Six inches had fallen overnight. Soon we would all be outside, rolling snowballs for snowmen, catching snowflakes on our tongues, and leaving snow angels in the yard.

"Do you have another shovel?" I asked Calvin.

He glanced up, the tip of his nose red, a rivulet of clear fluid beginning to leak from his nostrils. "Just the one," he replied, wiping at his nose before returning to the snow.

"Let me do that for you," I called after him. "Take a seat."

He paused, eyeing his progress. "I've been shoveling this driveway for almost forty years."

The sun began to rise above the tree line, illuminating the icy layer atop the snow that gleamed like diamonds and crackled satisfyingly with each shove of the shovel. The wind caught my hair, blowing strands across my eyes. Now, that was love, I thought—shoveling snow before daybreak while those you love are warm and cozy inside.

"Forty years is a long time," I said, rising from my chair. I walked along the narrow path he had shoveled and extended my arm. My slippers felt flimsy against the cold ground. "Sounds like it's my turn."

He chuckled, shaking his head as he handed over the shovel. "Make sure to get all the snow off the steps. We don't want anyone slipping on Thanksgiving." I passed him my coffee mug, and he perched on the folding chair to watch me work.

Calvin and Ronald were a lot alike. They seemed to be around the same age—both physicians, both presidents of their companies, both husbands to supportive wives and fathers to successful children. Yet they were ultimately nothing alike. Calvin felt protective while Ronald felt dangerous. Calvin felt settled; Ronald felt like a tempest, consuming whatever lay in his path.

Calvin coached me with a fatherly tone while I cleared the snow from the drive. After we finished shoveling, we joined the family for pancakes. Fox's parents excitedly discussed Thanksgiving plans, and Calvin mentioned showing his sons the new additions to Collins Radiology Center. It felt good to share conversations that excluded Ronald Aberdeen.

"It's still a bit understaffed," Calvin explained. "But I have three radiologist jobs posted, so soon—" He broke off in a sudden coughing fit. We waited for it to pass, but the hacking gave way to wheezing breaths. June set a glass of water in front of him. Calvin raised the glass to his lips, waving off our concern.

"He's been getting sick since August," June complained. "And each virus is worse than the one before it."

"Dad, you should get a chest X-ray," Fox said. He handed his father a Bloody Mary to quell the cough and poured another for himself.

"We'll see," Calvin replied. "Anyway, the new building is beautiful."

"Speaking of jobs," Allen said, "Fox, your new boss called my office the other day."

The pancake nearly fell out of my mouth.

"Aberdeen mentioned something about calling you," Fox said. "What did he want?"

"He wanted to see if I have any connections at Sloan Kettering." Allen took a bite of apple pie and chewed it thoughtfully.

"Why would he need a connection at Sloan Kettering?" I asked, feeling a tightening in my chest. I glanced down at Emily, who had crawled under the table to practice being a cat. I cut her pancake into small bites and pulled her back into her seat.

"He said something about switching gears."

Fox and I exchanged looks, eyebrows raised. "What does that mean?" Fox asked.

"I'm not sure," Allen replied. "But he mentioned getting involved with a research project."

"That's crazy!" I exclaimed. "Ronald can't go to New York. He just announced the merger!" My heart raced.

"Why do you care?" Fox asked, draining his glass and pouring himself another Bloody Mary.

Ignoring the rest of the family for a moment, I focused on Fox. "Why would he merge hospitals in Gilbert, just to turn around and leave for New York?"

"Who knows?" Fox replied, his speech slightly slurred. "Let's raise a toast to the end of Ronald Aberdeen," he continued. "The man is a creep. The hospitals will be better off without him."

"He's what we call a hustler," Allen added.

"Ronald is not a creep," I insisted. "He just promoted me to medical director." Silence fell, interrupted only by Emily's high-pitched meow.

"What now?" Fox finally asked.

"Medical director," I repeated. "He gave the PAL position to Karen and promoted me."

Allen clenched his jaw. "Opal, Aberdeen will paint you a rosy picture, then leave you in the dust."

Fox added with conviction, "You'll be stuck as the medical director of a hospital you don't want to work at while he's off sipping martinis in Manhattan."

"You were the one who wanted me to get that job."

"That was before the PAL," he replied.

"He promoted you too, Fox," I reminded him, refilling my own glass with orange juice.

"The difference is that I knew Aberdeen was using me to get to Allen," Fox replied. "But judging by your face, you thought Ronald actually thought you were special."

"This is what you wanted, Fox. I did this for you!" I cried.

"Why can't you be more like Katy?" Fox countered too loudly, pointing at our pregnant sister-in-law. "Why aren't you pregnant yet, Opal?"

Katy excused herself to another room.

"You're drunk, Fox," I argued. "And that's not fair."

Fox shoved a hand roughly in his pocket and came out with a packet of pills—my birth control. "I found this in our suitcase," he said miserably. "You have done nothing for me. You've been lying the whole time."

In an instant, the veil was lifted. Ronald wasn't the man I'd thought he was. He used me for Allen, and I let it happen. I lied, cheated, and ruined ten good years of marriage for him. I was a fool. None of this would hold my family together—not the promotion, not shorter hours, not nicer patients or more money. If I truly wanted to save my family, I had to get away from Ocean Hospital. My mind felt slippery, and I rubbed my eyes as I looked at Fox—my love, my everything.

"You're not wrong, Fox." Turning to Allen, I wondered if I'd be better off with Ronald gone. "Can you get Ronald into Sloan Kettering?"

"I know some people there. Gave him some names," Allen said.

I reached across the table, snatching the packet from Fox's hand and discarding it in the trash, alongside the dregs of pancake from my plate. Fox rested his heavy head on the table. I wrapped my arms around him, squeezing gently, rocking him.

"You should resign from Ocean Hospital," Fox slurred.

"I'll find somewhere else to work," I agreed.

TWENTY-SEVEN
RONALD

Now that almost twenty years had passed, Adam and Jerry Winterfeld had grown very old. Ronald realized this as he and Isabelle sat across from them in the Winterfelds' New York apartment, sipping from miniature crystal glasses filled with port wine. Ronald was surprised this soirée wasn't happening in a nursing home, but he had to pretend to like these men. He needed to be in the Winterfelds' good graces so Jerry wouldn't interfere with his return to research in New York. Ronald had a meeting with the director of Digestive Diseases at Sloan Kettering. But from the looks of things, Jerry might be dead by the time Ronald came back anyway.

When Adam Winterfeld sold Sunshine Medical to Ronald, he retired and bought an apartment in New York City, in the same building where Jerry had lived for years. Jerry remained tall and robust, while Adam had become thin and frail. Both men had rolling walkers parked under the windowsill. Adam spoke slowly, clearing his throat repeatedly.

"What have you done with Sunshine Medical, Ronald? That company always was a pain in my ass."

"Doctors Inc. has been very successful," Isabelle replied. "And we just merged with Santa Rosa Medical System." Ronald patted her hand.

A housekeeper appeared with four teacups on saucers, steaming with black coffee.

"Clyde Jewel always was a weasel," Adam said with a grin. "Now you're stuck with Bonne Santé. Good luck."

Anxious to change the subject, Ronald looked around Adam's apartment, past the old men's walkers and out the window. "It looks like you two are doing really well." They were clearly putting on a show of opulence for the Aberdeens' visit. The soirée had started with caviar and martinis, followed by braised lamb with mint jelly and roasted vegetables. Dessert had been an assortment of hand pies, truffles, and cakes.

"A reporter from a paper called the *West Florida Observer* contacted me," Jerry said.

Ronald set his jaw, and Isabelle stiffened beside him.

"Fucking *WFO*," Adam muttered, pulling a toothpick from his pocket and sticking it between his teeth.

Maybe the reporter had merely called to check facts. Maybe he was writing an article on Ronald's rise to power. But Ronald recalled his merger speech, after which the reporter had asked about his medical student, Trisha, and he knew in his heart what the article must be about.

In 2003, twenty-three-year-old Trisha Brown had been a third-year medical student on her surgical rotation at Good News Hospital. With long black hair and a dark complexion that could have been Middle Eastern or Italian, she caught attention that often eclipsed her biochemistry grades and hard work. Her scrub top strained across her chest, hinting at cleavage, while her loosely tied pants suggested a soft waist and pear-shaped bottom.

Ronald had noticed her immediately, and Trisha took a special interest in him. She was the first to arrive in the morning and the last to leave, eagerly trotting behind him throughout the day. Given her enthusiasm for surgery and the view down her shirt, Ronald had invited her to scrub in to all the interesting cases, allowing her to hold retractors and even suture. She had asked questions as he pointed out blood vessels and nerves. Adorable in her scrub cap, she lit up the operating room.

One evening, after the cases were finished and the residents had been dismissed, Ronald invited Trisha to sit with him in his office while he finished charting. He led her down a dimly lit corridor into the administrative wing, where few lights remained on. Upon reaching his office, he switched on his desk lamp, illuminating neatly stacked charts on a mahogany desk and a large window reflecting their figures against the dark sky. He yanked the window blinds shut with a bang that startled Trisha.

Ronald put a hand on her shoulder and led her through the threshold, shutting the door behind them. He'd motioned Trisha to a small chair beside the door and instructed her to study for her section exam while he finished his charting. As they sat in silence, she began sharing stories about her roommates, her family in Chicago, and her dinner plans. Ronald struggled with the desire to kiss her, fearing it was a mistake. But as she tossed her long hair over her shoulder, he finally rationalized that her rotation was almost over, and soon she would be back in Chicago.

Trisha stopped mid-sentence when he suddenly approached her and kissed her mouth. At first, she was rigid, almost motionless. She exhaled and her body went limp as he pressed into her. He took her hand and set it on the hard place in his scrubs.

"What do you think?" Ronald asked her.

She paused, carefully considering her words. "Am I done for today?"

"There's one more thing I need you to do before you go." He placed his hands on her waist and pulled her behind his desk, turning her to face the desk's surface. "Check this chart for me. See if the resident documented everything correctly." When she didn't move, he pressed gently between her shoulder blades, guiding her to lean over the chart.

He unclipped the pagers from his waist—first the service pager, then the OR pager, and finally the chief pager. In one swift motion, he yanked the tie holding up her scrub pants. They dropped to her ankles like the window blinds had dropped to the sill. He pushed down her blue cotton panties and discovered a swirl of dark hair at her lower back and the plump brown bottom he had imagined. Soon he was inside her, and, just as quickly, it was over.

The next morning, Ronald had scrubbed his arms in the OR sink beside her while she focused on her fingernails, taking the nail brush from finger to finger.

"Are we going to do this?" he'd whispered.

"Dr. Aberdeen, you're married," she'd protested.

"No one has to know."

Despite this, Trisha had withdrawn, avoiding his gaze. Refusing to speak to him, she became avoidant and sullen. Angry and humiliated, Ronald had assigned her to round on chronic-wound patients, forcing her to inspect their putrid infections and change soiled dressings until her rotation ended and she returned to Chicago.

She must have told the *West Florida Observer* everything. Ronald fidgeted now. Why stir up old ghosts? He studied Jerry's face, trying to guess what he'd told the reporter, but Jerry seemed disinterested.

"What did you say to them?" Ronald finally asked, stealing a glance at Isabelle.

Ronald's phone chimed with a text message. He watched as Isabelle's eyes flicked over to the screen. The text was from Opal.

> Fox and I are hosting a gathering on Saturday at noon. We would love for you and Isabelle to come.

He snatched the phone from the table and shoved it in his pocket.

"It was some reporter named Terry Knowls," Jerry said. "Asking questions about your girlfriend."

Ronald bit his lip. He should have been afraid for himself, for his reputation, but all he could think about was Isabelle. How after all this time, he continued to bring her pain. He didn't want to hurt her; he wanted to protect her.

"Isabelle, can you see if I left my pills on the bathroom counter?" He was trying to get her out of the room, but she was no fool.

Not only did Isabelle know about Trisha, but surely she had seen the new text message from Opal. "You check if you left your pills. I'm getting a drink," Isabelle snapped, pushing her chair back and stalking off to the kitchen.

"Come on, Ron," Jerry said, shrugging. "Even Isabelle must recognize that getting banished to Florida ended up being good for your career."

"I'd say you hit the jackpot," Adam added with a wink.

"Actually," Ronald said, "I want to talk to Jerry about my research."

"What research?" Jerry asked, perplexed.

"The early resection of gastrointestinal malignancies," Ronald replied, as if it were obvious.

"Ronald, when I said you were done in New York, I meant you were done for good. I killed that project years ago."

He sounded irritated, and Ronald winced. After all these years, he wanted to believe the research wasn't dead. That if he could convince Jerry to give him another chance, he could come back. But the finality of Jerry's words—it was like nothing had changed. He would always be the lowly intern, and Jerry would always be the chief.

Twenty-Eight
Ronald

Ronald had been fired from Good News Hospital in the Bronx in 2003 shortly after his affair with Trisha. That morning had started like any other. Ronald had climbed from a lowly medical student to chief of surgery, scrubbing into the most challenging and prestigious cases. His scalpel never betrayed him. He had published thirty-one articles, and his research promised to change the world. His days began before dawn, scrubbing, rounding, lecturing, scrubbing, and sleeping with a beeper next to his ear.

He was important. He was the most important. Once, people knew his name: Ronald Eugene Aberdeen. Once, his portrait hung in the lobby of Good News Hospital, a testament to his status; in it, his eyes did the smiling. It had replaced the portrait of the older, less handsome chief of surgery. The real Ronald, dressed in hospital scrubs and a surgical cap, had passed portrait Ronald every morning on his way to the operating room.

But that day, after passing portrait Ronald, the real Ronald hurried onto the elevator as the doors closed. Inside stood the chief of staff. Ronald smiled as the two ascended.

"Jerry, how are you, buddy? How's the wife?" Ronald extended a hand. The chief of staff gripped it firmly, his scowl deepening in his puffy face. Jerry's brow furrowed, and his eyes locked on the floor.

"What's wrong?" Ronald glanced at his reflection in the door. "Do I have something in my teeth?" But his teeth were perfectly white.

"My office, 9:00 a.m.," Jerry said, stepping out as the doors opened.

"I have a case," Ronald called after him.

"Bump it," Jerry replied without looking back. The doors shut and the elevator trundled on.

At 8:55, Ronald checked his reflection in the restroom mirror. He splashed cold water on his smoothly shaved cheeks and slicked back his hair. Pleased with the man smirking back, he looked himself over one last time before swinging open the door and heading to the chief of staff's office. Ronald had always been confident, but now he shoved down the knot that had formed in his stomach since the awkward encounter in the elevator.

He knocked on the door and waited. No answer. Trying the knob, he found it unlocked and slowly opened it. The large office was dimly lit by a small desk lamp, and Jerry's chair sat empty. Silence filled the room. Ronald flinched as a hand lightly touched his shoulder.

"You startled me," he barked, turning to the woman behind him. An elderly woman with gray hair and thick glasses had approached so quietly, he hadn't noticed.

"The meeting has been moved to the conference room. I'll take you there," she said flatly. They moved down the hall at her slow pace until they reached another closed door, marked B301. She began to pull it open, but Ronald reached over her and jerked it open.

"I've got it," he snapped. "Thank you."

B301 was a long conference room with a dark mahogany table surrounded by expensive leather chairs, their luxury stark against the shabby room. The beige walls were peeling, and three small windows at the back let in a hint of light from the alley outside. The rest of the illumination flickered from buzzing fluorescent lights overhead.

Jerry sat at the head of the table, flanked on his right by another man in a suit.

"Have a seat, Dr. Aberdeen," the chief of staff instructed. Ronald scanned the room. Three men in suits clustered at the other end of the table, whispering. He chose a chair in the middle of the table and sat down anxiously.

"Ronald," the chief continued, "this is Hector Goldman from our legal department." He gestured to his right. "And those are your union reps."

"Did you say legal department?"

"Ronald," Mr. Goldman started, "we've all done things we wish we could take back."

"Does anyone want to tell me what's going on? Do I need an attorney?" Ronald interrupted.

"Are you aware, Ronald," the lawyer continued, "that the number of workplace sexual harassment cases increased exponentially in the 1980s, and has continued to rise?"

"No one has accused me of anything," Ronald murmured, nearly inaudible.

"There is one young medical student who has," the lawyer replied.

Silence filled the room. Its weight lingered like the dirt on a grave as Ronald gathered his thoughts. He'd assumed the situation with Trisha was behind him; her surgical rotation had ended months ago, as had their fling.

Jerry interrupted, snapping Ronald back into the moment. "It's simple, Ronald. Resign, or I fire you."

"This is outrageous!" Ronald fired back, heat rising to his cheeks like a wave cresting before its crash to the shore. "That girl is lying! Whatever she said is a lie," he stammered. "She can't prove anything." Words slipped from his mouth through a sieve of horror. "I'm the chief of surgery—you can't just get rid of me."

Jerry leaned back in his chair, arms crossed and lips pursed, as if listening to Ronald was a nuisance.

"Come on, Jerry! You're going to toss me out like yesterday's garbage over some floozy medical student?"

No one in B301 spoke, not even Hector Goldman. Jerry coughed and looked down. Ronald swallowed hard, his temper sputtering and melting into fear like a thick rope tightening around his throat. What weren't they saying?

"There must be something I can do, right?" he asked quietly.

"Surely, there's a class or something for assholes like me. Can't I just pay a fine and move on? You don't need to fire me, for Christ's sake."

"A moment alone?" the chief requested. The attorney lingered, but with a look from Jerry, he left on the heels of the union reps.

"What the hell, Chief?" Ronald asked when they were alone. "You know I'm the best surgeon you've got. I'm not expendable. I can't be replaced. I've published more than anyone else on staff and I have three times as many cases."

"I know, Ronald. Calm down," Jerry said, pressing his palms into the table. "You're lucky I didn't invite HR to this meeting."

"Human Resources Gus?" Ronald scoffed.

"Good old HR Gus," Jerry chuckled and for a moment, they shared a laugh.

"You gave that girl a failing grade," Jerry continued. "For fuck's sake, couldn't you have just given her a gold star? Now she has a valid retaliation case against you."

"She seduced me, I swear! Why else would she come up to my office after business hours?"

Jerry shook his head in frustration, as if trying to shake the stupidity off Ronald. "Because she's your subordinate, you moron."

"But firing me?" Ronald pressed.

The silence swelled, the awkwardness thickening the air. Jerry let it linger, brushing a crumb off his tie and glancing at his watch.

"What about my research?" Ronald asked.

"I've taken you off the project," Jerry replied.

"The gastrointestinal malignancy project means everything to me! I'm so close to proving that early resection is key—"

"Ronald, stop," Jerry interrupted, raising a hand.

"That early resection is the key to saving lives!"

"Ronald, stop. I'm taking over the project." He cleared his throat and continued. "The landscape of this business is changing. Notice I said business. This is all just business." He emphasized the word "all," gesturing to indicate the hospital. "Soon, you'll be spending your days draining abscesses and wondering how to pay the mortgage on a salary less than what you'd make driving a cab. You've taken your surgical career as far as it will go. But I see greatness in you. I see a born leader."

"Leader?" Ronald asked, bemused by the melodrama.

"You were born to reign, not research. My brother owns a company down South," Jerry continued.

Ronald laughed. "No, Chief. I'm not going south of 3rd Street. You're not getting rid of me." He began to fidget in his seat, his knee bouncing anxiously. His eyes flicked to the door. Patients were waiting for him. He could almost feel the cool handle of a scalpel in his palm, and he suddenly yearned to sink it into the skin of his next patient.

"The company is called Sunshine Medical. It manages outpatient clinics and similar ventures. My brother wants out." Jerry chuckled. "He's even older than I am. Look, medical care is becoming big business, and you can get in at the ground level. Build it into whatever you want. It will be yours."

Ronald's knee stopped bouncing as he considered Jerry's offer. "So, what you're saying is I could either stay in New York and drain abscesses or go south and build an empire."

The chief set his jaw and looked Ronald in the eye. "Ronald, I'm telling you that you are done in New York."

And now, today, in the Winterfelds' apartment with caviar and wine, Jerry was confirming it. He'd killed the research project years ago. Ronald would have to use Allen. He touched his phone where Opal's text remained unanswered, suddenly anxious to leave.

"Lucinda!" Adam called. "Bring the cigars." The housekeeper returned with a box, standing beside Ronald and opening the lid. He took a cigar and held it to his nose as Lucinda distributed them to the Winterfelds, then cut and lit their cigars. The room thickened with smoke and toxic masculinity just as Isabelle returned from the kitchen, glass of wine in hand.

"I'll be at my mother's house," Isabelle announced.

"Ah, let me help you, Mami," Lucinda said trailing behind her. "I will call the driver. Sit. Sit."

"Tell the driver I'll be waiting outside," Isabelle said, picking up her Gucci handbag.

Ronald met her on the sidewalk, taking her hands. "I don't want you to leave."

"I don't want to stay," she shot back.

"The incident with Trisha was a long time ago," he said. "Please don't keep punishing me for it."

"You haven't changed at all, Ronald," she replied, stepping into the street to hail a cab. "You know the 'incident' with Trisha Brown wasn't an affair. It wasn't just 'sexual harassment.' It was rape, Ronald."

His cheeks flushed. "Isabelle, it was the nineties. That's just how it was back then."

She narrowed her eyes at him. "It was 2003." A cab pulled up and she opened the door.

"I've done everything you asked," he called after her. "I gave up my research. I took over Doctors Inc. and Santa Rosa. What more do you want?"

"I want you to back off Opal Collins," she said, spinning around to face him.

"You don't know what you're talking about, Isabelle," he argued.

"You're going to tear that poor girl's family apart," she said, climbing in and slamming the door.

Ronald didn't try to stop her. He should follow, but he felt tired, his head buzzing from the wine and cigar.

"Has anyone heard how Trisha Brown is doing?" Ronald asked when he returned to the apartment.

"After she threw you under the bus," Jerry said, "she worked her way up to chief of Colorectal Surgery at Cook County Hospital. I'd say she's doing pretty well."

"That's good," Ronald said, nodding. He thought about the dark swirl of hair on her back and how delicately she could suture.

"She probably had to sleep with a few people to get to the top," Adam said, and he and his brother laughed until they choked on the smoke from their cigars.

TWENTY-NINE
OPAL

I NEEDED A WAY OUT. I PRETENDED TO BE HELPLESS IN forming my own plans to leave Ocean Hospital and convinced Fantasia to rescue me again. It was only a matter of time before Ronald disposed of me. If I didn't have Ronald's protection at Ocean Hospital, Karen would eat me alive. I pictured her icy reign over Ocean Hospital—over me. Exposed, my protection having been discarded like my clothes at the Rest Rite, I looked to my friend to map out the rest of my life.

I was in luck. Fantasia already had plans to explore a cannabis dispensary her client recommended and readily agreed to help me. We pulled into the parking lot in a strip mall outside Gilbert.

"Is this the place?" Fantasia asked, checking the sign against the address in her phone.

Her hair casually spilled into her eyes. I was eager to have her to myself. "This is it. Hey, are things okay with Billy?"

Fantasia looked up from her phone. "Just a hitch," she said, looking back down again.

I turned off the engine. "He seemed pretty anxious to go golfing with Fox."

Fantasia shrugged and I dropped it.

A sign taped to the door of Harborage Artisanal Cannabis

instructed visitors to ring the bell, have their driver's licenses ready, and prepare to pay in cash. The dingy strip mall was mostly empty except for a group of old women in sneakers shuffling down the sidewalk as the shops opened for the day. We left the car in front of the dollar store where stuffed animals filled the window display, and walked three doors down. The place had an unassuming storefront with a green neon sign.

The realization that Ronald was planning his escape hit hard. I should have celebrated the jolt that sent me running back to Fox. I should have reveled in the opportunity to resurrect a second chance. Instead, I agonized over how to be the first to end the affair. I wanted to confront Ronald, but I needed to be away from him. I needed to stop thinking about him every minute of the day—but I also longed to see him. I'd considered inviting him to my house with Fantasia and Billy Maize; I wanted him to see me in my home with my family. Yet I'd worried my house was too shabby and my children too unruly. In the end, a few days before the gathering, I'd reached out to Ronald.

> Fox and I are hosting a gathering on Saturday at noon. We would love for you and Isabelle to come.

An hour later, Ronald's response had chimed across my phone.

> We're going to be in New York on Saturday.

Though part of me was relieved, the news sank me like a rock—not because I wouldn't be able to confront him about his plans to leave Ocean Hospital, but because Isabelle was real. His other life was real. He could slip through my fingers at any moment. The harder I braced myself to lose him, the more attached I became. I brushed aside his image in my mind and turned my attention back to Fantasia.

"I'm surprised that you and Billy didn't want to stick together today," I pressed.

"We aren't getting along," Fantasia admitted.

"Really?" I asked. "What's wrong?"

"Nothing's wrong," she said. "His little rock band is thriving, and I have more speaking engagements booked than I can count." Fantasia wore a maxi dress in a yellow floral pattern with slip-on mules. The casual way she pushed her hair back from her eyes made her even more attractive than when she wore it gelled.

"That sounds awful," I teased. I clipped my hair back in a twist and checked my deep-red lipstick in the window's reflection.

"I don't even know who we are," Fantasia said softly.

"You are a gorgeous exotic dancer," I replied. "I thought you were taking me to another strip club. Who knew you were an herbalist too?"

"I'm a jack-of-all-trades," she agreed, ringing the bell at the dispensary.

"Can I ask you something?" I called from behind her.

"Anything," she replied, turning to meet my eyes.

"How long have you and Billy been together?"

Fantasia smiled and answered proudly, "Billy was my high-school sweetheart."

I felt a pang of disappointment, as if her monogamy created a divide between us. "Have you only been with him?" I asked, trying to peer through the glass into the shop.

"I had an affair once," Fantasia said as we waited. My head snapped up in surprise. "I don't recommend it," she warned, a satisfied smirk creeping onto her lips.

I wanted to ask her about it. Who was it? What was it like? How long did it last? Did Billy know? But instead, I asked, "What are we shopping for?"

"In Jersey, I like to get the Airtight Indica," she replied, pressing her face to the glass. "But the Sleepy Sativa isn't bad either."

"Oh," I said. A woman named Harriette with more piercings than Fantasia held the door open with a warm smile. While Fantasia sorted out prescription-card questions, Harriette invited me to look around. I moved past the ATM at the entrance, glancing at clean glass shelves lined with jars. The sticky buds inside resembled the brussels sprouts we had for dinner last week. They were coated in a soft white frost, like flocking on a Christmas tree, and smelled far better. The jars had whimsical labels—Candy Cookie Kush, Glaucoma Killer—one especially tempting was labeled Dog's Breath. In front of the store, a cabinet under her register held vape pens, lighters, bowls, and little jars of gummy candies named Knockout Nuggets and Chill Pills. I showed Fantasia the Dog's Breath I had found.

"Okay, let's get started," Fantasia said commandingly. "We are not getting the Dog's Breath." I stood up straight and set down the jar I was holding. "We are looking for something that's seventy percent Indica and thirty percent Sativa."

"That's very specific," I said.

"I know. I'm kidding," Fantasia replied. "You can get some *Dog's Breath*." We moved through rows of buds named *Doctor's Orders, Hang Ten Hemp, Crunchy Munchy Kush, Tiger Tamer, Rosebuds.* "Opal," Fantasia said, pausing at the jar of Rosebuds.

I quickly set down a jar of Grandma's Brownies. "What?"

"A lot of doctors have depression and don't even know it. If you find yourself in a low place, a dose of Grandma's Brownies might not cut it," she said carefully.

"I'm one hundred percent better than I was at Moss Creek," I assured her. We reached a mirrored wall reflecting the garden of green medicinal bliss back at us. I looked at my reflection: a strong brow, tanned face, shoulders back, chest out. I had come a long way.

"When are you going to tell Fox?" Fantasia asked.

"Tell Fox what?" When she didn't respond, I added, "That sounds like a dumb idea." I hid my face behind a sample of weed.

"We need to talk about how to move forward," Fantasia said sternly, grabbing my wrist.

"About how to get me out of Ocean Hospital," I agreed, allowing her to detain me.

Fantasia took my other wrist and yanked me toward her until we were face to face. "Wipe the slate," she said, her minty breath colliding with my lips. "Tell Fox what you've done and walk away together."

"I think about telling him every day," I said, shifting my weight. "You're always right, Fantasia."

She let go of my wrists and wrapped me in an embrace, pushing me against the display case. Before I could come up with an excuse to procrastinate salvaging my marriage, my phone chimed with a text.

"I'm just going to check this," I explained. "In case it's about the kids." I sidestepped Fantasia and reached into my purse. It was Ronald.

> I came home early. Isabelle stayed in New York. Are you still free?

A kaleidoscope of butterflies tumbled in my gut, sending a soft, fluttering numbness to my fingertips as I looked from the text to my reflection to my dear friend who had traveled from New Jersey to be with me.

"Is it the kids?" Fantasia asked, touching my hand.

"No," I replied, quickly pulling my hand away and hiding the phone's screen on my chest.

"What is it?" She had canceled lectures to be here for me. We were supposed to get high together. But she was lecturing me about antidepressants. She was challenging my infidelity. I wanted to be away from her.

"It's work," I said, the words painful. "They need me to come in for a few hours." Just one more time with Ronald. Just for a few hours. Then I would stop. I replied to his text.

> What did you have in mind?

Fantasia looked at me with surprise and disappointment but said nothing. She gave Harriette her order and handed over some cash. The artisanal medicine was bundled in a plastic bag with the company logo, and we left. I dropped her off at home, explaining how to get into the garage where she could smoke alone. Then I ditched my dear friend for an old man in a sleazy motel.

THIRTY

Fox

Billy was gone. He took Fantasia and left. When they were at hole seven on the golf course, he had received a call from Fantasia. She was alone at Fox's house, surrounded by more weed than she knew what to do with. Fox found it strange that Opal agreed to fill in at work during a gathering she had so painstakingly arranged. Despite the trouble between them, Billy wasn't going to leave Fantasia alone, and no one would let all that good weed go to waste. So they packed up their clubs and joined her. Fox wasn't surprised when they left after getting good and stoned. Who could blame them?

Fox settled on the couch, the sour, grassy aroma of marijuana filling the house. Heightened by the lingering buzz, and having sent his children with Tanya for the afternoon, his imagination ran wild as he wondered what Opal was doing at that moment. He pushed himself off the couch and pulled a photo album from the shelf where it was collecting dust. Their wedding. Ten years and a lifetime ago. He flipped through pages of Opal's dress, the church in the woods, Pastor Bobby standing with them at the altar. His eyelids grew heavy and the album slipped to the floor.

After a few hours of napping, snacking on candy, sipping from a two-liter of Diet Coke, and staring blankly at the wall, he heard Opal's car pull into the driveway. Emily came through the door first, covering her nose, while Cal went to investigate the candy wrappers scattered across the floor. Before Fox could get off the couch, Cal had popped a piece of taffy into his mouth. Fortunately, it was drug-free taffy. The regular-kid kind.

Fox followed Opal's gaze when she finally came through the door and surveyed the scene: a half-eaten pizza on the counter, a lighter abandoned on the kitchen table, a trail of cheese crackers down the hall. A basketball game played silently in the background.

Fox and Opal used to watch basketball together when things were simple. He'd take her to the sports bar, and she would ask things like which team's uniform was cuter. Before long, he was taking her home to watch sports, and she'd ask the same silly questions with her head nestled on his shoulder. Fox would sit in wonder at this woman who had come into his life like a breath of fresh air.

In 2006, Fox wasn't thinking about holding his family together; he was just beginning medical school. He was the dorky guy from the Northeast, not knowing a soul at the University of Florida other than his roommate, Theo. They would lean against a wall in the main corridor, watching classmates hustle between lectures. Running a finger along the buttons of his dress shirt, Fox would feel the Florida heat seep in, sweat beginning to sting his armpits, melting into the white fabric. He'd yanked at his tie, freeing himself, and unbuttoned the top two buttons of his shirt.

Despite his father's achievements on the football field at Yale many years ago, Fox had been rejected by the Ivy League university, and he had settled on the University of Connecticut instead. That's where he'd met Theo. Tall, dark, and handsome Theo, who was from Florida and spent four years convincing Fox to follow him back for medical school. "Come to UF with me," Theo had said. "It's only four years. If you don't like it, you can go back and move in with your daddy. I hear there's an opening at Collins Radiology."

Fox would be forever grateful to Theo for instigating the move. In the corridor as students passed by, Theo would whisper to Fox his observations about each passing girl. "That's Misty Myers," he'd said under his breath. "She's a solid seven. I would date her. That's Becky—I don't know Becky's last name. She's more of a five."

"Who's that?" Fox had asked, pointing to a girl with chestnut hair and a relaxed smile.

"That's Opal Camry," Theo had replied, squinting as he studied her. "She's about a seven, maybe a seven point five." Opal wore a tank top and blue jeans; her tanned arms were golden brown, and her hair fell loosely over her shoulders. She was small but solid, and her casual confidence was intoxicating.

"She's a ten," Fox whispered. "Solid."

"Whoa there, Romeo," Theo replied, surprised. "Don't get your hopes up." Fox didn't answer; he was mesmerized by the girl who stood barely five feet tall but seemed larger than life.

"Look, buddy, Opal Camry is not on your level. Hell, she's not even on mine. If you want her, you'd better get in line. Every guy here wants to date her."

"How do you know all this?" Fox asked.

"The female student body is my favorite subject. As a serious student, I feel it's my job to know. Go talk to her."

"No."

"What do you mean, no? Go ask her out."

"Come with me. Introduce us."

"If I go over there with you, she's going to fall for my ravishing good looks and irresistible personality. I'll have to marry her, and then you'll end up hating me."

"Fine," Fox muttered, then did something he had never had the courage to do before—he'd decided to talk to a girl. Theo followed but trailed a few feet behind. When Fox reached the circle of people around Opal, he pushed right past them, standing directly in front of her.

Opal met his gaze, her dark eyes framed by strong, black brows. He had been caught staring. She smiled and nodded. Was he creepy? He turned to Theo for confirmation, but Theo had vanished. Opal marched straight to him with confidence.

"You're Opal Camry," Fox said. The chatter around them stopped; the corridor went silent, as he had interrupted whatever conversation they were having. His cheeks burned crimson, likely deeper red than his coppery hair.

"How do you know my name?" she asked.

"My friend told me," Fox replied, shoving his hands in his pockets. "He considers himself an expert on the female student body."

"That's disturbing," Opal said, raising an eyebrow. "I heard you're Fox Collins, son of Senator Allen Collins."

Fox smiled. It was his younger brother, not his father, who was gearing up to run for Congress when he graduated. "Well, you sort of heard wrong, but if you let me take you to dinner sometime, I'd be happy to clear up the details."

"Why did you wear a shirt and tie for lecture?" she teased, hooking her thumbs into the belt loops of her blue jeans, the fabric tight against her hips.

Fox took a deep breath. "I wanted to tell you you're a ten. A solid ten. Don't let anyone tell you you're a seven." Nervous laughter spread through the gathering crowd, more people inching closer to witness the spectacle.

"What?" Opal said, confused. "Who called me a seven?" A grin flashed across her face. Fox instinctively looked behind him. Theo had reappeared and was shooting him a look that said, *Stop now!*

He sheepishly sidled up beside Fox. "Opal, this is my roommate, Fox. Fox, Opal."

"We know," they said in unison.

Fox turned back to Opal. "Don't be charmed by Theo's ravishing good looks or his irresistible personality, Opal. Because then you might have to get married, and I'll end up hating him forever."

"I'm sorry," Theo said, pulling Fox away. "My friend is new to this."

"New to what?" Opal asked, amusement dancing through her voice.

"Talking to girls." Theo had him by the sleeve and was dragging him down the hall before he could embarrass himself anymore.

"Wait," Opal called, slipping her bag off her back. She unzipped it, reached inside, and pulled out a scrap of paper. Scribbling something on it, she handed it to Fox. "Then he's going to need some practice."

Her name and number were printed in wide, scrolling letters.

That's how it had started. As carefree as the wide, scrolling letters.

Fox longed for her to notice the basketball game or the wedding album on the floor. If he could just get her in his arms, they could exhale, and then face the decade of problems that had piled onto their marriage.

"Where are Fantasia and Billy?" Opal asked now, flopping into an armchair across the room. Was that cologne he smelled? Her cheeks were flushed.

"Cal and Emily," Fox called firmly. "Go brush your teeth and put on your pajamas. I need to speak with your mother."

Opal tensed. "I'm so sorry, Fox," she said after the kids had disappeared down the hall. "Alex was getting slammed and I didn't think I'd be gone so long."

"Fantasia and Billy found an early flight back to New Jersey," Fox interrupted.

"Oh, no," she replied, rising halfway from the chair as if she intended to join him but then thought better of it and sank back down. "Were they mad?"

"Wouldn't you be?" Fox replied. "I should go too."

She leaped from the chair. "What do you mean?" she cried.

"I think you've fallen out of love," he replied. "You've been so busy fixing yourself that you forgot to fix us." He rose from the sofa and turned toward the door.

"Where are you going?" she asked, hurrying to block his path.

"I'm staying with Theo tonight," he said.

"Fox, don't go. I need you," she pleaded. "You promised you would never leave me!"

With shoulders sagging and eyes lowered, he stepped closer to Opal and took her hands. "You smell like the activity room in a nursing home," he said.

She laughed. "You smell like a high-school kid whose parents left town for the weekend." She pulled him close for a kiss, but he stiffened and pulled back.

"The lies are killing us," Fox said, dropping Opal's hands. "But we lack the bravery required of the truth."

THIRTY-ONE
OPAL

"The lies are killing us," Fox said.

I couldn't hear what he said after that. The blood had drained from my face and left me lightheaded. The lies were killing me, indeed. He didn't know the half of it. I ached to tell him the whole of my past. I imagined the words coming out. This was Fox, I told myself. The one who promised to love me with all my warts. But in the end, who could love that kind of girl?

I couldn't tell Fox the truth, and I couldn't blame him for leaving. He dropped my hands and walked out the door. I collapsed into a heap of humiliation and confusion. My fingers plucked at the carpeting, blurred by tears. I deserved to be here. I deserved worse. I should have my face shoved to the floor with my pants around my ankles. Just like with Michael.

***

Once Michael had given me the clothes, his gifts began to come more frequently. As the months slipped by, he shared little treasures—each one more delightful than the last: a box of chocolates, a Nickelback CD, and a delicate necklace with a thin gold chain. Our small secrets thrilled me. Where the boys my age saw a Sasquatch with overgrown eyebrows, he saw a woman. Where my mother saw an unruly child, Michael saw me. I thought I saw him too. Like the way his hands would shake when we were alone.

One night, I let him get me alone, and everything changed. When midnight struck on December 31, 1999, the world held its breath as we rolled over into Y2K. A new year, a new decade, a new century, a new millennium.

The party that Michael had thrown at H.P. Elite Gymnastics began to wind down after the ball dropped. My plan was simple: I would clean up after the guests, then drive home in the car I had borrowed from Louis.

Michael sent Tracy and Gabby home shortly after midnight. "I'll stay and make sure everything gets cleaned up here," he had told them. Only Michael and I were left in the cavernous gym. I pushed a heavy vacuum over the carpeting. He bent down to pick up empty wrappers, bits of food, and stray water bottles. We worked in silence for a long time. Halfway through vacuuming the floor, I switched off the motor, put a hand to my back and winced, stretching a strained muscle. Michael noticed right away.

"Let me do that," he said, taking the vacuum.

"That's all right. You're old," I teased, taking back the handle.

"Fine," he replied. "I'm not going to beg for your vacuum. And just so you know, forty-two is not old."

I switched on the motor and continued pushing the vacuum along the floor. After a minute, he tapped my shoulder. I shut off the vacuum.

"I could do a muscle energy treatment for you," he said. "After you're done."

"What is that?" I asked.

"Basically a massage," he replied.

My stomach rolled over and I switched on the vacuum to slow my heart before answering. I continued to push the vacuum along the floor, quietly unpacking the meaning behind his words. If muscle energy was a medical treatment and he was a doctor, I most likely had misjudged his intentions. I was a child. He was my coach. He was my friend's dad. Why would he think any more of it?

When the cleaning was finished, I let him lead me to the back of the gym, past the locker rooms to the storage room where the trash was being stored and my timecard was waiting. I punched my timecard and slipped it back on the shelf. I sensed a change in his breathing. His breath was coming hard and, at times, erratic. I found that mine was too. He pulled a dusty mat from the pile and laid it on the floor.

On his instructions, I lay prone on the mat, the cold vinyl pressed against my cheek. He straddled me, lifted my shirt to my neck, and unfastened my bra. His hands went to work. I sighed as he took big, firm handfuls of muscle and squeezed. His strength surprised and delighted me. It wasn't until his fingertips drifted to the parts of my breasts exposed at my sides that I panicked. Under my shorts were tattered unicorn panties soiled by thin white tendrils of adolescence. A cold, wet spot had been forming there all night. I couldn't let Michael see that; it was humiliating.

I squirmed and he pressed my face against the mat. With one hand obnoxiously held over my mouth, he used his other to yank my shorts to my knees. I squeezed my eyes shut as my underpants were exposed. He pulled at the panties, his fingers going right to the wet place. While he seemed to be unmoved by the dampness, I thought I was going to die. The underpants were pushed down, and his brutal fingers found where I was wet. Stubby fingernails tore the soft flesh inside me, leaving long gouges that would bleed for days. With a grunt, he pulled his hand away and quickly left the storage room, leaving me facedown with my panties between my knees.

I rolled over and slowly dressed, trying to take stock of what the fuck just happened. Was this how an adult relationship worked? Was I supposed to feel humiliated? Was I supposed to bleed? Was I being a baby? I crept into the hallway, eager to hear what Michael would say, but he was gone. I was left alone to sort out the gouges, which had created rivulets of blood that blossomed pink in my cotton panties. I was left alone to make sense of Michael's betrayal of Gabby and my role in it. I was left alone to write the narrative of my guilt in silence.

***

Many years later, I found myself alone again, the weight of my guilt over Ronald pressing into my chest. The mess of candy wrappers and pizza boxes stared at me in judgment. Fantasia was gone. Billy was gone, and now Fox was gone too. Of course I was alone. Of course Fox stopped loving me. I'd stopped loving myself. It was by God's grace alone that Fox returned later that night.

Thirty-Two
Opal

New capri pants couldn't fend off the chill inside Ocean Hospital. When last I was there, I was the lowest-producing peon in the company. I was coming back as the new medical director. Shivering, I threw on my white coat for warmth.

"I need to talk to you about something," Tom said as he entered the room behind me, setting down his patient list.

My stomach dropped. "Actually, Tom, I need to talk to you too."

Tom grimaced and took off his glasses. "Oh, okay," he said. "What's going on?"

I took a deep breath. "I've been promoted to medical director."

"Oh, we know," Tom said, raising his eyebrows.

"What does that mean?" I asked, sliding into the chair next to him.

"Opal, what I'm about to say is none of my business," he began.

"Wait," I interrupted. "I'm looking for a way out."

"You don't have to say anything when I'm done," Tom continued.

My heart quickened as I picked up his patient list and pretended to inspect the names.

"You haven't been yourself lately and I worry about you. You're like a daughter to me," he added.

"Tom," I said firmly. "What is it?"

"You need to back off Aberdeen."

"I have backed off Aberdeen," I said carefully.

He took the list from my hands and set it down, forcing me to look him in the eye. "Come on, Opal. You're suddenly medical director, and Fox is head of Radiology?"

"I think it may be time to bring my skills to another hospital. Any ideas?" I asked.

"If there's anything going on between you and Ronald, you need to end it. Whatever you do in your personal life is up to you, but professionally, Opal, don't do this."

I sat, deadpan, but my insides churned. I wanted to leave Ronald. Why was it so hard? I kept waiting for my heart to cool down, to stop missing him, to stop loving him. Nothing yet. I was powerless against his pull.

"You've worked so hard to get to where you are," Tom continued. "You've survived college, medical school, residency, and five years on the job. That's sixteen years you've worked to get here." He covered my hand with his. "You're good at your job. If you screw this up, it all goes away." He gestured emphatically. "A little canoodling, or whatever you're doing, might seem harmless, but fair warning," he said, pointing toward the administration offices, "they will rain down on you. We work by a code of ethics, and you do not want to violate that. The damage to your career is not worth it. Not for someone like Ronald Aberdeen." He twisted his face in disgust at the mention of his name. "He'll use you, hurt you, then throw you away. People like him are untouchable. People like us are expendable."

Tears welled in my eyes, threatening to spill down my cheeks. "Help me get it right, Tom. I want to fix this. For Fox."

Tom softened and rested a hand on my shoulder. "Can you picture the look on Karen Chamberlain's face when she found out she was being assigned to the PAL position?"

I let out a laugh despite the tears. "I've been picturing that for a long time." I wanted to let the tears spring forth, to free themselves from my madness. Every day I told myself I would stop, but I didn't know how. There was a devil inside me, drawing me back like an addict chasing a high. This would be easier to excuse if I were an addict, but my struggle felt like a defect of character. I had always been that kind of girl. "There was a doctor who used to mentor me," I told Tom. "I could leave Ocean Hospital and work for him."

"I'll tell you what," Tom said, picking up his patient list. "I'll hang onto this. You go make that call."

Tom was right. I should have marched into Ronald's office and quit months ago, but I was a fool. I thought a little adoration would fix me. I thought a few hours at the Rest Rite Motel would work like Miracle Cream to soothe my burned-out career, balance my load, and invigorate my marriage. Now I spent my free time sneaking off with Grandpa instead of mothering my children, and my husband had one foot out the door.

I was going to call Michael McMillan and escape Ocean Hospital. I peered down the corridor, hoping to avoid anyone from administration.

Finding a quiet desk away from the nurses' station, I folded myself into the chair and dialed the hospital phone. "Is this Michael McMillan?" I said into the receiver, my eyes darting up and down the hall, my heart racing.

I shouldn't be doing this. I didn't care.

"This is Dr. McMillan," came the voice on the line, bringing me straight back to my childhood. I never imagined I would speak to him again, or that his voice could sound so charismatic.

"It's Opal Camry," I said in a low voice, using the maiden name he would remember.

"Opal!" Michael exclaimed. "It's been about a thousand years. How are you?"

My gaze landed on a tall man in a suit rounding the corner. Ronald. Fuck. Why was he at Ocean Hospital? I grasped the phone and dropped to the floor, pushing myself under the desk. "Can we meet in person?" I whispered into the receiver.

"Is everything okay?" I could hear the concern creeping into his voice.

Polished shoes strode heavily in my direction. "Can you meet me at the Roasted Bean at five o'clock?" I asked. Before Michael could answer, a text chimed on my phone. It was Ronald.

I hope those capris are wrinkle resistant.

LOL, just testing the fabric.

I laughed out loud and crawled out from under the desk, the hospital phone still pressed to my ear. "Just give them another dose of Ex-Lax and we'll see if everything comes out all right," I said, pretending to speak to a nurse before quickly hanging up on Michael. I looked at Ronald and shrugged.

"Who is Michael McMillan?" he asked. "And why do you need to hide under the desk to talk to him?"

"Just an old friend," I said, biting my lip.

Ronald studied me with suspicion before grunting and continuing down the hall.

Thirty-Three

Opal

THE BACK OF A BALD MAN'S HEAD GLEAMED UNDER THE lights when I arrived at the Roasted Bean ten minutes early for my meeting. The dome of Michael's skull, rimmed by a crown of white curls, reflected the light. He was a step ahead, controlling the scene as usual.

I approached carefully, my footfalls deliberately soft. But as if sensing his prey, he twisted in his chair, his sagging jowls framing a wide grin.

"You look great, Opal," he said as I slid into the seat across from him, smoothing my eyebrows. I hadn't heard his voice in years. My eyes flicked between his hairline, his face, his hands.

I had made those hands shake once. *If people found out, I could lose my wife, my job. Tracy could be taken away from me.* But his hands were steady now.

"Um, same," I replied, awkward and unsure, scanning him for traces of the past. I half expected him to pull a gift from his pocket. Another token of flattery to add to the list. Images I'd tried to bury clawed their way back. The gift that haunted me most. The gift.

I could still see his trembling hands as he'd held out that white paper package.

"Do you see what you do to me?" he'd asked then, inspecting his hands and their tremulous betrayal of his feelings. Inside, a foil packet—a prescription filled out in Gabby McMillan's name.

"That's how incredible you are, Opal," he'd explained, dropping his hands as the weight of his admiration burned into his lap. "I prescribed you birth control pills. . . just in case."

I should have been appalled. Instead, I had imagined I was the most powerful girl in the world. A goddess watching a wealthy doctor crumble before me.

And now, I was the one crumbling.

I inhaled the sharp Roasted Bean coffee and rubbed my eyes. Two untouched cups sat on the table, their steam curling between us, and Michael stirred the air with casual small talk.

"I see you're married," he said, pointing to the ring on my hand.

"Yep. Opal Collins now," I replied, toying with a sugar packet to keep my hands busy. "My husband's great—chief of Radiology at Health Solutions South."

"No kidding? Are you a doctor too?" he asked.

I nodded, his surprise grating my nerves.

"Well," Michael said, leaning back in his chair and snatching the packet from my hand. He lifted my chin with his finger. "What can I do for you, Dr. Opal?"

I shrank from his touch. His fat gut bulged against the buttons of his shirt and his belt complained with the strain.

"I'm looking for a job," I said evenly. "Is Better Health hiring?"

"Ah." A flicker of interest lit his eye as he tapped his lips. "What department? Let me guess—ER?"

"I'm interested in a supervisor position in the hospitalist division," I corrected, fidgeting as my confidence wilted under the weight of the memories. A blend of aversion to his geriatric Michaelness and disappointment in myself took over.

Michael scoffed. "Well, Opal, I work in the ER."

"I just thought you—"

"I don't know any of the hospitalists," he cut me off, waving dismissively. "Well, except for one guy who's always asking if I—ah, never mind. Sorry, kid."

My chest deflated. Of course he couldn't help me. Our connection had burned out years ago, and with it, any possibility of leverage. It had died with the same explosive power it had started with.

"Do you remember how we got caught?" My lip curled, my tone accusatory.

Michael raised his hands defensively. "Whoa! There was nothing—"

"My mother. Who else could shred my dignity with a snap of her fingers? But you couldn't run fast enough."

It had started as the best day, but, God, it had ended as the worst. Victory had tasted so sweet from the top of the podium. I had just won the gymnastics state championship. I glowed, rushing back into the bleachers with my gleaming trophy in hand.

"Mom," I had shrieked, pushing the trophy into her lap when I reached her, ready to bask in her pride. "I won first place! Do you know what this means?"

"That you're going to be unbearable for the next week?" she quipped, snatching my joy from the air.

My face faltered. "It means I can compete at nationals," I mumbled.

"Congratulations, Opal," Louis offered over the top of his newspaper.

But my mother hadn't been smiling.

"Opal, sit down." Before I could savor another second of victory, her tone froze me in place beside her. From my duffel, she plucked the blue plastic case holding my pills. The label was clearly visible.

"Why do you have birth control prescribed to Gabby McMillan?" she'd demanded.

My throat dried. I couldn't lie. "Dr. McMillan gave them to me," I whispered.

"Why do you need them?" Her words cut sharp and loud.

"He said I should—"

"You need to leave Gabby and Michael alone," she sneered. All you're going to do is ruin them. After everything that man's done for you?"

The blood drained from my body, leaving me lightheaded and numb. I sank to my mother's feet and buried my face in my hands.

"Girls like you," she continued slowly, "get men like him in a lot of trouble. Is that what you want?"

The words washed over me like acid and echoed in my chest as I wilted on the bleachers. Men like him.

"How would Gabby feel? How would Tracy feel?"

I said nothing as tears dripped through my closed fingers and dampened my knees below.

"I knew you were. . ." My mother paused, hands splayed out as she weighed her words. "A slut. But this? Even for you, Opal—"

I had shriveled to the floor weeping, and Louis was silent except for the rustling of his newspaper turning to a more interesting story.

Michael had disappeared after that. Why now, after all this time, did I think I should ask him for a job? Nothing had changed. He was about to reject me again. I struggled to focus on what he said now; his words sounded far away. He rustled a Roasted Bean sugar packet, and I came sharply back to focus. "Sorry, kid," he repeated.

"No problem," I said, my reply curt as I rose.

"Wait," he called. His hand shot out, grabbing mine across the table. I sank down reluctantly. "We could. . . catch up?" His wink disgusted me.

"Michael," I said in a low voice, retreating from his touch, "we're both married."

His grin broadened. "Gabby and I divorced years ago."

"Divorced?" Was that really a surprise? "This was a mistake," I said flatly, pushing my chair back.

Michael stood, a mocking air of formality settling on him like a shabby suit. "You've changed, Opal. You're old." He turned on his heel and was gone, leaving me alone in the Roasted Bean with a prickle of shame lodged in my throat. I stared at two unwanted coffees, with no escape plan.

THIRTY-FOUR
OPAL

The chaos at Ocean Hospital hit me the moment I stepped into the bright fluorescent light of the back office, long before my shift officially started. Expecting I'd find Tom in his usual shadowy sanctuary, a trusted advisor after the Michael failure, I was blindsided. Someone had switched on every light, and they stabbed at my sleep-deprived eyes.

"I'm Dr. Sylvia Baker," came a voice, unfamiliar and crisp. I blinked away the glare to find a young Black woman in a white coat, seated confidently at the corner computer. Her voice was rich with authority. "They sent me from Bonne Santé."

"Opal Collins," I replied, lowering my bag and extending a hand. "Where's Tom?"

"I'm Tom Rogers's replacement."

The words hit like a punch to the gut. "What does that mean?"

"Ask Karen," Sylvia said with a shrug, her disinterest as cutting as her professionalism.

"Karen is the patient advocate liaison," I argued, my voice rising. "I'm the medical director." Why didn't anyone tell me this was happening? A confused sort of panic was rising in my chest. "Did you work Tom's shift last night?"

"No, I worked my shift last night," she replied, impatient and poised to leave. "Can I tell you about the new ones? I've got to get my kid on the bus."

A chill swept through me as she folded herself seamlessly into the space Tom used to own, as though it had never belonged to him. Pulling myself together, I grabbed the list, glancing at it half-heartedly. "And Nassrin?" I pressed.

Sylvia tilted her head, trying to recall. "The Middle Eastern doctor? Big smile, no hijab?"

"That's her. She should've been here by now."

"Fahadi and Tang were chatting last night," Sylvia said, her voice flat, "when the court served Fahadi with a notice of intent to sue for malpractice. She took it. . . hard."

Malpractice? Where had that come from? "For fuck's sake, what is going on?" I snapped. Was Nassrin being sued? It was thing we all feared the most. Why hadn't she called me?

Sylvia stiffened. "Nassrin said she was going to call you later."

I forced myself to breathe deeply, pinning on a brittle smile. "Welcome aboard, Dr. Baker," I said, flipping over her patient list like it was on fire.

Once Sylvia left, resentment that had been simmering in my chest began to roil. I clenched my fists, waiting for Karen to show up. When her stupid hair-sprayed bangs came bobbing through the hall, I stalked to her office, barely pausing long enough to knock before shoving the door open.

Karen sat behind the desk with Ronald in a chair beside her, his arm wrapped in a blood-pressure cuff, the bell of her stethoscope pressed firmly to his brachial artery. My heart, already frozen, nearly stopped when I caught sight of him. She held up a finger for silence as my pulse slammed in time with the gauge's tiny needle.

Karen deflated the cuff with a hiss and scowled. "Your pressure is two hundred and twenty over a hundred and twelve!" she barked at Ronald.

I barely registered his high blood pressure. "Where is Tom Rogers?" I demanded.

Karen's glare sharpened. "Opal, shut the door."

I hurled it behind me and stood, arms crossed, waiting.

Ronald spoke first, his tone calm, detached. "Doctors Inc. has parted ways with Tom. I'm sorry, Opal. I know you were close."

"How could you?" I cried. Ronald stared straight ahead, and Karen dipped her head in silent complicity.

"It's business," Ronald replied with a shrug, gesturing as though to indicate the whole hospital.

"This is his livelihood!" I fired back.

"Speaking of redistributing assets," Ronald continued with maddening calm, "I need you to inform Alex Tang he's being detailed to Bonne Santé."

"You fired Tom and now you're sending Alex away?" My voice cracked with disbelief. "Why?"

"His numbers are stellar," Ronald replied, pulling the cuff from his arm as Karen cleared the desk. "Bonne Santé has a heavier patient load."

"So, you want to squeeze every last RVU out of him?"

"No," Ronald said slowly, as if explaining himself to a child. "I want you to send him where I can squeeze every last RVU out of him."

"Business, right?" I muttered, spinning to the door.

"Don't look at me, Opal," Karen called after me. "I'm just the patient advocate liaison. Being medical director isn't so easy, is it?"

I whirled back to face her. "You know, I came here early to talk to Tom about resigning. The conversation's going to be a whole lot easier now."

Karen stiffened, but Ronald barely blinked. He waved Karen away, then gestured for me to stay. "Close the door," he said. "I don't accept your resignation. Again, I'm sorry. I know you're upset about Tom."

"Bring him back and fire me instead," I countered, standing firm with my back pressed to the door.

Ronald locked eyes with me, amused. "You're not going anywhere, Opal. I promise."

"I am," I insisted. "You're about to leave for Sloan Kettering—or God knows where—and you're going to dump this mess on me."

A look of surprise flickered in Ronald's eyes, but he kept his voice even. He leaned back in his chair. "Sit," he said.

I stiffened, but his calm disarmed me. I sank into the chair across from him, fists clenched in my lap.

"If you resign," he said simply, "I can't promote Fox to chief of staff."

"Fox doesn't care about chief of staff."

Ronald's mouth twitched. "In fact, if you're gone, I won't have any reason to keep him on staff at all. Wouldn't you agree?"

My breath caught. "Ronald Aberdeen!" My voice cracked with a mix of fury and panic. "You wouldn't."

"There's no retaliation here, Opal," he said with an exaggerated sigh. "Just business."

In desperation, my mind raced to Fox—watching him walk out the door like Tom, taking with him the life we'd built together.

Ronald rose slowly, opening his arms. "Come here."

I stayed rooted.

"Opal." His voice softened. "Come here." He reached for my hand, tugging gently until I stood. His arms folded around me, his chest warm against my body. I rested my head against him, breathing in the comfort of his cologne. He raised my chin and kissed me, and I slipped back under his spell.

"Go on now," he murmured. "Patients are waiting."

I pulled away, my shoulders hunched, gaze downcast.

"I will quit you," I whispered as I walked out. But the words felt less like a promise and more like a prayer.

THIRTY-FIVE
OPAL

I stalked away from Karen's office, desperate to escape the corporate monster I'd created. Heading toward my patient's room, I collided with Sylvia, who was retrieving a forgotten phone.

"Did Dr. Aberdeen detail you here?" I asked before she could side-step me. "If you're not aware, he can be—"

Sylvia cut me off. "Ronald wants me here."

"Dr. Aberdeen?" I probed.

Her lips curved into a knowing smile. "I've known Ron forever." She brushed past me without breaking stride.

Sylvia Baker was here to replace Tom—on paper, at least. But I couldn't shake the feeling she wasn't just here for Tom's job. One, two, three: Tom, Nassrin, me. Dominoes falling in sequence.

Shaking it off, I braced myself and entered Mr. Jarvis's room. If Sylvia was the creeping shadow of my eventual replacement, Mr. Jarvis was the immediate punch in the gut the universe must've thought I needed to balance things out.

Most patients are an odd sort of wonderful: imperfect oysters with the occasional pearl. But sometimes, a Mr. Jarvis will wash up like a rotten fish, stinking everything up. On a typical day, you carefully throw the smelly fish back into the sea. Not on a day like today.

"Can anyone in this place do anything right?" Mr. Jarvis bellowed as I knocked and stepped in.

"What's wrong, Mr. Jarvis?" I asked with forced calm, moving to his bedside.

He sat there, burly and sweating in his boxers, his face red and scrunched with righteous indignation. "I want this kidney stone surgically removed. Right now."

"Oh. Ouch. What did the urologist say?"

"That I have to wait and pee it out!" He shook his head in disgust. "Moron."

I glanced at his notes. "Looks like your stone is about two millimeters," I said with what I hoped sounded like good news. "You probably don't need surgery."

Mr. Jarvis swung his legs over the edge of the bed and stood, looming over me like a furious bear. "I don't need some incompetent quack telling me what I need."

He took a step closer. I instinctively stepped back.

"I can adjust your pain medications," I offered, scrambling for a peace treaty. "We can make this a little easier—"

"Oh, sure. Mask the pain while this stone shreds my insides! Get me hooked on some pills, right? Typical." He sneered at me, his disdain dagger sharp. "Can I get a real doctor in here?"

Another step forward. Another step back. My hand found the door.

"Mr. Jarvis," I warned, keeping my tone steady, "you are a guest in this hospital. I need you to conduct yourself accordingly."

"I'm reporting you!" he roared, his voice shaking the walls.

I smirked, swinging the door open. "Let me give you the name of the patient advocate liaison."

Safely outside, I logged into his chart and typed up the encounter. Tom won't believe this, I thought before the realization hit. Tom wasn't around to help me endure the likes of patients like Mr. Jarvis. I couldn't just call him up for a laugh. Tom was gone. Alex was going. And Mr. Jarvis? He was the icing on an already monumental shit-brick cake.

I leaned back in my chair, imagining myself in a quaint bakery. I would lean over the display, inspecting each delicious cake. The air would carry the scent of warm sugar and dough. Smiling, the baker would ask, "What can I get you?"

I would reply, "What about that cake there? The brown rectangle?"

And the baker would frown and say, "That's our shit-brick cake. It's only for really bad days. Are you sure?"

"I'm sure."

The baker would nod, pulling out a piping bag. "Would you like the Jarvis icing? We're running a special."

"Perfect," I would say, watching as she spread watery icing over the shit-brick cake before handing it to me.

Back in reality, I finished Mr. Jarvis's note and closed his chart, burning with anger and satisfying passive revenge.

Thirty-Six

Opal

I walked into the office, feeling raw and red-eyed, only to find Alex snipping at the bonsai with mechanical ease. It irritated me how calm he seemed when my insides felt carved out. He glanced up as I came closer, his scissors still in hand, a leaf dangling precariously.

"Alex, we need to talk."

"Sure, Opal," he replied, setting the scissors down.

Before I could inform Alex of his impending doom, his transfer to Bonne Santé, a frazzled nurse burst through the door. "Dr. Collins, they need you on 3A."

"What is it?" I asked.

"It's Gloria," she replied. "She can hardly breathe. I want her in the ICU, and she won't go. She says she'll only talk to you."

"Go," said Alex, retrieving his scissors. "We can come back to this."

Rushing to the ward, I steeled myself to console Gloria. But when I arrived at the room, everything was in order.

"What's wrong, doc?" Gloria asked as soon as she saw my face.

"This place is fucked up," I replied, closing the door behind me. I guess I was going to make this about me, after all.

"That's what I've been telling everyone!" Gloria agreed with a husky cackle. "No one is listening!"

I managed a smile, which fell quickly as Gloria's laugh devolved into a wet cough. I rushed to the chair beside her bed. She had shriveled into a much smaller version of herself since the last time I saw her. She hid her body under a blanket, and her head sank into the pillow. The only light came from the television mounted over us on the ceiling, muted, oblivious to the depth of our grief. It played a megachurch service.

"How long do I have to live?" Gloria asked from her pile of bedding. Her words were blunt, but the edges were softened by her wheezy delivery.

I swallowed. "Well, the hospital's been your second home lately. Your oxygen levels. . ." I grasped at my throat to get past the lump, but her gaze bore right into me, expectant. "The steroids aren't working anymore. And. . ." I shifted, refusing to crumble. "There's not much time, Gloria."

"Ah, so I'm at the end of the line, huh?" She smoothed out the canula under her nose, trying to cover an unmistakable grin. "Well, Doc, at least you finally said it. Only took you five visits and three panic attacks to spit it out."

The corner of my mouth twitched—her humor was infectious, even now. My devastation must have shown because Gloria patted my hand, her papery skin cool against mine. "Don't feel bad, sweetheart. I've known for a while. Should I be in hospice?"

I nodded, unable to get the word "yes" to leave my mouth.

"It's okay, honey," she said. "Come here." Gloria beckoned me to sit beside her on the bed. She untangled her wrinkled hand from her oxygen tubing and clutched mine. Her touch sent a cascade of tears down my cheeks.

"I've been ready for a long time. I've just been waiting for you to be ready."

I shut my eyes, departing from my role as her physician, or perhaps finally embodying it. "You knew?"

"Of course I knew." She wheezed again, her breath shattering into another coughing fit. When it passed, she rasped, "I've been livin' too long on borrowed time. The bank called last week, Doc. I'm being repossessed. Just wasn't sure you were ready to file the paperwork."

I sighed. As the televised church service ended, an infomercial for Miracle Cream began to play silently. I grabbed her remote and restored the volume, buying a moment to pull myself together.

"Look at me, Doc," she croaked, her voice rattling louder than before. "I'm dying. I've got one foot in heaven, the other in a bedpan. Still, I don't hide from my messes."

Her thin lips turned up in a wry grin. "You, though? You came in here lookin' like you'd rather tackle Satan than deal with. . . whatever it is you're running from. Troubles don't run, honey. They sit there, all polite, and wait for you to trip over them."

"I'm not running," I lied.

"Ha!" Her retort came quick and sour. "Don't bullshit the dying, Doc. It's bad manners." Her hand tightened slightly on mine. "Whatever it is—it's time. You hear me? Time to fix it or fight it. But stop showing up with hollow eyes and checkin' out before the conversation even starts."

"It's fine," I conceded. "I just need some Miracle Cream."

"There's no Miracle Cream for me," Gloria said, pointing weakly to the TV, where the smiling woman dabbed lotion on her flawless skin. Her voice softened. "No Miracle Cream for you either, Doc. Just grit and God, and whatever's left when you finally get out of your own way."

I smiled softly. My tears blurred her face. "I'm going to miss you, Gloria."

She gave a somber nod that softened into another grin as she patted me once more. "Like I said, honey. Get yourself ready to miss a lot of things. I'm only the warm-up act."

The room seemed smaller and quieter, except for Gloria's rapid, shallow breaths. But she wasn't afraid. It was me—the one clinging to things she'd already let go of.

"I have to tell Dr. Tang he's being sent to Bonne Santé."

"Oh, thank God. No more Dr. Tang smoking lectures. Now, skedaddle. What are you still doing hanging around a corpse like me?"

I wrapped her in a hug cut short by that awful coughing again. We parted ways, and I returned to the office, red-eyed, finding Alex amongst a pile of scattered bonsai clippings.

"Ronald and Karen are detailing you to Bonne Santé," I announced miserably. "They made me the messenger."

Alex blinked. Then, with deliberate precision, he clipped a dangling leaf from the bonsai. "Huh. Sounds about right," he said, setting his scissors down and leaning back in his chair as if it were just another day.

It wasn't what I expected. No anger. No sadness. Nothing.

"That's it?" I asked. "You're okay with this?"

He tilted his head, his expression unreadable. "Opal, everything's changing. It's a sinking ship." His voice lowered. "Tom left. Nassrin got sued. She's next."

I grabbed Alex's arm. "No."

"Some bullshit about blood cultures," he replied. "I'm better off leaving too."

I winced. Alex's words resonated, unsettlingly rational. Too rational. People were so damn rational about leaving. Gloria wasn't rational. She'd held on until I was ready to let go. I wanted some of that.

"Are you going to miss it here at all?" I pressed.

"Would you?" he shot back. His tone was soft, yes, but also distant. Polite. Polished. We weren't arguing, but we weren't saying the things we really wanted to either.

"Can I have a hug?" I asked. "I could really use one."

Alex wrapped me in his arms, awkward and unnatural. His hands rested lightly on my shoulders before he let go. No warmth lingered. I laughed at the absurdity of it.

"Thanks, Alex," I said as I broke away. "That momentary void of intimacy you call a hug is exactly what I needed. I'm ready to get back to business."

THIRTY-SEVEN
OPAL

WEST FLORIDA OBSERVER
Worldwide Pandemic Reaches West Florida

COVID-19, the deadly respiratory illness that has been sweeping the world, has reached west Florida and hospitals are instituting new protocols, including mandatory masking policies and all but eliminating visiting hours. Schools are shutting down, with teachers announcing they don't plan to return until it's safe. People are being urged to stay home and avoid large gatherings. Weddings, graduations, and even funerals have been cancelled throughout Gilbert and the surrounding areas...

Gloria became a pariah the moment COVID swept through our corner of the country. Her breathing hadn't changed; she still had the familiar shallow rasp of a woman nearing the end, but no hospice provider in the area wanted to touch the foreboding cough. By mid-afternoon, I was on the phone with the medical director of my third hospice unit of the day, desperation creeping into my voice as I pleaded for someone—anyone—to take her case.

A chime sounded from my computer, and an email popped up on the screen. Ronald. My stomach twisted. I almost didn't open it. Ronald brought more chaos—the tiniest word from him could upend my precarious world. My cursor lingered over the subject line before I double-clicked.

Attention all supervisory staff within Health Solutions South:

We are in the midst of an unprecedented health-care crisis. COVID-19 promises to devastate more human life than we have seen thus far. Ocean Hospital and Bonne Santé will continue to provide the utmost care for our patients and our community.

However, in an effort to contain the virus and preserve the health of our patients and staff, all supervisors will now work from home until further notice. This directive takes effect immediately. Proceed directly to Information Technology to obtain your laptop and other office necessities.

We understand this may be difficult for those employees who are compelled to be in the hospital on the front lines. To you, I implore: Do the right thing. Serve your patients from home.

Sincerely,

Ronald Aberdeen, MD

President and CEO, Health Solutions South

"Excuse me," I said into the phone, cutting off the hospice director mid-sentence. "I'll need to call you back."

I hung up and dialed Fox.

"Did you see the email?" I asked, the words spilling out before he could even say hello.

"It appears we're working from home, babe," Fox said, his voice calm, almost relieved. "I'm already packing my bag."

My thoughts drifted to the Blue Moon, the strip club we had visited a hundred years ago. Between rum, weed, and the naked flesh of strangers, Fox had implored me to slow down, come home, and focus on my family. My heart should have been singing. My every wish was being granted, as if I had released a genie from its bottle. I was the medical director and I was going home. Why did I have no song in my heart?

"This feels wrong," I said, pacing the room. "I can't abandon my patients. I can't abandon Gloria. She's dying, Fox."

"You need to be at home," he said gently. "Your son has asthma. Your husband too."

My throat tightened, along with my resolve. "Fox, this is it. Becoming a doctor—giving my life to this profession—it was all for this. I ended up on the front lines of the pandemic for a reason. I can't run and hide."

"Opal," Fox pressed, "this is our chance to put our family first. Remember? We said our careers could wait. Don't choose your patients over your family. Not this time."

I sighed, tapping my pen on the desk, then shoving it between my molars. "You're right. But will there be any doctors left for the bedside?"

I heard Fox chuckle softly. "Yes, Opal. There are plenty of excellent doctors there. Let them stay. Come home."

I stared at my desk, littered with sticky notes and patient lists that had suddenly become irrelevant. Swallowing the lump in my throat, I replied, "I'm on my way."

I shoved my stethoscope into my bag, wondering if I would ever take it out again. Slinging it over my shoulder, I walked to Gloria's room to say goodbye. Her eyes fluttered open as I approached, but she didn't speak. I placed a hand on her arm, the warmth of her skin a quiet reminder of all the years I'd spent fighting to protect lives like hers.

"Goodbye, Gloria," I whispered.

She only nodded, her breathing a soft, uneven metronome.

The halls of Ocean Hospital seemed foreign as I made my way out. The smell of antiseptic, the hum of fluorescent lights, the quiet urgency in every footstep—they had been my constants for years. What world did I belong to now?

Ronald Aberdeen was waiting by my car.

"Goodbye, Ronald," I said, my voice unnaturally clipped as I passed him.

"Goodbye, Opal," he said, his tone softer than I'd expected. We paused, the space between us thick with unspoken words. He took a step closer, then stopped himself. "I did this for you," he said finally. "For your children."

I nodded, my throat too tight to speak.

"Thank you," I managed, though I wasn't sure I meant it.

He stepped back, and I climbed into the car. As I drove away, I glanced in the rearview mirror. Ronald stood there, hands in his pockets, watching me leave. I wondered if he had the same weight on his chest that I did—the weight of betrayal.

THIRTY-EIGHT
OPAL

After a whirlwind morning, I went out searching the town for Ronald. He wasn't replying to my texts or voicemails. Things were coming to a head.

"Dr. Aberdeen is out of the office," Miranda said without looking up from her computer at the corporate office.

"But I just came from Ocean Hospital, and he's not there," I argued, leaning over the reception desk. "Is he at Bonne Santé?"

My morning had been a chaotic chase for Ronald Aberdeen. The man I couldn't seem to escape was suddenly nowhere to be found. Covid brought the world to its knees, but for Fox and me, the sudden halt turned out to be a hidden blessing. Working from home with our kids underfoot had somehow replanted our family. We were growing stronger, like the oak tree in our yard, sprouting fresh leaves after its bout with sudden oak death. Then, this morning, everything changed.

Fox walked into the living room in scrubs, a pager clipped to his waist.

"What's going on?" I asked, juggling Emily, who was tugging on my arm, and Cal, who was on the brink of spilling cereal everywhere.

"I'm being sent back to Interventional Radiology," he said, fishing for his keys on the sideboard.

"Sent back?" I pressed, trying to peel Emily off me. "You're leaving?"

"I don't want to leave you," he said, finding his keys, "but someone promoted my partner to head of Radiology. He's remote now. So, yeah, I'm back in the hospital."

"Ronald demoted you?" My voice rose over the sound of cereal dancing across the floor. Cal's "Oops!" rang out from the kitchen.

Fox shrugged, grabbing his bag. "It's complicated."

Complicated? He was putting himself, and us, at risk. If he got sick, what would that mean for Cal, whose lungs could barely handle spring pollen, let alone a pandemic?

Still, Fox was about to leave me at home to clean cereal glue off the floor, juggling work and playing elementary school teacher. I set my jaw and waited until his car was out of sight before hastily bustling the kids off to Aunt Amber's in order to comb Gilbert for the traitor. The anger was exhausting, and I was running on fumes.

At the corporate office, Miranda finally looked up, her tight twist of hair pulling her expression into perpetual disdain. She motioned me closer and whispered, "I'm not at liberty to discuss Dr. Aberdeen's whereabouts, but if I were you, I'd check his home."

I stared at her, debating if I should say what I was thinking. "I'm trying to resign."

She pulled out a sticky note and scribbled an address. "About time, Dr. Collins," she said, sliding it over.

The manicured streets of Ronald's neighborhood were enemy territory. The lawns were too green, the tree tunnels too perfect, and I became an intruder in my own life. I inched down the street, my hands gripping the wheel. A woman walking her dog waved, and I forced a weak smile in return. When I found the house—a pristine, camera-watched fortress with neatly trimmed hedges—I wanted to turn back. But I didn't.

I knocked, and the door opened before my knuckles left the wood.

"Isabelle," I said, startled by the woman standing in the doorway. Her sharp eyes froze me in place. "I . . . didn't realize you were home."

"What do you want?" she asked, her voice cold. She shifted to block my view inside the house.

"I'm looking for Ronald. Is he here?"

"Dr. Aberdeen is in his office. Make an appointment."

"Please, Isabelle. I need to see him."

"Over my dead body," she snapped, stepping onto the porch.

I backed up, hands raised. "I'm just trying to resign. That's it."

Her laugh was bitter. "You think I don't know what he's doing with you?"

"It's not like that," I insisted, retreating to my car. "That day at the taco stand. . ." I trailed off. How could I explain that? "I'm sorry, Isabelle. You're right. I'll make an appointment."

I climbed into the driver's seat, fumbling with the ignition. Isabelle followed, motioning for me to roll down the window. I hesitated but complied.

"Let's not kid ourselves, Dr. Collins," she said, her smirk cutting through the air. "You're no Trisha Brown."

I stilled, my hand frozen on the gearshift. "Who is Trisha Brown?"

This time, her laugh was almost gleeful. "Trisha Brown is the talk of Gilbert, and you're the only one who doesn't know?"

My stomach dropped. "I don't know, Isabelle."

"He raped her," she said, her tone dripping with venom. "That's what everyone's saying. You still want to find him? Have you tried that sleazy motel the two of you like so much?"

THIRTY-NINE
OPAL

THE REST RITE WAS QUIET, THE LAZY HEAT BETRAYING MY urgency as I kicked up a plume of dust pulling into the lot. One of the R's on the neon sign was out again. Ronald had finally returned my text with one telling me to meet him at the Rest Rite. I stormed past his car, my hands trembling, and banged on the door to room seven.

"Why are you here?" I demanded the moment the door opened. "I didn't agree to meet you today."

Ronald rested on the bed, shirtless, his pants slung over the chair. He raised his hands in mock surrender. "Hey, I just came to buy Bernie his sandwich."

"Why is my husband at Bonne Santé today?" I snapped. "You couldn't stand seeing us thrive? You had to rip us apart?"

"Opal," he said gently, motioning to the chair, "have a seat. Let's talk."

"Who is Trisha Brown?" I asked instead, slamming the door behind me.

Ronald cringed, looking away as he crossed his legs. "You can't believe everything they print in the papers."

"Print in the papers?" I pressed. "What do you mean?"

"Who told you about Trisha?" he asked, standing to step into his pants.

"Isabelle."

He froze. "Oh, fuck. . . you've been talking to Isabelle?"

"I've been looking all over for you," I said, my voice rising.

"Well, you found me," he said quietly, tugging his belt tight.

"You've brought nothing but ruin to my life. Now that I know about Trisha Brown, it all makes sense."

He reached for my hand, his touch disarming. "Stay, Opal. We don't have to make love. Just stay."

"You break everything you touch," I whispered, crossing my arms. "I'm done, Ronald. I'm done with you and with Ocean Hospital."

"Did you tell Fox about us?" he asked.

"No," I admitted. "But I'm going to."

Ronald stepped closer, his voice soft. "If you haven't told Fox, then you're not done with me yet."

I should've pulled away, but I didn't. "That's not true," I whispered.

"You could have called. You could have met me in my office. You came here," he said, gesturing to the bed. "You came to the Rest Rite because you're not done with me."

I hated that he was right. I hated the rush of excitement in my chest when he pushed me onto the bed. I hated the way my body betrayed me as his lips brushed my neck, as he told me about Trisha Brown—the medical student who loved him and whom he had loved in return. He told me about everything he'd risked, everything he'd lost for that love. And instead of ending things, instead of setting things right with Fox, I let him consume me, our clothes ripped off and tossed aside. I let it happen like I always did. I fucked Ronald Aberdeen and then I fell asleep, our tension spilling to the ground with my orgasm.

***

"Opal," came a man's voice later, syrupy behind my veil of slumber. The air outside the blanket was crisp. A fluorescent light blinked somewhere far away.

"Opal, wake up!" The hand on my back shook me harder. I opened my eyes to find Ronald's face inches from mine, his concern cutting through my grogginess.

"Your phone keeps ringing," he said, handing it to me.

I stared at the screen. Fifteen missed calls from Fox. Three from Amber. One from my mother. My heart sank.

"Something's wrong," Ronald said. "You need to call Fox."

I hit the call button with shaking fingers. "Honey, what's wrong?" I asked when he picked up.

"Cal had an asthma attack at soccer practice," Fox said, his voice breaking. "You were supposed to bring his inhaler. We're at Bonne Santé. Where are you, Opal?"

"I'm on my way," I stammered, yanking on my leggings.

"From where? You were supposed to take him to practice."

"How bad is it?" I asked, dodging the question as I shoved my feet into my sneakers.

"They had to tube him," Fox said, choking on the words. "He was gray, Opal. He was fucking gray."

My tears fell freely now. "I'll be there in twenty minutes," I lied, knowing it was at least thirty. In an instant, I cared nothing for Ronald, or Ocean Hospital, or my devious path to my happiness. All I cared about was Cal.

"The doctor said he probably won't survive the night," Fox continued.

"The doctor can't know that—"

"And if he does, he could have brain damage."

"Are you sure I have his inhaler?" I asked, desperate for a reprieve from the guilt crushing my chest.

"Whatever's going on with you," Fox said, his voice hardening, "we'll sort it out later. But I'm staying at the hospital tonight."

"I'll stay with Cal," I said quickly.

"No! I can't be around you right now," he snapped. "Our marriage is broken, Opal. If you haven't noticed."

"I know," I breathed. "I'm sorry."

I hung up, the weight of my failure crushing me. Ronald held out my keys, already dressed. "I'll call Dr. Davis," he said. "He's a damn good pediatrician and an old friend."

I shook my head. "It's best if you stay out of this."

"Go take care of your son, Opal," Ronald whispered. "I'll check on you soon."

My hand trembled as I opened the door of the Rest Rite Motel. My chest turned to ice as I stepped back into the real world. It wasn't only my marriage I had destroyed. I might have just killed my son.

FORTY

OPAL

Cal's nurse entered to check his vitals, followed by a jovial respiratory therapist who swapped out the albuterol and began another round of nebulizer treatments. They had planned to keep him intubated overnight, but my very-much-alive son had yanked out the breathing tube out of his throat before I arrived. Now he lay under the watchful eyes of the pediatric ICU nurses.

I sat on the bed behind Cal, stroking his hair and kissing the top of his head, grateful he couldn't see my swollen face and puffy eyes. Everyone else had seen them when I rushed into the waiting room, conspicuously late, under the judgmental gaze of my family.

"Why don't we let Dad have a turn visiting now?" the nurse suggested.

I avoided Fox's glare as we switched places. Sensing the weight of the air between us, the nurse left the room. I lingered, holding Cal's tiny hand, even as Fox took my seat on the bed. I could feel his eyes burning into me as I stared at Cal's fingernails.

"You're supposed to leave now," Fox said, his tone carefully neutral for Cal's benefit, though the bitterness was clear.

"I'm waiting to hear from the nurse," I whispered.

"This is your fault, Opal," he hissed. "Or should I say Momma? You were supposed to pack his inhaler. You were supposed to be at practice!"

His words found their mark, but I reacted like a guilty person caught in the act. I threw it back at him. "My fault? You're the one obsessed with that damn oak tree! You should have cut it down."

Fox scoffed. "The pollen didn't forget the inhaler. You did."

Cal's face fell, and he coughed. Fox covered his ears, shielding him from our words like it could undo the damage. "You haven't been the same since you took that promotion," he said. "You let it consume you."

His misconception should have brought relief. How difficult would this conversation be if he knew I'd been basking in the afterglow of an orgasm at a sleazy motel? But I wasn't relieved; I was furious. "This is what you wanted, Fox," I shot back. "I did what I had to do. I'm not sorry."

The bedside monitor flashed red. *Ding-dong, ding-dong* went the alarm as Cal's heart rate spiked.

I knelt beside him, burying my face in his neck as the alarm pierced the air. I hated myself. I hated what I'd done to my son, to my family, to myself. This version of me was trash.

The nurse returned, her expression calm as she guided me out of the ICU without a trace of judgment.

"I'll see you out there," I told Fox.

"I'm staying here tonight," he said, not looking up.

In the waiting room, I collapsed into one of the hard plastic chairs and pulled Emily onto my lap. She clutched a bag of crackers, half of which tumbled to the floor as she peppered me with questions.

"Is Cal going to die? Is he coming home tonight? What are we having for dinner? Does Jesus let you bring stuffed animals to heaven?"

"Emily, let's go for a walk," Amber said, taking her hand. I handed her the empty cracker bag and they disappeared down the hall, leaving me alone with my mother.

I paced the waiting room, drifting to the window. My mind replayed the image of Cal struggling to breathe. I covered my face and let the tears come.

My mother placed a hand on my back. "Did you call Dad?" I asked.

"I haven't had Joe's number for years," she said.

"Seeing him again would be good for me."

"Don't give him the opportunity to disappoint you, Opal."

"At some point, you're going to have to stop punishing him for leaving," I snapped, though I wasn't sure if it was the stress or her insufferable calm that fueled my anger.

She laughed, surprising me. "Is that what you think? That he left me?"

"He left us, Mom. But I forgave him years ago."

"Your father didn't leave me. I left him."

I turned to face her, confused. "What?"

"Your father had an affair," she said with a shrug. "I didn't realize you didn't know."

"You left him because he cheated?"

"Of course. I couldn't very well stay with him after that."

"People do, though," I whispered.

"Opal, you would leave Fox in a heartbeat if he had an affair."

"Maybe. . ."

"And you'd be right to leave."

Before I could respond, Amber and Emily returned, Emily bouncing excitedly.

"She wants to visit the teddy bears in the gift shop," Amber explained.

"The toy store," Emily corrected.

I handed my mother a fifty from my purse. "Have Emily get something special for Cal," I said, kissing my daughter on the cheek.

Once we were alone, Amber turned to me, her voice sharp. "Opal, what happened? Your son almost died, and no one could reach you."

"Bad reception," I offered weakly.

"Don't bullshit me. Is something going on with you and that Richard Abernathy?"

I almost laughed. "Ronald Aberdeen," I corrected. But my lack of an answer was confirmation enough.

"Opal..." She trailed off. "I don't know what to say."

"I know, Amber. I know. I—why can't I stop thinking about him?"

"What's so special about him?"

"Nothing," I admitted. "He's just smart, successful, powerful—"

"Yeah, Opal. You just described your husband. Is he older? He's old, isn't he?"

"He's not that old."

Amber's voice hardened. "You need to stop, Opal. Look what you've done." She stared out the window.

"This isn't Cal's first asthma attack," I argued.

"You've abandoned your children, humiliated your husband, and made a fool of yourself."

I closed my eyes against her truth. "Okay. It's done. I'll never do it again."

"That's not good enough. You need to tell Fox."

I scoffed. "Why does everyone keep saying that?"

"It's the only way."

I jabbed a finger into her arm. "What about your secret, Amber?"

"What secret?"

"I've seen the way you look at Wendy Windsor," I said. "I've known you my whole life."

"Opal, stop."

"You're in love with her. You're a couple."

"Leave Wendy out of this," Amber said firmly.

"Why don't you come out? What are you afraid of? Mom? You should be. She can be very judgmental. Is it Pastor Bobby?"

"Enough, Opal!" Amber drew the attention of a ward clerk. She clenched her fist and fished a copy of the *West Florida Observer* from her handbag. "This is from a few months ago, when your hospitals merged."

Mega-Merger Announcement Clouded by Scandal

Regional health-care giants Doctors Inc. and Santa Rosa Medical System today announced their plans to merge. News of the mega-merger was meant to give hope for those in the community without reliable health care, but who is leading this merger, and is the leader fit to be king?

Dr. Ronald Aberdeen, president of Doctors Inc., is set to take over the conglomerate when Clyde Jewel of SRMS retires in January. But scandal clouded Aberdeen's rise to the top. Ronald Aberdeen purchased Sunshine

Medical from Adam Winterfeld in 2003. Prior to that, he was chief of surgery at Good News Hospital in New York City under the leadership of Jerry Winterfeld, Adam Winterfeld's brother. Aberdeen was dismissed from Good News Hospital in 2003 after allegations of sexual harassment. Dr. Trisha Brown, a former medical student of Aberdeen's, accused Aberdeen of soliciting sexual favors in exchange for work on prominent cases. Brown alleged that when she refused, she was demoted to menial tasks and was assigned a failing grade.

In place of reprimand, it appears that Aberdeen was handed the keys to the castle.

"My God, what have I done?" I whispered through the lump in my throat.

"Right now, you need to focus on Fox," Amber said. "Fox, Fox, Fox. If that doesn't work, quit your job."

"You're right," I agreed, tearing the newspaper in half.

"I am?" she asked, surprised.

"I have to figure out my next move," I said.

"Gabby McMillan is a doctor. Go work at Gabby's hospital," she said without hesitation.

The newspaper pieces fluttered to the floor around me. "Amber, you're right!" I exclaimed.

"Take Fox with you."

I wrapped Amber in a hug. "What would I do without you?"

"Fuck Ocean Hospital," she said. "Fuck Bonne Santé and fuck Ronald Aberdeen."

FORTY-ONE
OPAL

It wasn't hard to track down Michael's ex-wife. When Gabby McMillan inched open her door, her warmth collided with the weight of my guilt, a burden I had carried for years. I adjusted Emily on my hip, her small fingers clutching my sleeve. Cal remained in the ICU. Gabby's eyes met mine, and for a moment, neither of us moved. Then, with a smile that hadn't aged a day, she flung the door wide and gestured us inside.

"Come in, come in," she urged. She rested a hand on my elbow, her touch soft and familiar, as though no time had passed. The new smattering of freckles across her shoulders was the only sign she had aged at all.

"This is my daughter, Emily," I said, setting Emily on a chair after Gabby led us down the narrow hallway to a cozy kitchen. I lowered my eyes to my feet and mumbled, "My son, Cal, is in the ICU after an asthma attack."

"Oh?" Gabby's surprise was gentle. "I'm sorry to hear that."

"Mommy forgot his inhaler," Emily added helpfully. I cringed, heat rising to my cheeks, but Gabby's expression didn't falter.

"Have a seat, dear." She motioned to the honey-colored dinette. I dropped obediently into the chair beside Emily, though my eyes lingered on the hallway's gallery of photos. One caught my attention—a picture of her daughter, my friend Tracy with a family of her own. How long had it been since we'd spoken?

Gabby poured coffee into mugs and set out a plate of cookies, her tone light as she remarked on Fox's promotion. Her gaiety was a thin veil covering the tension between us, but that was always her way.

Noticing my gaze lingering on the photos, she plucked the portrait from its nail and sat beside me.

"Tracy's husband, Frank, works for the attorney general," she said, pointing to the man in the photo. "And these are my grandchildren, Alexis and Henry. They live in Tallahassee."

"Wow, Gabby. They're beautiful." I pulled my phone from my pocket, scrolling to a photo of Emily and Cal. My stomach somersaulted, and my cheeks burned as the small talk gave way to silence. The time for difficult conversations had arrived. I returned my phone to my pocket and wrapped my hands around the warm mug, running my thumb over the painted pink flowers.

"I'm looking for a job," I said, my voice squeaking unnaturally. "I thought maybe I could come work for you."

Gabby laughed heartily, covering her mouth with her hands. "Opal, I retired from St. Agnes two years ago when they closed the inpatient program."

A rush of embarrassment flushed my face. "Oh! I'm sorry. I think I've wasted your time."

"Michael said you might call," she said gently. "He mentioned you'd been to see him."

I swallowed hard, my gaze fixed on the table. "Gabby, I have to apologize."

"There's no need," she said quickly.

"I took something from you," I replied evenly, though my throat tightened.

"Opal," she began, shaking her head. "That was a long time ago. Leave the past in the past." Her hand flitted through the air between us, brushing away my words.

I drew in a deep breath and exhaled slowly. Placing my hands over

Emily's ears as if she didn't already know I was a terrible person, I said, "Gabby, I slept with Michael."

Gabby's hand clenched around her cookie, squeezing until it was dust, crumbs tumbling onto the table, knuckles white. She opened her hand and stared absently at the impressions her fingernails had left in her palm.

"You were a child," she murmured, not looking me in the eye.

"I'm still sorry." My voice cracked as my throat betrayed me. I took her hand in mine, and she finally looked up. There were tears in her eyes.

"Michael manipulated you, Opal. Please stop saying you're sorry."

"It's a little late to forgive myself."

"Let him carry the weight!" Gabby shouted. She stood abruptly, swiping at the crumbs on her hands. They dropped to the floor, where she let them lie.

I wanted to argue, to cling to my shame as I had done for so long. But her words cracked open a place inside me I had never seen. Would I find forgiveness there?

"He was the adult. He was supposed to protect you, not hurt you." She spun on her heel and leaned over the sink, not bothering to rinse the cookie crumbs from her hands. She needed only to turn her face away from mine.

"You were the one who got hurt," I told her.

"Do you know," Gabby continued, "that he would throw entire parties just to be around you?"

"I'm sorry?" I watched her spine curl above the sink, her shoulders hunched and sagging.

"Come on, Opal. A New Year's celebration at a children's gym?" she said, her tone rich with cynicism.

My mind raced through the tally—each time he had placed himself in my path. The secrets. The gifts. Gabby was right. He had manipulated me as skillfully as a marionette's puppet master.

"Did you know he was doing it?" I asked reluctantly. I didn't want to accuse her of complicity, and I didn't want to know it if she was.

"I don't think I knew it then," she replied. She twisted to regard me. "But when the other girls came forward—" She shrugged. "I left."

Her words hung heavy, and a chill crept into my chest. "Other girls?" I asked, the question barely a whisper.

Gabby disappeared down the hall and returned moments later, handing me a folded newspaper yellowed at the edges. I unfolded it, rearranging the mugs to spread it open.

"There," she said, pointing to a small headline buried in the lower margin of the *West Florida Observer*. "It's from five years ago."

Too Little, Too Late: Coach Continues to Work Amid Allegations

Local physician and assistant USA Gymnastics coach Michael McMillan is facing accusations of sexual abuse from a growing number of young women and one young man.

The accusers say McMillan engaged in inappropriate sexual activity of a predatory nature while acting as the coach and team doctor of H.P. Elite Gymnastics. Complaints against McMillan filed with USA Gymnastics and SafeSport are mounting. So, why is McMillan still coaching children?

I skimmed through the article, unable to focus. Emotion seeped through my heart, creeping up my throat, clouding my brain, dripping into my gut. It was a mixture of sadness for my successors, anger at Michael for failing us, and remorse for doing nothing to stop him. Had I been complicit in my silence? I glanced at Gabby, who was now perched beside me. Studying the anguished question on my face, she took my hands in hers.

"Go see your father, Opal," she said, giving me a squeeze. "He alone challenged Michael back then. He can explain this better than I can."

"But. . . I. . ." I stammered.

"No more guilt, Opal. No more guilt. No more shame."

FORTY-TWO
OPAL

Gabby convinced me to go and see my dad. She thought he'd be the perfect person to tell me about redemption after what he'd survived—divorce, alcoholism and losing his kids. Years had passed since we spoke. Before I could talk myself out of it, I was knocking at his door.

"Hey, Dad," I said, stepping inside. It was as if I were facing a stranger. His face had softened, gray hair replacing the military buzz cut I remembered. He still tucked his shirt neatly, but now it stretched over a soft belly. His eyes, though—those were unchanged. Family. They held my reflection, my roots. I relaxed into familiarity as he shut the door behind me.

"Hey, Opal," he greeted, pulling me into a warm hug. The cedarwood scent of his aftershave lingered as he stepped back to study me. "My beautiful little girl, all grown up," he said softly, leading me into a tidy room that doubled as a kitchen and living room. He gestured to an overstuffed armchair near a cracked leather sofa. The small space was clean but worn, like him. A single photograph rested in a frame. It was of my father with his arms around Amber and me. I could see where he'd worn the edges, suggesting he'd taken the photo out of the frame a thousand times to hold it.

"I'd offer you a drink, but all I have is flat ginger ale. What's on your mind?"

"I'll get the ginger ale," I stalled, heading to the fridge. Inside, I found condiments, lunch meat, and the half-empty soda.

"I've been sober over twenty-five years, honey," he called. "You won't find anything."

"I'm not here for that," I said, returning with two glasses. I sat and faced him. "I'm lost, Dad. And I hoped you could help."

He laughed, a deep, throaty guffaw. "You thought I was the right person to be your life coach?"

"No, but I figured no matter how badly I screwed up, you'd understand."

"I guess I earned that," he said.

I was there to talk about what happened with Michael, but I couldn't get the words to leave my mouth. Instead, I blurted out, "I had an affair with my boss." Then I filled my mouth with a swig of ginger ale.

His eyebrow shot up. "Oh?"

"I have to quit my job now, and I assume you know a thing or two about stepping out."

"That's not fair, Opal," he remarked, setting his glass down. "You don't understand—"

"Mom told me about your affair," I interrupted.

He sighed, rubbing his chin. "I loved your mother—I still do—but I made a terrible decision. When she left, I made another."

"Alcohol," I said quietly.

He nodded. "I thought those mistakes defined me. But I was wrong. There was still good in me, Opal. I needed to forgive myself to find it again."

"You've always been a good father," I replied.

"Thanks, honey." He stood as if to end the conversation. "This isn't you, Opal. Your affair doesn't define you. There's another Opal in there. It's time you found her."

As he walked me to the door, my phone rang. I glanced at the screen. Better Health Hospital? I picked up the call. "Hello?"

"Opal Collins?" a man's voice asked. "This is Dr. Edwards from Better Health emergency room. Dr. McMillan gave me your number."

"Oh?" My chest tightened at the mention of Michael's name.

"You probably don't remember me, but we met years ago at a New Year's Eve party in the gymnastics place."

"Oh," I said, my voice faint. "Yes, Dr. Edwards. Hello."

"Michael said you're looking for work. We have an opening in urgent care. Are you available Wednesday for an interview?"

Was this real? A chance to escape Ocean Hospital had landed in my lap. But what would that look like? Memories swirled: Michael's touch, his gifts, the weight of my mistakes. I peered at my father and the simple world he'd built from the rubble of his own life.

"I'll have to call you back, Dr. Edwards," I said, hanging up. I wondered what my dad would think about me working alongside Michael. Turning to my father, I asked, "Do you remember Michael McMillan from my gymnastics team?"

His brow furrowed. "Your gymnastics team? From the '90s?"

I nodded. "I called him about work."

His eyes narrowed. "Did he touch you?"

"No..." I faltered. "Okay, yes."

The glass in his hand shook. "What happened?"

Painfully, awkwardly, I told him everything—the attention, the gifts, the party, the affair. As the last words left my mouth, he shot to his feet and stormed down the hall.

"I'm going to fucking kill him!" he shouted.

"Dad, no!" I ran after him. "It was my fault—it was twenty years ago!"

He stopped in his bedroom, kneeling in front of a drawer. "How old were you? Fourteen?"

"Sixteen," I whispered. "But. . . he said he fell in love with me when I was fourteen."

"Fuck!" he yelled, shoving through the drawer's contents. "I knew that man was a creep. I told your mother!"

"You knew?" I asked, stunned.

"I saw the way he looked at you at that gymnastics meet. I asked your mother about him." He yanked the drawer open wider, shoveling out handfuls of earplugs, phone chargers, pencils, and coins. "I fucking asked your mother about him!"

"She found the birth control he gave me," I admitted, my voice shaking. "She called me a slut."

"Goddammit!" he yelled.

Still kneeling in front of his bedside table, my father covered his face with his hands. Clawing at his scalp with neatly trimmed fingernails, he wore his wounded soul on his sleeve.

Then he froze, hands gripping the edges of the drawer. Slowly, he turned to face me, his expression shattered. "None of that ever should've happened. Michael never should've touched you, and your mother never should've said that."

He pulled a pistol from the drawer. My breath caught. He held it with both hands, aiming at the wall, checking the sights.

"Calm down!" I begged. "What are you doing?"

"It wasn't your fault, Opal," he said softly, squeezing the trigger. The click echoed in the quiet room. "You liked it because you're human. That doesn't make you a monster. You're not worthless. You're priceless."

"Stop! Stop! Stop!" I cried, tears burning my cheeks. But the words you're not worthless hung in the air, a lifeline. But killing Michael wouldn't change the past.

I rested my hand on his shoulder and whispered, "I don't want this, Dad."

His arms went slack and his shoulders slumped. He set the pistol back in the drawer and closed it gently. I began to cry, and he wrapped his arms around me. "I'm sorry I scared you, Opal," he murmured. "I should have protected you back then. Let's start over."

Permission to start over was like a light in the dark part of my soul. Finally, after all these years with the skeletons, I realized it wasn't my fault. It was time to throw them off my shoulders and rise.

It was time to let go of Ronald too. I wasn't so blameless with him. As my father and I sat on the bed, I turned my phone over in my hands, understanding I needed to answer Dr. Edwards. My gaze shifted from my phone to my father.

"Do you want me to take care of McMillan for you?" my father asked.

"No," I replied. "I need to do that myself."

Forty-Three

Opal

Cal's asthma attack had wrecked me. After visiting Gabby and my father, I turned all my attention to my son, and avoided returning the call about the job at Better Health. If I weren't trying to be a better mother, I'd have drowned myself in gin and tonic and disappeared into the dark corner of the universe I deserved.

We binged on crackers, then cookies, then ice cream—whatever was within arm's reach. Dishes stacked in the sink. Laundry towered. Every day, I listened to my mother knocking, her voice calling my name. I ignored her. Ronald stepped in, covering my shifts so I could stay in the hospital until Cal left the ICU. He booked us a room at the Pelican to avoid memories of the Rest Rite. Ronald yearned to be the perfect paramour, but in my heart, I was no longer his mistress.

Grateful for the pandemic's school closures, I hoarded Cal under strict quarantine, clutching him like my lifeline. On the bathroom floor, cradling Cal's head as I slipped the nebulizer mask over it, I avoided Ronald and Ocean Hospital. But the impossibility of escape meant difficult choices had to be made. Even my greasy hair and the threadbare bathrobe clinging to my unwashed skin couldn't stall me anymore. The thought of calling Michael McMillan sent vomit creeping up the back of my throat, but I needed out. This time, I wasn't taking the easy road.

Michael answered on the first ring. "Opal Camry!" he exclaimed. "I found you a job, after all, in the ER."

"I know." My voice was blunt, and I ran a hand over the stiff hair covering my legs. "But we should never work together. Not after. . ." Say it. But words betrayed me, and I couldn't finish.

"Oh, stop." He brushed off the comment as if time had erased the scars. "You'd be in urgent care—a sandbox compared to the real ER. You wouldn't even see me." He sighed. "Tomorrow's a new day, Opal. Pick yourself up. Let me know your decision."

I urged myself to be courageous. "I'll meet with Dr. Edwards Wednesday."

As the day drew closer, I pretended things were normal. I read comics to Cal. I played Barbies with Emily. I made eggplant parmesan, Fox's favorite, and tiptoed around him, still uncertain how to approach him after the argument in the ICU. He stepped carefully around me as well.

I carried my past like a bad tattoo: impossible to erase and demanding an explanation when discovered. I kept it hidden, even from Fox. I convinced myself it was for the best. If returning to Michael was my only escape from Ronald, then I had to do it.

The next morning, I shaved the forest from my legs, watching the black stubble circle the drain like ants marching away from battle.

The battered sweater I'd interviewed in years ago hung in my closet, the stain on its shoulder a badge of a woman I had long outgrown. Beside it hung the blazer that had tried to eat me. I trashed them both, slipping into a maroon silk blouse. Tying its scarf around my neck, I squared my shoulders in the mirror. My reflection suggested I was ready to move on with my life. Better Health and Dr. Edwards might offer salvation—if I dared face them.

When I arrived, Dr. Edwards greeted me with a warm handshake and led me on a tour. We passed doctors and nurses in the halls. The rhythm of the ER hummed against my nerves. At the mention of Michael, my stomach knotted. "Is Dr. McMillan working today?" I asked, feigning nonchalance.

"Off today," he said, easing the tightness in my chest.

In his office, I glanced absently at the photos taped above his monitor. My phone buzzed with a message from Gabby. I flipped it facedown and focused on Dr. Edwards.

"I remember when Michael used to coach Tracy's gymnastics team," he said as we settled ourselves. "A million years ago." He chuckled. "I always knew I liked you."

There was a knock at the door. A tough-looking, thick-waisted woman popped in. As she launched into her announcement of a stroke alert en route, I peeked at Gabby's text.

> Did you see the news article yesterday about Michael? Unbelievable.

> No. What article?

Dr. Edwards jumped up from his chair and said a quick, "Be right back," as he followed the nurse.

A moment later, a link appeared from Gabby with a picture of Michael in his white coat smiling a million-dollar smile.

Local Doctor Saves Cheerleader at Riverside High-School Football Game

I clicked on the link and began to read.

Riverside High School cheerleader Chelsea Hansen is calling Dr. Michael McMillan a hero today after the doctor's actions following her near-devastating fall.

Hansen, 16, tumbled from the top of a cheerleading formation called a pyramid, striking her head on the ground below. As Hansen lay unconscious, Better Health ER doctor McMillan sprang into action. Stabilizing the young woman's spine, McMillan assisted paramedics in getting Hansen into a collar and onto a backboard.

Now, Hansen, who is expected to make a full recovery from a minor concussion, is calling McMillan a hero. "Thank God he was there!" Hansen said. McMillan insisted it was all instinct, not heroics.

But McMillan has a long history of being a hero to young women. Years ago, he worked as a volunteer coach for his daughter's gymnastic team, H.P. Elite. He later volunteered his coaching and medical expertise for the cheerleading squad at Riverside High School. Three cheers for Dr. McMillan: hip, hip, hooray!

Michael had gone too far. He was no hero. He was a predator. He didn't save girls; he ruined them. I couldn't work here, not with him.

As if Michael could sense my magnanimous shift, he called me right on cue.

I answered sharply. "I'm not taking the job."

A beat of silence. "Well, hello to you too, Opal. Can I ask why not?"

"You know why."

"Ancient history. Irrelevant," he countered.

The cheap static of his voice through the phone grated my nerves. History. That was his word for it. History?

"You were supposed to protect me, and you hurt me," I snapped, surprising even myself.

"Opal, you're fine," he growled, anger cutting through his charm. "Nothing happened."

As his words assaulted me, I let my fingertips drift to the smooth skin above my ankles. The razor hadn't just prepared my legs; it held symbolism. It had stripped away the rough part that was just surviving, revealing the part strong enough to fight.

Dr. Edwards burst back into the office, his sudden presence grounding me. My heart pounded as I shoved my phone to the center of the room, letting Michael's words fly into the space between us.

"Opal?" Michael's voice was crystal clear. "You're fine because nothing happened."

"I'm angry, Michael," I said with a calm I didn't feel.

"I'm so confused right now, Opal. You wanted the job, and now you don't? You'll never work again. I'll have you blacklisted. You need me."

"I was sixteen years old. You were in your forties!"

"I was forty-two. So what? You wanted it. You threw yourself at me."

Dr. Edwards rubbed his chin, his face frozen in between rage and disbelief. "Opal—" he started, but words faltered.

"Let me be clear. Sixteen. Sixteen years old when. . . when you held me down. You were my coach. I was your athlete." My voice cracked. "My mother's little girl."

"I specifically waited until you weren't little, so don't give me that." His pathetic attempt at self-defense continued to dig his grave.

"You were careless with a decision that devastated me for years."

Dr. Edwards had heard enough. His eyes were red, and he was shaking. So was I.

"McMillan!" he roared, plucking the phone from my hand. "This is Dr. Edwards."

"Opal? What the hell is going on?" Michael's tone abruptly shifted to panic.

"Never show your face in my ER again."

"Dr. Edwards, let me explain—"

"You're fired." Dr. Edwards jabbed the button that ended the call and held the phone to me.

"I had no idea. I'm sorry."

"It's okay," I replied. "I can't believe you fired him."

"It was all you."

I was relieved, as if I'd finally come up for air, but a weight remained. My escape had disintegrated. Still, I smiled—a genuine smile—for the first time in ages.

FORTY-FOUR
OPAL

I HAD ONCE BEEN A BRAVE WOMAN. I WAS LEARNING TO BE A good mother. Now, it was time to become a better wife. But before I could face Fox, I needed guidance—someone who loved me and could point me back toward grace.

"Opal Antoinette Collins!" boomed Pastor Bobby's familiar voice. The gravel crunched beneath my tires as I eased into the parking lot of the old church. The pine-scented air was thick with dew, and puddles from the morning rain sparkled in the hazy light. This place held pieces of me: childhood Sundays, my wedding day to Fox, and now, hopefully, my last thread of hope to stitch my family back together. The chipped white paint and missing letters on the sign were an aged weariness that mirrored my own. But in the storm of my life, it had stood firm. I prayed I could do the same.

Pastor Bobby swung his legs out of a nearby Honda and struggled to his feet. He wobbled as the cane held in his hand shifted in the gravel. His hunched back forced a great round belly to hang over his belt and dangle over the wet ground. He was older now, but his face still shone with the kindness I remembered. A wave of relief washed over me. He would know what to do. He would remember me and want to save me.

Pastor Bobby would say, Why, hello Opal. It's good to see you. I'm glad you're back. Is everything okay? And I would confess that it was not. I would tell him that nothing was okay, and he'd pull me into his weathered arms, listen to my brokenness, and tell me all would be well.

"Come on now," he called across the empty lot. "Get your ass over here." I stepped out, my legs trembling. He pulled me into a warm embrace. "What's wrong, Opal?"

"Everything," I replied. "I had an affair. I need to tell Fox."

His eyebrows disappeared into his forehead. "Well, damn. That's a big one."

I let out a nervous chuckle, but he wasn't finished.

"How long has it been since you last went to church? And now you think I can sprinkle a little Jesus on you to fix this?" His cane beat the gravel for emphasis. "Opal, you're a mess. I'm afraid you're too late."

"I should go," I whispered, fighting back tears.

"Now, hold on," Bobby softened, gripping my arm. "Let's talk this through." He gestured toward the building, leading me past the echoing sanctuary and down a hall I'd never visited. His office overlooked thick woods, where green leaves glistened in the clearing sunlight. "Sit," he said, motioning to a chair more luxurious than I'd seen in the rest of his worn church.

"This has to stay between us," I replied, my voice thin.

He raised a brow. "Should I call Fox? Get him here?"

"No," I murmured, staring at my chipped pink nails. "Not yet."

"Well, then." He exhaled heavily. "My way, now." Then he shuffled off, mumbling something about an information packet. Left alone, I focused on the window. Outside, sunlight pierced through a breaking cloud. Maybe it was a sign. Maybe I wasn't entirely lost.

Bobby returned with black coffee and a sheaf of papers bound with a rusty staple. "Here, it's all in the packet: sin, guilt, redemption, blah, blah." He dropped into his chair. "Now, talk."

So I did. It spilled out of me, as messy as the rain-splattered parking lot outside. I told Bobby about Michael and about Ronald. My thoughts, my mistakes, my collapse. He listened without interrupting. I admitted I was broken.

"Opal," he said finally when I had finished. "From a clergyman's viewpoint, let me clarify."

"Okay," I agreed, wringing my hands.

"I've known you since you were a little girl. I recall the girl who played Mary in the Christmas recital. The girl who insisted on delivering care packages to every shelter east of Gilbert. The young woman who chose the church's thrift sale over her friend's party. You are a woman who knows Jesus."

I nodded, not meeting his eyes. He rifled through a Bible—his own Bible, from the appearance of the tattered pages and prolific notes in the margins—and tapped on a passage.

As far as the east is from the west, so far has he removed our transgressions from us.

As a father has compassion on his children, so the Lord has compassion on those who fear him; for he knows our form, he remembers that we are dust.

The life of the mortals is like grass, they flourish like a flower of the field; the wind blows over it and it is gone, and its place remembers it no more.

He leaned back and folded his hands. "You feel burnt to ash," he said. "But God didn't snuff out your flame, Opal. That wind blowing through your mess will not put you out—it's going to scatter your embers so they can spark something new. You're gonna burn brighter for this."

I clenched the mug as his words seeped into me.

"Start with Fox," he added. "He deserves the truth." He stood then and stretched. "I've got some business to attend to. Settle in; look over the packet."

I nodded, a mind's image of Fox tightening my throat. "Are you going to tell him?" I asked.

"No," he whispered without looking back.

He left, the door creaking open behind him. I tried to focus on the words on the page, but the sound of giggles broke through my spiraling thoughts. Two children raced down the hallway outside, their laughter warming the musty air. I knew them, somehow. The recognition prodded at me until a woman's voice called after them.

"Nicholas! Abigail! No running."

It was no use; the children were much faster than her. When she appeared in the doorway, she stopped, startled by me standing there. "Oh, hi. I know you! You were my mom's doctor, right?"

My brow furrowed. "Who's your mother?"

"Gloria Halloway," she said. "We met at Ocean Hospital."

I gasped. "Yes! Of course. I remember. How is she?"

The woman's smile faltered for a moment, and my stomach turned. "We're here to plan her funeral."

The word hit like a hammer. Not yet. I swallowed hard. Tears sprang to my eyes before I registered the news. "I'm so sorry, ma'am. Your mother was one of my favorite patients."

"Don't be sorry. She's not dead yet!" The woman laughed. "That old bat is here planning her own funeral. Seems that you told her she should get her affairs in order."

I clutched my chest and laughed, my relief soon joined by Gloria's raspy voice as she rounded the corner. Gloria's walker screeched against the floor as her oxygen backpack jostled with her movements. She wore clean white slacks and a T-shirt bedazzled with jewels that took the shape of a sea turtle. She had neatly combed her thin hair and wore lipstick. I had never seen her in anything but a hospital gown, lying in a hospital bed.

"Jesus fucking Christ!" Gloria exclaimed, eyeing me.

"Mom!" her daughter admonished, though she was smiling. "You can't say that in church!"

I rushed out to hug her—awkwardly—with her walker between us. But I didn't care. Seeing her alive, alert, and as sassy as ever was the balm I needed.

"You look like hell," Gloria croaked, pulling back.

"You look like spring," I replied softly.

"You aren't here planning your funeral too, are you?" She wagged her finger at me. "This shit is expensive!"

"Not quite," I admitted, heat flushing my cheeks. "I'm figuring out how to tell my husband I had an affair."

"Psh. What a bummer." Her grin widened. "The solution is obvious. I know what we need."

"Thank God someone does."

"A girls' night!"

"Gloria, you just want an excuse to party, but I'm going to allow it."

"You're damn right," she said. "And don't even try to rain-check me."

FORTY-FIVE
OPAL

Fantasia opened the oven door, fanning the smoke rising from a dollop of cheese. She slid the pepperoni pizza out of the oven and dropped the pan on the stovetop, letting it cool before picking up a pizza cutter wheel and slicing it. She and Billy had officially separated.

She'd dyed her hair platinum blond, styling it in her signature gelled waves. Her lopsided hair attempted to tell the world she was okay, but I knew better. She was breaking. Fantasia had come to stay with me before moving in with her sister in New Haven. Fox had left to tend to Billy up north. I missed Fox fiercely, a fervor for our love having washed over me. I needed us to be right again like I needed to breathe, but tonight wasn't about him.

Gloria's idea for a girls' night was just what we needed. The pizzas were ready, chips filled bowls, and the women would arrive soon. Fantasia cleaned the pizza cutter in the sink as I carried the snacks to the table.

"Hey, Opal," she whispered. I turned, and she caught the sleeve of my blouse in her hand, pulling me close. She had a body both firm and yielding. Her lips felt natural against mine.

Fantasia had been sleeping next to me since coming here. Her sturdy arms had wrapped around me for comfort at night. Now I understood this was for comfort too. If things had been different, I would have ventured beyond the kiss, but I had no appetite for romance now.

I pulled back gently, my voice low. "Fox."

Her lips parted slightly, then closed again. "Okay," she agreed, returning to the sink.

I poured tortilla chips into a bowl, setting it beside a candy dish piled with M&Ms. "Are you okay, Fantasia?" I asked.

"Sure," she said, forcing a smile.

A knock at the door broke the tension. Amber and Wendy let themselves in, bright-eyed and eager. I hugged them as headlights approached in the driveway. Gloria. Throwing on a cardigan, I ran outside to meet her. An old green Camry idled as her daughter jumped out to help, and together we guided Gloria and her portable oxygen inside.

Her daughter kissed her cheek with a teasing smile. "Don't smoke too much," she warned. "And watch your language. Not everyone likes it so spicy."

"You're welcome to stay," I offered.

"Thanks, but not today," she said before leaving. Once inside, I added an extra folding chair to the table, and the party began.

Fantasia shook Gloria's hand with a grin, then pulled a plastic bag from her pocket, dropping it onto the table beside the chips. Inside were green, fuzzy marijuana buds, their sharp scent filling the air. "Grandma's Brownies," I read aloud with a laugh as Fantasia placed a blue glass bowl beside it.

"My girl!" Wendy whooped, high-fiving Fantasia. Amber arched a brow, confusion flickering in her expression.

"It's okay," Wendy murmured, cupping Amber's cheek. "I'll take care of you."

Gloria's wet, raspy voice cut through. "Let's light that pipe already." She reached for the buds and began packing some of the sticky greens into the bowl.

I glared at her. "Absolutely not."

"Don't be a buzzkill, Dr. Collins," Gloria replied. "Where's the lighter?"

"I'm serious. I don't want any dead bodies in my house."

She groaned but held up her hands in mock surrender. "Fine." Fishing in her pockets, she produced a second bag, this one labeled Feeling Peachy. I peeled it open, revealing sugary peach gummies infused with that unmistakable herbal smell.

Wendy burst into laughter, declaring Gloria her "soulmate," and soon hands passed the bowl and gummies in tandem, laughter curling like smoke through the room.

Marijuana was inhaled. Weird peach-salad gummies were consumed. Fingertips buzzed. Minds relaxed. Five women suddenly became comediennes, and in my kitchen, the world was funny and good. We had another pizza baking in the oven. The M&Ms were long gone.

"Ladies," Fantasia announced with a clink of her fork on her wineglass, "we are gathered here today to find a new job for Opal."

"Hear, hear," Amber toasted, downing her chardonnay.

"Ideas?" Fantasia asked, looking around expectantly.

Bonne Santé, Better Health, and St. Agnes were out of the question, leaving me with exactly nothing within a thirty-mile radius of Ocean Hospital. Moving farther for a job I didn't want would mean selling my grandmother's house—a prospect that sat heavy in my chest.

"You could get me hired in the strip club," I replied, petting Fantasia's shoulder. "Dancing with you."

Fantasia patted me on the head. "You're not a dancer," she said gently. "You're a retired gymnast who's given birth to two kids. What are you going to do? Cartwheel across the stage? No one wants to see that."

The table erupted in laughter, and a warm, giddy joy loosened the weight in my chest.

"You should apply for a Connecticut medical license," Wendy suggested.

"Why?" I asked, surprised.

"Fox's parents are there," Amber chimed in. "Maybe a fresh start wouldn't hurt."

"It's freezing there," I huffed.

"Gilbert may have us," Wendy said of the women, "but it will always be filled with temptation."

"A mother does what she needs to for her kids," Gloria intoned with the sharp exactness of someone who believed it herself. Her words hit deeply, but before they could take root, Amber hijacked the room.

"I don't want to be a teacher anymore!" she blurted, her voice unsteady but earnest. The kitchen fell quiet as she turned to Wendy. "I want to quit my job and marry you. I love you."

"You don't have to quit your job," Wendy said. "I don't care what people think."

"Honey, you just promoted my mother to assistant principal," Amber retorted. "Look where that got Opal."

She grabbed Wendy's hand. "I never wanted to teach. I only did it because it's what my mother expected. I want to be happy, for once."

We surrounded them, laughter folding into hugs until Amber's nervous confession seemed to lift the air itself. Wendy pulled her close, kissing her softly.

"Is someone lighting that bowl, or do I have to make another speech?" Wendy teased, her sharp humor breaking the mushy moment.

As the smoke weaved into fantastic clouds in my kitchen, I let myself imagine New Haven—Fox, his parents, the clean slate. Gloria's words replayed in my mind. *A mother does what she needs to for her kids.* I'd repair the wreckage, lean into the discomfort of hope, and let a new life catch fire.

FORTY-SIX

RONALD

THE MORNING LIGHT CREPT BETWEEN THE LINEN CURTAIN panels, stretched across the room, and found the bed where Ronald shielded his eyes. A dull, familiar ache throbbed behind them—the pain that greeted him every morning. This morning was no different. He reached to the familiar spot beside the bed, his fingers closing around the pill bottle and glass. He swallowed in a practiced motion. Isabelle stirred, pushing the sleep mask from her eyes. He didn't need to look to know she was awake.

Grimacing, Ronald swung his legs over the edge of the bed, pushed himself up, and forced the day to begin.

At his corporate office, the pain eventually receded. The pills and coffee worked their magic, as always. Ronald sifted through emails, quickly replying to a few and deleting most. His phone pinged with three messages from Karen Chamberlain. She wanted him to help her friend land a hospitalist position. Ronald felt little interest.

Meanwhile, Opal hadn't texted in three days. He wasn't surprised, though it gnawed at him. She'd seemed distant, unhappy. Was she losing interest in him? His mind, as usual, flicked between being ignored by Opal and his still-unfinished efforts at bonding with Allen, her brother-in-law.

Thoughts of his past achievements tugged at him—a triumphant return to New York research, the life he dreamed of reclaiming. It reminded him he still needed to arrange another meeting with Rebecca, his daughter. The company was already signed over, but he wanted to ensure she remained involved.

Ronald was two clicks away from attaching a file called Timesheet to an email when pain exploded through his skull like a sudden clap of thunder. His hands flew to his face, clawing and clutching at his temples. The searing, dizzying agony enveloped him, dragging him into what felt like another dimension. It was terrifying.

The sharp, wet sounds of retching carried down the hall to Miranda. She rushed into his office, alarm written all over her face. She grimaced in the dark room, stifling with the sour tang of vomit. Ronald sat hunched over his desk, his large hands covering his head. He had switched off the fluorescent light and pulled the blackout shades over the window.

"Dr. Aberdeen! Are you all right?" she asked, her voice trembling.

Without lifting his head, he replied weakly, "I'm fine. Thank you, Miranda."

"Do you need me to call an ambulance?"

"Of course not," he rasped.

"You should go home," she urged, her voice soft but insistent.

A pause. Then, "Close the door. You're letting in the light."

Quietly, Miranda shut the door and returned to her desk. If Isabelle had been the one to find him instead of her, things would've been different. Isabelle would've pushed past his resistance, shattered through his displays of stoic pride, and forced him to acknowledge the danger glaring back at him. But it wasn't Isabelle. It was Miranda, unwilling to disobey. Ronald had left no room in his schedule to deal with his own fragility.

Like an affirmation, the pain began to ebb, slipping away like a receding tide. Ronald steadied his breath. In and out. The spinning slowed until the room settled. In and out. The nausea vanished. He was fine again. He thought of Opal and was abruptly seized with the need to see her. There were things he needed to say, things he couldn't leave unsaid.

Bright light flooded the office when he raised the blackout shades. The air felt lighter. All the paper he found bore the sharp-printed logo of Doctors Inc. He pushed a button on the phone. Miranda answered, swiftly providing a sheet of flowery stationery. Relieved, Ronald scrawled a message to Opal in dark ink before calling Rebecca. She agreed to come to Gilbert that week.

"I think I'll go home, after all," he told Miranda as he hurried out the door. It wasn't even 10:00 a.m. He saved Opal's home address in his phone, letting the car's GPS guide him to Bramblewood Estates. He hoped she was home. He hoped she would answer. He waited until he was in her neighborhood to make the call.

The phone call pierced the silence of the drive. "Absolutely not!" Opal snapped. "You cannot come here. You cannot be at my house!"

Mailbox after mailbox blurred past as Ronald realized he was driving too fast. Women jogged on the sidewalks; others pushed strollers, casting wary glances at the dark storm clouds rolling in. He slowed as the GPS directed him to turn, easing into the neighborhood's winding streets.

"I won't stay long, Opal," he assured her. "I just need to see you."

"Ronald, we need to talk," she replied, her tone ominous. "Let's meet at the Roasted Bean. I don't want you at my house."

The erratic driving left his head spinning, though he wasn't sure if it was the remains of this morning's migraine or something deeper. He felt unsteady as he parked in front of a modest white house. The well-tended lawn shimmered like a restless sea with every step he took.

Before he could knock, the door opened, and a hand yanked him through the threshold.

"You cannot be here," Opal bit out. She wore a loose cream sweater with the sleeves pushed up, paired with knit pants of the same shade. Her skin glowed several shades darker than her outfit, and her hair knotted high on her head. Her stormy eyes pinned him in place. His heart squeezed painfully as he looked at her, momentarily forgetting why he had come. His hand brushed the sealed envelope in his pocket.

"Are you okay?" Opal asked as Ronald stood limply in the foyer. Ronald's silence hung between them.

"Come on," she said firmly, grabbing his sleeve and leading him down the hall. "I don't want you standing in front of the window."

Photographs lined the walls. They passed a child's bedroom, then another, before entering the last door at the hall's end.

Inside was a bed, neatly made, flanked by two nightstands. Across from it stood a window framing a sprawling oak. The tree had shed its leaves, its bare branches clawing at the overcast sky. Ronald envisioned it in its full majesty—draped in emerald leaves and Spanish moss. A pang of melancholy rose in his chest as he took in the sight. There was beauty in its brokenness.

"Sit," Opal instructed, tugging him toward the bed. He sank down, though neither spoke. For a moment, Ronald traced the curve of her profile as she climbed into bed beside him one last time.

FORTY-SEVEN

Fox

Seeing Billy unravel after leaving Fantasia made Fox appreciate Opal more. By the time he returned from New Jersey, he was certain he'd put everything back the way it was. Opal seemed eager—almost too eager—to prove she still loved him.

The next morning, Fox swept crumbs from the table, kissed the kids on their heads, and searched for his wife. It was his turn to take call, and he was already running late.

Out back, Opal stood under the oak tree, her palm resting gently on its trunk. Her face was pale.

"The tree looks dead," she breathed.

"It's March. Everything bounces back in March," he replied, brushing her concern aside.

"Fox," she began, moving her hand from the weathered bark to his shoulder, "I need to tell you something."

"I'm on call, babe," he said, dropping a quick kiss on her hand. "Text me later."

"It's important," she said, her voice tightening.

With a sigh, Fox turned to face her. She pressed herself against him, arms wrapped tight, her words muffled against his chest. "I think we should move to New Haven."

Fox smoothed her hair and kissed her head. His heart soared. He had waited years to hear her say it, but he kept his voice level. "We can talk when I'm off. Six a.m. tomorrow." When he pulled away, her tears caught him by surprise. But he had to go. Call was call.

****

Later, Fox finished a procedure in the sterile hum of the suite when an overhead page crackled. He ignored it until Devon, his nurse practitioner, appeared at the door.

"Dr. Collins," Devon said, "the operator's been overhead paging you."

Fox frowned, shrugging off his gown. His pager—it wasn't clipped to his waist.

"Shoot," he muttered.

At the nurse's desk, he called the operator. "Fox Collins here. What's going on?"

"Ah, yes. Dr. Collins. The emergency room is trying to reach you, and they have notified us you have not responded to your pager. Is the pager working, or do you want it forwarded to another number?"

Fox groaned inwardly, patting his empty hip. How had he left without it? "Yeah, sure," he said, rattling off his number.

The ER called minutes later about a patient's malfunctioning dialysis catheter, but Fox's mind snagged on his mistake. He always had his pager, always called back, always came through. What was wrong with him today?

"You should run home and get it," his partner suggested after the consult. "I can cover you for fifteen minutes."

"You sure?" Fox asked, hesitant.

"It's no problem. I, for one, want to know if you backed over it with your car. That happened to my buddy in residency, and he said the pager popped like a grape. They found pager parts in the parking garage for weeks."

Reluctantly, Fox agreed and retraced his steps, eyes scanning every corner, crack, and shadow for the misplaced device. Rain dotted his windshield as he sped toward home. Windshield wipers danced arrhythmically as storm clouds broke.

Halfway home, he remembered. The junk drawer. He'd stuffed the pager there last night to keep Emily's busy hands off it.

FORTY-EIGHT
OPAL

I STOOD IN THE KITCHEN, DAZED AND UTTERLY disappointed in myself. A few hours earlier, I had stood under the oak tree with my palm pressed to its trunk. "I had an affair," I told the tree, rehearsing for Fox. The tree didn't respond. "It meant nothing. I didn't love him."

A squirrel bouncing along the branches caused a fantastic scampering sound that spoke the emphatic reply of the tree—*That isn't true.*

I frowned at the dried-up oak. "Well, how would you tell him, then?"

I jumped, startled by Fox's sudden presence in the yard. *I had an affair*, I willed myself to say. Instead, I said, "The tree looks dead."

"It's March. Everything bounces back in March," he replied.

That was good. I could use that. We would bounce back too. "Fox, I need to tell you something."

"I'm on call, babe," he said, kissing my hand. "Text me later."

My heart squeezed itself into my throat. "It's important."

Say '*I had an affair*,' I willed myself. Instead, "I think we should move to New Haven" left my mouth.

I failed, but Fox was right. Call was call, and it wasn't fair for me to lay this on him now. Soon enough, I would tell him.

Still wrapped in the panic of near confession, my gut wrenched a little while later when my phone trilled across the kitchen counter. Who was torturing me now? My breath caught. The phone kept ringing.

It was Ronald. He wanted to see me.

"Absolutely not!" I snapped. "You cannot come here. You cannot be at my house!" I yelled with a force neither of us recognized as he insisted he was nearby.

I closed my eyes, forcing calm into my words. "Ronald, we need to talk. Let's meet at the Roasted Bean. I don't want you in my house."

Before I could reach for my keys, the doorbell rang.

Ronald stood in the doorway, disheveled, his face pale, hair unruly.

"Are you okay?" I asked. "Get in here."

I scanned the street behind him—empty, but that meant nothing. I grabbed his arm and pulled him inside shutting the door with a soft but firm click. The curtains shifted. I pulled him through the living room that felt too exposed and down the narrow hall into my more secluded bedroom.

Sitting him on the edge of my bed, I hesitated before perching beside him.

"I won't stay long, Opal. I just need to see you," he said, voice strained, eyes hollow.

"I know about Trisha Brown," I announced, flat and sharp.

He flinched. "Opal, I'm sorry. That. . . that was years ago. I'm not that man anymore."

"Is that so? What about Allen? You fucked me to get to him. You made me feel special so you could trap me in this stupid job and fuck me whenever you want! You are exactly the man who fucked over Trisha Brown."

Ronald moved a hand over his stomach and dry heaved. I jumped back. "Opal, I love you."

"I loved you too," I shouted, frustration tearing through knots in my chest. "But I can't do this anymore." I watched the weight of my words drizzle over him, his brow furrowed, eyes glassy. "This isn't okay. You're my boss. Were my boss."

He reached for my hand. "I'll quit too."

"Ronald, I'm not that kind of girl anymore," I said firmly, standing and folding my arms. A flicker of triumph sparked in my chest. There, I'd said it.

His face fell, dragging something in me with it.

"Then. . . let me kiss you goodbye," he whispered.

His lips brushed mine. Something felt off. Sloppy, disconnected. My stomach turned as a slick trail of saliva escaped his mouth, clinging to his chin.

"Ronald. . . what's going on?"

"I'm. . . not," he replied.

His speech was off. Half his face was limp. Dread rose in my chest and leaked out to my fingertips, which slid through the drool on his face.

"What's wrong?" I asked, my voice trembling now.

"I'm not doing well."

FORTY-NINE

RONALD

"We have to stop doing this," Opal said, her words colliding with Ronald's quiet. "I love you."

"I know," he replied, his voice soft and resigned. "I know. It's okay, Opal. I'm quitting too."

He kissed her, her lips trembling against his. She pulled away, squinting at his face. "Are you okay?" she asked, her voice sharpening.

"I'm. . ." *What?* The word hovered out of reach. "Not. . . doing. . . well."

"There's something wrong with your pupils," she said, pushing up his eyelids with gentle fingers. "The left one—it's bigger." Alarm flashed across her face.

"They've always been that way," Ronald mumbled, his words forced. He pulled her into an embrace. His grip felt weak, trembling. A wave of nausea surged through him just as thunder cracked too close, rattling the house. The sudden noise made Opal jerk away, flicking on the lamp beside her. The light struck his face, skewed and unforgiving. His stomach churned violently as a tidal wave of pain crashed through his skull.

He wasn't okay.

"Ronald!" Opal cried. Fear replaced the frustration in her voice. "What's happening?"

Ronald found himself unable to answer, although he was sure she knew. The words were on the tip of his tongue, but instead of being spoken, they vanished like a candle's snuffed flame. He reached for the letter in his pocket, but his right hand refused to obey. He couldn't manage to form a simple movement.

"Ronald, you're having a stroke," Opal said, her tone calm only on the surface. Her hands were anything but steady as she laid him flat on the bed, lifting his legs to straighten him. Ronald patted his pocket clumsily with his functioning left hand, desperate for her to notice. But she didn't see. She was already sprinting from the room.

Seconds later, Opal returned, her phone pressed tight against her ear. Ronald fumbled again for the crumpled envelope, but she pushed his hand aside, her focus on the voice on the line. "I need an ambulance," she blurted. Panic strangled her words.

Vomit crept up his throat, choking him, trickling into his lungs. He sputtered weakly, and Opal gasped, rolling him onto his side. The corner of the envelope dug into her arm. He watched her eyes dart to his pocket, and she pulled the envelope free.

Open it. Read it now, he thought. The words inside held everything he couldn't say. But she tossed it to the floor as she barked into the phone.

"It's a stroke. Sixty-seven-year-old man, last seen normal at 10:35 a.m."

The room pitched, walls closing in, as the darkness at the edges of his vision spread. He struggled to picture his brain inside his head. Was the steady throb of pain behind his eye actually a trickle of blood? But the image vanished along with his vision as the neural pathways that used to connect one thought to the next were gently extinguished. His comprehension of the details melted into one voice. Death hurts.

"It's Dr. Collins. Connect me to the ER. Quickly, please."

The voice was tinny, the octave too high against his faltering ears. A breathless pause followed.

"Dr. Lin? It's Opal Collins. I'm sending you a stroke alert." Her voice cracked. "It's Ronald Aberdeen."

The words "Ronald Aberdeen" caught his attention, but their meaning slipped away as his body became a puddle, expanding to fill the bed. Or was it his soul that had leaked out?

"He's not doing well," she continued, before her voice gave way to sobs.

There was a thud; something had slipped from her hand to the floor. She climbed into the bed with him, lowering herself onto his chest, her tears soaking his shirt.

And then a spark of something familiar crossed his mind, crystal clear before receding. A brain scan. A bleed. His brain must be shifting across the midline. Ten millimeters. Eleven.

"There's still time," she whispered, her words desperate. "You're okay. You're going to be fine."

It was the last thing he heard before the darkness swallowed him. *Sweet girl.* His pain dissolved into nothingness. *You can't save me.*

FIFTY

Fox

An unfamiliar car idled in the rain outside the house when Fox pulled up. He eyed it suspiciously, but the pounding rain kept him from investigating. Instead, he hurried inside, shaking off the chill. The distant wail of sirens prickled at his nerves as he opened the drawer where he'd left his pager.

Rain, sirens, the faint sound of exercise equipment—the mix put him on edge. Not seeing Opal or her guest in the living room, Fox walked cautiously toward the chirping pager and read the new message.

The number belonged to Bonne Santé's ER. His pulse quickened as he dialed.

"Wei Lin paged you. Let me get him for you."

Fox moved slowly down the hallway to the bedroom, his heart hammering. Whose car was in front of his house? The idea of his wife, Opal, being in their bedroom with another man cut through him. He stopped in the hall, hearing her labored breaths. His blood froze.

"Fox, it's Wei," came the voice on the line. "I'm sure Opal told you, but Ronald Aberdeen is en route as a stroke alert. Doesn't sound good. If it's a large vessel, he might be coming your way."

"What?" Fox's gut tightened. Whatever he'd expected, it wasn't that.

"Opal called it in," Wei continued. "Just thought I'd give you a heads-up."

Numb and confused, Fox hung up and pushed the bedroom door open. His eyes first fell on the bed, the sheets rumpled and wet, the room giving off the pungent scent of vomit. Then his gaze locked on Ronald, his skin ashen, sprawled motionless in the mess. Opal straddled his body, pressing frantically on his chest, sweat and tears dripping onto him as her hands rose and fell in sharp, desperate compressions.

Fox remained frozen in the doorway, his pager dropping from limp fingers to the floor. The wail of the nearing siren grew louder. His shoulders sagged under the weight of too much bad news.

At some point, his body moved, though he couldn't recall deciding to, and he was at the bedside.

FIFTY-ONE
OPAL

Was this justice for what I had done?

Anger tangled with anguish as I pounded on Ronald's chest. He had defied me, burned down my resolve to prove a point. And now he was dying in my bed, taking any hope of reconciliation with him. My fear spilled into rage. I looked up and saw Fox in the doorway, his face unreadable. Would I lose him too?

Determination ignited in me. I would save one. Maybe both. Sweat stung my eyes as I met Fox's gaze.

"We need to move him to the floor," he said flatly.

Together, we wrestled Ronald's heavy, lifeless body from the bed. His weight dragged our arms, and we struggled to get him onto the carpet. Fox took over compressions with steady precision.

I wiped vomit from the corner of Ronald's mouth and tilted his head back before pressing my lips to his. Fox's jaw tightened at the sight, his wince striking sharp. Even now, even like this, his anger simmered beneath the surface.

"How long?" he asked, his voice sharp-edged.

I shrugged, unable to speak.

He paused to check Ronald's pulse, his fingers pressing against the slackened neck. I crawled away, bile rising in my throat. In the bathroom, I vomited into the trash can before collapsing against the wall, pulling my knees tightly to my chest.

Fox returned to his task. I'd seen it too many times. My sobs came fast, useless, as I watched him stop, then pluck a feather from the pillow.

"Fox, no!" My voice cracked under the weight of disbelief. "No, no, no."

"Opal, he has no pulse. His pupils are fixed and dilated." He brushed the feather across Ronald's eye. No flinch, no blink. "He's dead."

The siren stopped abruptly outside, and the front door rattled under the force of sharp knocking. "EMS!" someone shouted.

Fox rose, his steps weary as he left to let them in. He returned moments later with two paramedics and a gurney. Calm and professional, he explained Ronald was dead.

One paramedic knelt to confirm. "Time of death: 11:04 a.m.," Fox said, his voice hollow.

The paramedics left the body untouched. "Are you next of kin?" one asked.

"No. He was our boss," Fox replied.

The paramedic's brow furrowed as his eyes traveled from Fox to me, then to the bed. "Hmm. Interesting."

"Someone needs to call the next of kin," added the other paramedic.

I spoke without thinking. "Isabelle," I whispered.

"I'm not calling Isabelle," Fox snapped. "This is your mess. You call her."

And so it was. Our old marriage was as dead as my lover. The unraveling had begun.

My voice cracked with bitterness. "What would I say, Fox? 'Don't worry, Ronald's at my house, but you don't have to kill him—he's already dead'?"

"I don't give a fuck what you say," he shouted, the sharpness tearing through the room.

The paramedics cut us off. "We'll notify an officer to contact the next of kin." They left, leaving the gurney untouched.

"Wait!" Fox called. "Aren't you going to take the body?"

The second paramedic turned to them. "You have to call a funeral home and request a removal."

I stared at Ronald's body lying between us on the floor. Silent. Still. The weight of who I had become settled over me like a second skin.

"I can't believe you," Fox whispered.

I couldn't answer. "I—we—I tried to tell you earlier."

"But why was he in my bed?"

"He came to tell me something," I replied. "I told him it was over. I didn't want him here, but he came, I ended it, and he died."

"Damn you!" The words exploded from his chest, apparently having been impatient to escape. "You're pathetic," he spat, a side of him coming to light that neither of us had seen before. "We were trying for a baby, Opal!" he shouted, his face pained. "What would have happened if he—"

I was silent, pondering my lack of excuses.

"That's why you hid your pills." Fox slid down the wall and sat beside me. "How stupid could I have been?"

Fox walked out after the undertaker finally removed the body. I followed him to the barn. He tore through the tools, tossing aside shovels and spades until he found what he was looking for: the ax.

The rain had slowed, but fat drops still dripped from the oak tree overhead. Fox stood under its canopy, gripping the ax. Without a word, he swung it into the trunk. The blade bit deep, sinking into the wood.

With a mechanical rhythm, he swung again and again, sweat running with the rain down his face. Blond gouges marred the bark as he struck it over and over until his strength gave way.

In the end, none of it mattered. The tree was already dead.

FIFTY-TWO
OPAL

CHOP AFTER CHOP, FOX SWUNG WITH FURIOUS PRECISION but seemed to get nowhere.

"It's already dead, Fox," I said, breaking the tense silence.

He turned, brow slick with sweat, chest heaving. "You made a fool of me," he panted. His eyes burned into mine. "You made a fool of yourself."

"I'm sorry," I whispered. I trailed my fingers over the jagged slashes —the rough edges of bark and the sharp, woody splinters. I had tallied the damage a thousand times. I never imagined it would run this deep.

Fox dropped the ax. The thud should have made me flinch, but I held steady. "I want a divorce."

I didn't move, afraid the truth in his voice would shatter me. Instead, I stared at the battered trunk. "I'm taking the kids," he continued, voice flat, detached. "I'll be in New Haven, working for my father."

That got my attention. "You're not taking the kids," I said sharply.

He scoffed, a bitter edge in his tone. "You almost killed Cal. They're safer with me."

His words struck like a blow, each syllable reinforcing every doubt I carried. I wanted to scream at him, argue, tear his accusations apart. But how could I, when the mirror of my failures stared back at me?

I studied him instead. "You need a Connecticut license to practice medicine there," I replied, my tone quiet but pointed.

He let out a slow, almost mocking breath. "Opal, I've had a Connecticut medical license for years."

The ground caved beneath me. I stood and brushed the dirt from my pants. "How long have you been planning to leave?"

Fox sighed, straightening his posture. "I wasn't planning anything," he said. "I just. . . needed a safety net." He turned away, walking across the yard, not toward the house, but skirting it, as though it wasn't home anymore, but another structure to walk around.

I had rehearsed this day of reckoning in my head a thousand times. I pictured what it would be like to lose them, even as I lay in Ronald's arms. But I was wholly unprepared for the devastation I had caused. "Wait!" I called, the desperation spilling out. "I can fix this."

He stopped, just beyond reach. "Opal. I just don't want to."

I froze, a gaping emptiness rushing over me. In a daze, I darted toward the house, rifling through forgotten drawers. When I returned, my hands were full of Cal's inhalers. "Here," I said, thrusting them into his hands. My throat tightened. "Make sure he always has one."

Fox hesitated before taking them, transferring the small devices into his pocket. "Don't worry." He handed one back to me. "He's still your son."

My knees sank into the dirt as he turned and walked out of the yard and out of my life. A stranger. He was clutching his pager. Probably going back to work, as if dismantling a family fit neatly between patients.

I remained there, weighing the inhaler in my palm. The tears came unbidden, hot and relentless, until there were none left. Only after the sobs subsided did I slump back into the house, hollow. At the kitchen table, the letter from Ronald waited, unfolding like a slow-moving storm.

Opal,

You've asked me why we're doing this, and I have struggled to find an answer. Maybe we do this to feel young and invincible. Maybe we do this to take control of our destiny. Maybe we do this because we are weak and cannot resist the temptation to feed our fragile egos. I stay because you make me feel young and vibrant rather than old and slow. I stay because you are kind. You are soft. You have a beautiful heart. The consequences of our actions terrify me, yet I could not quit you.

But I must quit you, Opal. Somewhere along the way, I fell in love. It's not the same as the love I have for Isabelle. You won't wake up next to me every morning, treasure my secrets, care for me when I'm old, or bury me when I die. My love for you is free from those burdens. I only want to be near you. My love for you has grown to the point that I love your marriage to Fox too. He is perfect for you, and I'm rooting for your happiness. I understand now that I shouldn't allow your happiness to depend on me. I should not have let you love me.

Goodbye, Opal. I will never stop thinking of you. You'll be in my thoughts for the rest of my life. If you think of me too, I hope it is warm and with love.

—Ronald

FIFTY-THREE

OCEAN HOSPITAL DOCTOR FIRED AFTER BOSS FOUND DEAD AT HER HOME

Health Solutions South announced Wednesday that a local physician has officially been fired from her position at Ocean Hospital in Gilbert, Florida, after the former president of the health conglomerate was found dead in her home.

HSS sources allege that Dr. Opal Collins, 35, was having an affair with the now-deceased former president of HSS, Dr. Ronald Aberdeen. Aberdeen, 67, was found dead Monday in the home Collins shares with her husband, HSS physician Dr. Fox Collins.

The manner of death has been ruled as natural causes.

Sources close to the Collins couple have said this was a love triangle gone bad. HSS hasn't confirmed whether Fox Collins plans to resign.

Opal Collins's former supervisor, Dr. Karen Chamberlain, who has been named acting president of HSS, said, "Dr. [Opal] Collins was always one step behind. It's so unfortunate that she chose to get involved in an unsanctioned relationship with Dr. Aberdeen in order to get ahead."

Opal Collins was recently promoted to medical director after the merger between Doctors Inc. and Santa Rosa Medical System that became HSS.

Collins's former coworker, Dr. Nassrin Fahadi, said, "Our job is to take care of patients, and Dr. [Opal] Collins did that better than anyone. She is and will always be a wonderful physician."

Fahadi continued, "Practicing medicine is an extremely difficult and stressful profession. I think Dr. Collins was just dealing with that stress in an unhealthy way. My heart goes out to the Aberdeen and Collins families."

Dr. Thomas Rogers, who was fired from Doctors Inc. in 2019 for undisclosed reasons, said, "Garbage in, garbage out. Dr. Collins never stood a chance of improving her working conditions at Ocean Hospital while the greed from the top was choking the people at the bottom."

He added, "I'm glad Aberdeen has been exposed, even if it's posthumously. My only hope is that exposure brings change to a company desperately in need of redemption."

Aberdeen recently left the entire Health Solutions South conglomerate to his daughter, Rebecca Aberdeen, naming her president in a will signed only days before his death. Aberdeen's widow, Isabelle Aberdeen, said her husband was about to step down from the company to retire and that he'd planned to volunteer his time doing cancer research. This comes on the heels of allegations of past sexual misconduct by Aberdeen involving his then medical student, Trisha Brown.

Opal Collins has declined multiple requests for an interview.

FIFTY-FOUR
OPAL

BEFORE THE MEDIA GOT WIND OF RONALD'S DEATH, HEALTH Solutions South technically was still my employer. My resignation had died with Ronald, and I didn't trust Karen Chamberlain to protect me when the fallout hit. Despite my grief, when the time came to get back to work, I forced myself to confront her in the office that was once Ronald's. My purpose was simple: resignation.

Karen didn't fit into Ronald Aberdeen's chair. The ergonomic neck cushion brushed the frizz of her hair, and her feet dangled just above the floor. After I breezed in confidently, it appeared as if the chair was trying to eat her.

I didn't bother knocking. Karen narrowed her eyes as if I were an unruly teenager, but I ignored her, proceeding to the wall of windows. The city sprawled ahead of me as I stood with my back to her in silence.

"Opal, have a seat," she said in the tone she used to fake cheerfulness. I turned, met her gaze, and took a seat in one of the acrylic chairs. My expression remained blank. She leaned forward to shove her toes into her burgundy heels, a clumsy effort, before pulling open the filing cabinet to retrieve my file. Her chair betrayed her, snagging a strand of her blond hair. She grumbled, and I didn't bother to tell her about the crooked smear of red lipstick streaking her front tooth like a crayon had gone rogue.

"Let's take a look, shall we?" she said, setting the file on the desk and flipping it open. "This is some of your patient feedback."

"I know," I replied evenly. My eyes flicked to a syrupy note from a patient's family member. "I've seen it. Anyway, I considered quitting before Ronald died."

Karen didn't look up. "Hmm," she murmured, tugging a paper loose. "Here's the one I want to discuss." She tilted the page toward me. "Do you recall a Mr. Jarvis?"

I raised an eyebrow. "Shit brick?"

Karen flinched but kept going. "Now, I understand some patients are. . . difficult," she said, her voice measured, "but Mr. Jarvis got a hold of his chart and didn't appreciate the way he was. . . described."

"It's an objective reflection of the encounter," I replied calmly.

Karen shot me a tight-lipped smile. "Let me quote. 'I don't need any more piece-of-shit doctors at this piece-of-shit hospital telling me what I need.'"

"That's what he said," I replied. "Those were his words."

"Opal, you can't write things like that. Patients don't like it when you're mean."

My shrug widened into a stretch.

"It puts us in danger of a low Press Ganey score," she added, her voice taking on an edge.

"That sounds like a Mr. Jarvis problem."

Karen flipped the paper onto the desk. "Well, Mr. Jarvis is demanding we amend his record. He wants you to say something nicer."

I glanced back out the window. "No."

"Yes!" Karen shouted, slamming her fist on the desk.

I absorbed all the venom in the room and used it to pierce her with my eyes. "Karen, we are doctors, and we are women. This isn't about Mr. Jarvis taking an inch. This is about the men who have taken miles. No, I will not rewrite his chart."

Her breath snagged audibly. For a moment, silence passed between us, heavy with animosity. Then, with a resigned sigh, Karen tossed the paper aside.

"Fine. You don't have to amend it."

"Thank you," I said coldly, folding my arms over my chest.

Karen hesitated, her fingers tapping the desk before she spoke again, her tone devoid of fake cheer this time. "You're terminated, effective immediately. I'll amend the chart myself."

My mouth tightened, but I held steady. "Wow, Karen," I finally said. "Ronald isn't even in the ground yet."

FIFTY-FIVE
OPAL

RONALD'S FUNERAL WASN'T HELD AT A CHURCH—NOT because the Aberdeens were not religious, but because the Pelican was the only venue in Gilbert big enough to contain the swarm of mourners. I pictured Isabelle and her daughter cloistered in the funeral home: choosing flowers without me, service hymns without me, his casket without me. They were probably poring over family photos, curating memories that pointedly erased me. In their eyes, I wasn't insignificant. I was worse. I was a stain.

I knew better than to go to the Pelican. It wasn't just about sparing my reputation or Fox's. Showing up would be twisting the knife into Isabelle's grief, adding fuel to the wildfire of media speculation. I should have stayed home, screaming into the scratchy bath mat on my bathroom floor like I had every day since Ronald died, or packing for New Haven where my kids and a new life waited.

But I couldn't. Death made him pull my heart stronger than he had even in life. I needed closure. Or something.

I scrubbed myself clean under scalding water until some of the grief sloughed off me like dead skin. With shampoo in my hair, I resolved to face whatever came next. Soon, I was pulling on a black sweater, fixing my eyebrows as if they could somehow armor me, sliding into expensive shoes that pinched more than I'd admit.

Amber and Wendy drove me. Their chatter filled the car while my mind drifted elsewhere. The Pelican was a madhouse. The line for the valet took twenty minutes. We found ourselves sandwiched between an Aston Martin and a Mercedes from the street to the porte cochere. The atrium thrummed with people dressed in black suits, black dresses, and black cravats mingling with inappropriately high spirits. Their laughter felt obscene, as if my lover weren't lying dead in the next room.

The Pelican staff weaved their way amongst the guests, several of them with notepads. Reporters began to whisper when they saw me. I dropped my eyes, unwilling to meet theirs. Someone muttered and snapped a picture from the corner of the room. I ducked into a mercifully empty restroom and dialed my mother.

"I'm at Ronald's funeral, Mom," I said, checking for feet under the stall doors. "Mom. . . can you come?"

"I read the article, Opal." She sounded tired of me, a sigh heavy at the end of her thought. "It occurred to me you might need space to figure yourself out."

"I'm going through hell, Mom. I need— I don't know—a hug."

"We aren't home this afternoon, sweetheart." She said it as if confirming a dental appointment. "Did you reach out to a lawyer about getting the kids back?"

"Are you serious? God, Mom. I need someone."

"You've got yourself into quite the mess, dear." I could imagine her shaking her head, that special brand of disappointment only my mother could shine my way.

"And I need you to stop judging me for once!"

She clucked her tongue and let her breath out slowly. "Opal, I knew you would go off the rails, but I never expected it to be this bad."

"That's why I need you!"

Static silence flooded the line. "Why can't you be more like your sister?"

Something cracked in me. "I'm trying. I am. Flaws and all. Take it or leave it."

She exhaled slowly. "Why don't you get the number of that divorce lawyer I used? Louis and I—"

I hung up first.

Amber met me with a squeeze of the hand outside the restroom. Wendy, the other. "Come on," they murmured, pulling me where I least wanted to go—forward. The ballroom was a sea of plush purple carpeting, flowers in whites and pinks cascading around the casket like storm clouds colliding. Amber found seats in the back row. I slipped off the heels that had been pinching my feet and sank my toes into the soft rug.

"If you're going to say goodbye," Amber said, pointing at the line filing past the casket, "I can go with you."

A rich sheen gleamed on the mahogany casket. Isabelle had spared no expense. The open side revealed Ronald's face, but it wasn't him. Rosy cheeks, waxy pallor, hands unmoving. That wasn't my Ronald. That wasn't life.

Amber nudged me toward the casket when it was my turn. Isabelle and her daughter stood like sentinels beside it, graceful and gaunt in their mourning. Isabelle's dress plunged daringly low, and a gold chain with Ronald's wedding band rested against her chest like a final stab at remembrance. Her daughter, older than me by years, mirrored her grace. I barely glanced at them. They weren't who I'd come for.

My hand hovered over the casket, trembling. I wanted to touch the polished wood—or the suit jacket he wore. One last connection. But her voice sliced through my grief.

"Do not lay a single finger on my husband, Opal."

Isabelle's voice was a polite blade, sharp and brittle. I froze midair, then yanked my hand back. Amber moved to grab my elbow, but it was too late.

Isabelle's smile gleamed but her words were venom. "I pity you, Dr. Collins," she said, flipping through scorn. "You thought you could use my husband to claw your way up. Now look at you, back where you started. In the trash."

Her daughter murmured a quiet, "Shhh," but Isabelle plowed forward. Wendy gasped quietly beside me.

I don't know what came over me, but I didn't cower. Perhaps she was right to pity me, but I pitied her more. "I'm sorry, Isabelle," I said.

Sorry he'd tangled himself in my life. Sorry we were left with this wreckage. "But do you hate him too? You should. It wasn't okay. He was my boss." Isabelle glared at me, but I ignored the malice in her eyes. "He was my boss," I repeated. "He gave me orders and look what happened. He died a hero and I'm being thrown out with the trash."

Her shriek—"Leave!"—followed me out the door. Camera bulbs flashed. The press had gotten wind of the drama unfolding at the casket.

Amber and Wendy whisked me into the car. My head tilted against the window, eyes on the pandemonium in the rearview mirror. Neither of them spoke. The valet untangled the Aston Martins and Bentleys, and soon the world outside was silent. Except there wasn't peace. Not really. Something far bigger loomed. The covid pandemic.

It was coming for us all.

FIFTY-SIX

OPAL

THE NEW HAVEN AIR FELT LIGHTER, CLEANER—FREE OF THE
sticky humidity that clung like regret. Here, the ghosts of Ocean
Hospital and Ronald remained, but they whispered less. They'd better
stay quiet. I needed my kids back.

Fantasia snaked the car through Yale's campus until we stopped at a
charming old house carved into apartments. A woman leaned in the
doorway, taller than Fantasia with a kind, round face framed by long
brown hair streaked pink. A hole gaped at the knee of her jeans as
Fantasia rushed to greet her, pulling me along.

"Opal, meet my sister, Maxine."

Her warm handshake was unexpectedly comforting, bringing tears
to my eyes. This beautiful stranger was taking me in.

"What's wrong?" Maxine asked softly.

"Nothing," I said, shaking my head. "I'm happy. I'm finally in the
same city as my kids." It had only been days since I left Gilbert, but it
felt much longer.

Fantasia squeezed my hand, piling my luggage into the corner of the
living room. The decor carried Maxine's personality—a needlepoint
Welcome sign with cats hung beside a Machine Gun Kelly poster. She
whisked an armful of mugs to the kitchen as I sank onto the sofa with

my laptop, pulling up physician jobs at Yale New Haven Hospital. She reappeared with wine and glasses, setting them down with the ease of an old friend.

"I work with the Risen Savior shelter," she said, filling the glasses. Her voice was sly and melodic like her sister's. "I meet people living on the streets. Sometimes I bring them back to the shelter if they're interested. Reverend Boomer runs it—I'm mostly his sidekick."

"I'd hoped to do social work as a kid," I said, taking a glass. "But some jerk thought I'd make a good doctor."

Maxine laughed. I took a long sip of wine, distracted by thoughts of my children. What should I say the next time we meet? What should I say to Fox? As if hearing my thoughts, my ringing phone interrupted us. Fox's name was on the screen. I swiped without hesitation.

"My dad died." His announcement was abrupt.

"What?"

"Covid," he murmured.

"No. No, that can't be right," I argued, falling into the corner of the sofa.

"He refused to close his radiology clinics for the quarantine. The hospital wouldn't allow visitors. In the end, he died alone."

"Fuck," I breathed. "How is your mother? How are the kids?" I asked.

"Scared as hell," he replied. "We're having a small funeral tomorrow. Family only."

"I'll be there."

I unpacked the same black sweater and Louboutin shoes I'd worn to Ronald's funeral only weeks ago. When the time came, Fantasia drove me to the funeral home and wished me luck.

The service for Calvin was intimate, if not painfully small. If not for Covid, many more would have come. The contrast to Ronald's lavish funeral struck me; this was a humble goodbye for a man who deserved so much more. Those not here included radiologists at Collins Radiology, receptionists, technicians, old classmates, old football friends, neighbors, and cousins. All of them would have to grieve privately.

Fox nodded a greeting, but his hair was disheveled and his eyes were red. I never loved Fox more than I did at that moment. I wrapped my arms around him, and he froze like a pillar of salt. Regret washed away my flicker of hope. Was it his father or the end of our relationship that made him look like a walking corpse? Maybe he didn't know either.

"Let me take the kids," I suggested.

"You can take them to the back with Katy," he replied, squeezing his eyes shut. I glanced behind me and found my sister-in-law bouncing her new baby girl on her knee.

I kept my children occupied playing cards until "Amazing Grace" floated through the parlor. The melody carved into something fragile in me as I held Emily's hand. She watched me cry, her face folding in fear. I grieved for her grief, for June's and Fox's, and even for the ghost of the love we'd lost.

My precious Cal saw my tears and came in for the kill.

"I know what divorce is. Divorce is two houses," Cal said, his voice thin but sharp. "And neither one feels like home."

"Oh, honey." I reached for his shoulder, but he pulled away.

"If Dad left because you needed a boyfriend, why didn't you love me enough to not need him?"

"Cal, it isn't you. I love you more than the moon!" I promised, taking him by the hand.

"What did you need a boyfriend for, anyway?" he asked, turning his back to me.

Just then, Fantasia shuffled in quietly with Maxine on her arm. The funeral director glared at them crossly, checking a list but saying nothing as the women squeezed beside me.

The service ended, and we waited for the hearse. I stayed tucked in the back, trying to remain inconspicuous, but to my dismay, June approached. My heart beat wildly. We hadn't spoken since Thanksgiving, when everything was okay. I'd torn her son's family apart, and I braced myself for her wrath. Astonishingly, she grasped my hand, urging, "Don't go back to Florida. Stay with me for a while. You can have Fox's room."

My heart squeezed in my chest. She should have hated me, but she kept loving me like an actual daughter. I wanted to say, *Yes, of course I'll stay with you*, but I couldn't make this about me. "That's really generous, June, but I can't be a burden right now."

"You can still call me Mom," she said. "You haven't signed the divorce papers yet."

"Actually, Opal, there's something I want to discuss with you," Maxine interrupted. I turned to her curiously. "The shelter has a medical clinic attached to it. Medical residents ran it, but Yale pulled them because of the pandemic."

"Go on," I said, still clutching June's hand.

"Reverend Boomer wants to hire a doctor to manage the clinic," Maxine continued. "It pays shit, and you would have to do community outreach with me in the streets—"

"I'll do it!" I exclaimed, turning to my mother-in-law. "I'll stay with you."

I wrapped Emily and Cal in a hug, squishing their tiny faces. "Mommy's back," I whispered into their hair.

After the others left for the procession, Fantasia pulled me aside. "What about Fox?" she asked.

"I want to fix it. I want my family back," I replied, realizing I was ready to let go of Ronald's ghost. "But Fox won't talk to me."

"Have you confronted him?" Fantasia asked.

"Confronted him? I fucked him over. I don't get to confront him."

"If you want this to rise from the ashes," Fantasia said, her voice low enough to be a warning, "you'll need to light the fire."

FIFTY-SEVEN
OPAL

Within a few weeks of working for the Risen Savior Shelter, I realized Maxine was right. This job was gritty, raw, and very cold. But the rush in my chest warmed me as I ducked into the overpass. There was someone under there, and I hoped to get him to the shelter. I had to nudge the heap of blankets to know if the man was dead. I had seen dead bodies before. The bodies were always quiet, like this one. Was he sleeping under there? Since the incident with Ronald, I no longer had the stomach for spending time with the dead. Squinting at the blankets, waiting for their rise and fall, wasn't giving me answers.

Despite approaching noon, the blankets remained still and the light dim. I had to decide if I would nudge him with my toe or shake him with my hand. I stooped as I approached to avoid hitting my head on the concrete. Graffiti, once vibrant, decorated the walls, now faded by layers of dust. The scent of exhaust mingled with the scent of urine. Maxine was in the car, and I ensured she could see me from the driver's seat. I glanced back once and confirmed she had the engine running. Exhaust billowed from the car in warm plumes that turned white in the chill. I faced the tousled blankets again and knelt beside them. I laid my hand on the red wool blanket and felt something solid beneath.

"Johnnie?" I tried, but the sound of the cars whizzing by overhead drown out the sound, and the bundle of blankets didn't stir.

"Johnnie?" I yelled. The blankets lay beside an overturned suitcase with the handle still extended. Scattered plastic food wrappers rustled in the breeze, although the overpass sheltered most of the wind. Empty beer bottles littered the edges of the alcove, some broken.

"Who's asking?" came a man's voice.

I jumped back, both startled and relieved. "Opal," I replied loud enough for him to hear.

An arm stretched from under the blankets, and the man slowly propped himself up. He turned to face me, legs still covered by his linens. He cleared his throat, then spat thick, white phlegm on the concrete beside him. His forehead was creased with deep furrowing lines. There were bags of puffy flesh below his eyes and his temples caved in like sunken goals and dreams. Both his and mine. A bulbous nose sat atop a white beard that was discolored by a yellow ring around his mouth. Different shades of dirt blotched his skin. His eyes were apathetic as they took me in.

"Where are you from?" he asked.

"I'm from the Risen Savior shelter. I run the clinic there," I replied. "I'm here for a wellness check." I had checked on the wellness of many people under many bridges since taking Maxine's offer.

"I don't suppose you brought any beer or cigarettes, then?" He tossed the blanket from his lap—his feet were bare. Now that he had shifted, I could see a pair of dirt-stained socks laid out to dry behind him. I could smell them now too.

"My friend Maxine is a social worker," I went on. "She got word you were staying here. We enjoy getting to know the new guys. You might not know about the shelter or the clinic." I reached into my jacket pocket and pulled out a slip of folded paper. I bent forward to give it to him. He waved my hand away.

"No, thanks."

"No problem," I said, quickly pocketing the pamphlet. "If you change your mind, we're over on Temple Street, right by MLK."

As Johnnie began asking about the food options at the shelter, I noticed Fox approaching on foot coming from the direction of the parking lot. "You got food there?" Johnnie asked.

"Always," I replied, distracted as he picked up a sock and worked his foot in.

"Hot food?"

"Sometimes," I said, turning to find Fox right behind me.

"Opal, what are you doing here?" he asked me. And to Johnnie, "Sorry, sir. Excuse me."

"I work for the shelter clinic now, Fox," I said. "I told you that."

"But. . . under the bridge?" he asked, his brow twisted.

"I've never felt so complete," I explained. Johnnie stood up, quickly gathering his suitcase to leave us. He averted his eyes as he hurried away. "You made Johnnie leave," I accused.

"I can get you in at Yale," Fox said, pulling his hands into the sleeves of his expensive sweater. I gazed down at my dirty sneakers. Fox belonged in a Yale world. I belonged to this one.

"Fox, we need to talk," I said, lowering myself and taking a seat on the ground. He rolled his eyes, dropping reluctantly beside me.

"I know I screwed up." He crossed his arms over his chest. I pressed on. "It upsets me you gave up so easily."

He scratched his head. He rubbed his eyes. He touched his nose. He rested his chin on his fist. He didn't look at me.

"You didn't fight for me, and you didn't fight for us. You were just gone. You tossed our marriage into the dumpster and walked away."

"Opal, I'm not the kind of person who can stay in a relationship like that," he mumbled.

"I'm not either, Fox. I don't disagree, but I don't want our old relationship back. That version of our marriage is gone for good. But I think we have the potential to grow something entirely new, and a thousand times better."

"How?" he asked sarcastically. "You're a liar and cheater."

"I was a liar and cheater," I agreed. "I need to share something difficult with you. I want you to see me—the entire package. The worst that can happen is that you still say no."

"Okay, fine," Fox said, stretching out his legs and blowing warm air onto his icy hands. He listened as I described my past. I told him about

Michael and why I kept it a secret. A part of me stayed broken, even after he came into my life. Fox was perfect. I told him it was hard to live up to perfection. I told him I'd confronted Michael, Ronald, and Isabelle. I told him I was sorry. I told him I was becoming a new person —and that I would like a chance to get to know him again.

When I finished, my back was sore and my right leg was numb. The sun disappeared behind a cloud, causing the temperature to drop further. Fox took a breath. "You should have shared your past with me a long time ago, Opal," he said, leaning forward in the cramped space and taking my hand. My heart leaped as he pulled me up, but then he dropped my hand, breaking the weak connection.

"Fox, I can't take a job at Yale," I said. "Thank you, though. Thank you so much."

"I'm sorry, Opal. We're done," Fox whispered. He walked away, back toward the parking lot. Then he stopped, turned to me and said, "You were never broken in my eyes. You were always perfect to me."

EPILOGUE
OPAL ONE YEAR LATER

MAXINE AND I BECAME WELL ACQUAINTED WITH THE unhoused men and women of New Haven. We were known as "the Miracle Workers" because we cared for all the Johnnies and Bernies—a nickname we embraced. Reverend Boomer was a different animal than Pastor Bobby. He was old and his breath smelled like cardboard. He never laughed until I started doing impressions of the acolytes or the lady who played the organ on Sundays.

Maxine gave me the name of the doctor who prescribed her antidepressant, and I finally took the leap and made an appointment. Dr. Rodriguez was younger than me and passionate about mental health. When I explained my trepidation about treating my depression, she waved away my concern and said simply, "We'll keep that out of your chart and between you and me." I thought it would take weeks to feel something. I was wrong. The first pill hit my bloodstream, and a light switched on. The light flooded the darkness within me. I could see everything clearly. The medication didn't change my identity; it reached deep into the hole where I had retreated and pulled me back to life.

Fox and I never got back together, but he remained a dear friend. I would always regret the way I lost him. Despite the heartache I'd caused,

I realized that burning my life to the ground paved the way for this life. The one I was made for.

Covid fizzled, and schools reopened. Cal joined the soccer team, and Emily started taking gymnastics lessons. Despite my concern over the battered reputation of the sport, gymnastics was in her blood. It was no surprise that she was good at it.

Nassrin and Tallahassee were married, and it wasn't until I received the wedding invitation that I learned his given name was Greg. Soon they were expecting a baby. The malpractice suit was dropped. She began working at a clinic, inheriting a group of patients from a doctor who was retiring. Tom and his wife moved to Gainesville, where he became an anatomy professor at the medical school. Alex continued to work for Ronald's daughter at Bonne Santé, where he made enough money to buy a big house on the Gulf of Mexico. Gloria's daughter called me when Gloria moved to the hospice house, her lungs finally giving up. I spoke with her daughter daily, both before and after Gloria passed away.

My parents stayed in Gilbert, although my father was looking for a job in New Haven so he could be near me. Amber quit working as a teacher, and shortly after, she and Wendy had a coming-out celebration. My mother had a hard time with Amber and Wendy's relationship at first. She said she couldn't be seen at church with that kind of person. But once Pastor Bobby found out about Amber and Wendy, he drove to Amber's house to congratulate them. Amber spent her time working on the old blueberry patch full time. Eventually, she and Wendy moved into my old farmhouse and turned the blueberry patch into a U-Pick tourist attraction. The farm's success led the county to grant them a back entrance from the highway, preventing pickers from driving through Bramblewood Estates. Amber and Wendy hired a tree service to grind the oak tree's stump and had bougainvillea planted there instead. Although an explosion of purple flowers covered the bougainvillea's branches, it was the thorns that made it perfectly imperfect.

THE END

———

Don't stop now. Scan the QR code or visit https://books.jcbcbooks.com/ib1aewbt51 to keep reading a bonus scene.

Isabelle takes place in 2003 when the consequences of Ronald's early betrayals come raining down. The scene is told from his wife Isabelle's perspective. Isabelle is one of my favorite characters, and I love writing in her point of view.

To find out what going on currently, visit https://books.thatkindofgirl.shop/

If you enjoyed *That Kind of Girl*, a great way to show your support is by leaving a review. Reviews help more people find and enjoy the book. Consider taking a moment to leave your review today.

About the Author

Jacey Bici writes Women's Fiction with a humorous twist. When she's not saving the world with Dad Jokes, you can find her in the Emergency Room of a Veterans hospital where she works as a doctor. She is honored to be immersed in genuine stories from real-life heroes.

Acknowledgments

Thank you to my readers who make it possible for me to share my work and continue to create new stories.

Thank you to my husband, Brian, for believing in my dream. Without your support, my stories would be dust on a shelf. To my children Brian, Kendra and Tyler who keep me accountable.

Thanks to my editor, Pam Hines for patiently growing me into a better writer and sifting through the many drafts that eventually became *That Kind of Girl*.

Thank you A.N. Deeb for generously sharing your wealth of knowledge on publishing.

To editors Jennifer Safrey and Sara DeGonia, your eyes are exactly what the story needed.

To James and Stefan at Spiffing Cover Design, your work is beautiful. I'm forever grateful for the art that brought the story to life.

To SRQ Headshots for photography in "About the Author."

Thank you to the many hundreds of patients who inspire me with your own stories.